THE HUNKPAPA SCOUT

A WESTERN TRIO

WILL HENRY

CENTER POINT PUBLISHING
THORNDIKE, MAINE

This Center Point Large Print edition
is published in the year 2009 by arrangement with
Golden West Literary Agency.

The text of this Large Print edition is unabridged.
In other aspects, this book may vary
from the original edition.
Printed in the United States of America.
Set in 16-point Times New Roman type.

ISBN: 978-1-60285-465-9

Library of Congress Cataloging-in-Publication Data

Henry, Will, 1912-1991.
 The Hunkpapa scout : a western trio / Will Henry.
    p. cm.
 ISBN 978-1-60285-465-9 (library binding : alk. paper)
 1. Western stories. 2. Large type books. I. Title.

PS3551.L393H86 2009
813'.54--dc22

2009000343

TABLE OF CONTENTS

RED BLIZZARD

I

It was a brittle-cold December day, wine-clear and still as a buzzard's shadow. Perez, cutting the trail of the moving village about noon, had known at once this was the first sign of the hostile concentration he'd been expecting. A dark man, lean as a tendon, Pawnee Perez, was senior civil scout with Colonel Harry Fenton's garrison at Fort Will Farney. His narrow head moved constantly as he rode, the slant, black eyes never still, ceaselessly roving every quarter of the landscape—for upon accuracy of those chert-hard eyes depended the lives and safety of the northernmost Army post along the bloody Virginia City Road.

Perez's face was not one to go well with an unexpected meeting in the dark. It was thin, with high cheekbones of saddle-leather swartness. A short, spade beard pointed the long jaw. The mouth was as wide and iron-lipped as a Cheyenne dog soldier's—a big mouth, a merciless mouth, an Indian mouth. When you saw Pawnee Perez, you thought of one thing: a lean, high-withered buffalo wolf, alert, nervous, dangerous.

Sioux-reared, Perez was a Pawnee half-breed, fathered by a Basque fur trader, mothered by a Pony Stealer squaw. He was a strange, friendless man with the fire of one ambition burning in his dark breast: to belong, by force of achievement, to the white race of his father. Behind him now, forty miles south and west, lay Fort Will Farney. Ahead, somewhere in the weird snow tumble of the Wolf Mountains, must lie the suspected concentration of Sioux and Cheyenne hostiles which report had insisted were gathering there under Tashunka Witko for the long-threatened wipe-out of Fort Farney. The concentration's existence and intent would be proved by the nature of the village Perez was now following. If that village were headed by the chief he figured it was. . . .

All day Pawnee Perez had run the trail out, coming, an hour short of sunset, in sight of the distant, tenuous spirals of cooking-fire smokes. Pausing briefly, he studied the twisted land ahead. Then, clucking softly to Sosi, his mud-yellow gelding, he put the little horse back on the trail. Half an hour's cat-footed going up a side valley paralleling the village track had topped them out on a low ridge overlooking a sight that drew in the scout's breath with a whistle as sharp as a bullet's passage.

Below him spread some 200 Oglala Sioux lodges, the peaceful smokes of their fires lazily wisping out of the teepee smoke holes, crawling blue-white up into the thin air of the winter twilight. But it was not the number of the lodges that brought the half-breed's breath sucking in. It was the pony herd.

Perez could identify any sizable Sioux village by its horses. If he could see the horse herd, he could tell whose village it was—and he could see this herd. He knew these horses as you might know your neighbor's dogs. Turning to Sosi, whose muzzle he held tight-wrapped, he whispered: "Ho, ye, Sosi. Do ye recognize yer friends down there?"

The little buckskin flicked his ears nervously, his strange, glass-blue eyes watching the grazing animals below.

"Mebbe we kin get old Iron Head to uncover his ears now." The scout referred to Colonel Fenton. "Wait'll we tell him who's sneakin' into the Wolves with five hundred warriors. *Aii-eee*!"

Swiftly Perez worked his way off the back side of the ridge, hand-leading the yellow pony down the icy going. At the bottom he paused as a keening wind whipped suddenly through the stillness of the gully. "Our Sioux friend across the ridge there ain't the only one that's comin'," he muttered, removing the nose wrap from the gelding's muzzle. "Do ye smell what I smell, Sosi, old friend?" Sosi threw his sooty nose into the freshening wind, snuffling softly, then laid his ears back, swinging his rump to the wind, hunching his back like a snow-drifted steer.

"Aye, ye smell it, all right. That's *Wasiya*, eh, Sosi?" For answer the gelding hunched his back yet more, nudging the man with quick bunts of his black nose. *Wasiya* was the Sioux name for the

9

Blizzard Giant. *Wanitu* was winter, but *Wasiya* personified the season. He carried the Big Snows in his frozen chest.

"Let's make tracks away from here, Sosi." The half-breed's words were grimly subdued. "Happen I don't like the smell of that wind any better than I do the looks of that camp."

The fort was dark when Perez galloped Sosi up to the stockade at midnight. Sergeant Orin Duffy was on the guard detail. The scout answered him abruptly when his challenge came down through the darkness.

"It's Perez. Open up!"

"Holy sleepin' Mary," muttered the sergeant. "I was jest gettin' me beauty rest."

"Hope ye enjoyed it," called the scout, loping through the stockade gates. "Ye ain't gonna get another fer some time." Inside, he pulled up the gelding, dismounted.

"What's up, Mister Perez?" The Irishman frowned, noticing Sosi's steaming flanks. "Faith, now, ye've ridden the poor little beast 'most to death."

"Yeah. I got to put him up and rub him off. While I'm doin' it, ye'd best roust the colonel outen the hay. Tell him I've got somethin' that'll curl his wig six ways from Sunday. Best get the other officers, too. He'll want them."

"Yes, sir!" answered Duffy. "Right away!"

"And get John Clanton over there, too!" Perez called after the sergeant as he hurried off. "*I'll* want *him.*"

"Yez bet I will. I'll have the lot of them over there in three minutes."

Duffy was as good as his word.

As the half-breed neared the C.O.'s office, a tall shadow lounged up through the darkness and the guttural voice of John Clanton growled: "What's in the wind, Pawnee?"

"A blizzard, fer one thing, Hawk," Perez answered, using the name the admiring Sioux had given the other scout.

"Ye're not ridin' that muckle-dun pony of yers into a green lather jest to bring in a weather report." Clanton's words were dry as dust. "I kin smell that snow same as ye. It's comin', and it's comin' big, but that ain't what's got yer nostrils flared out."

"Ye're wrong." A wolf grin flicked its twisted way across Perez's swart features. "I got a blizzard to report, all right. Jest a little different color than usual, that's all."

"Color wouldn't be red, would it?"

"It would. We got a red blizzard comin', that's fer certain, Hawk."

"Ye sure?"

"Sure as a schoolmarm's got a soft leg."

"Anybody we know?" The white scout's voice was as casual as though asking the time of day.

11

"Tashunka Witko," said the half-breed, turning for the colonel's door.

"*Aii-eee*," breathed Clanton softly, as the yellow light closed behind Perez.

When he entered Fenton's office, every officer on the post except the O.D. was present: Major Stacey, Captains Bolen and Tendrake, another captain Perez didn't know, and the three lieutenants.

Colonel Fenton was in a poor mood. He was a man who enjoyed the rigors of his own discipline, one of those rigors being lights out at nine and a good ten hours' sleep. His statement to the scout was challenging: "You'd better have something important, Perez. I don't like my garrison routed out in the middle of the night for no good reason."

"There's plenty good reason," muttered the scout, "but ye won't like it. Tashunka Witko and five hundred Oglala Bad Face braves are camped forty miles north and east of here. They're headin' fer the Wolf Mountains."

"Who in hell cares?" Major Stacey had been called away from company more intimate and glandularly attractive than that of his sleepy-eyed fellow officers. "What's five hundred Indians, more or less?"

"Yes, Perez," agreed Colonel Fenton. "What about it? Hang it all, man, you didn't get us out of bed to tell us you'd found five hundred Indians." On his words, the office door opened soundlessly

12

and the other scout, Clanton, slid in to stand against the wall.

"I allow ye didn't hear me," replied the half-breed evenly. "I said . . . Tashunka Witko. If that don't wake ye up, nothin' will."

"Oh, quit talking like a damn' Indian, Perez." Their enforced association had done nothing to diminish Stacey's dislike of the half-breed. "Who the hell is Tashunka Witko?"

"Yes," echoed Colonel Fenton stiffly. "Are we supposed to be excited?"

"I am," announced Perez simply.

"Well?" The colonel's query soaked up a shade of the scout's seriousness.

"Tashunka Witko is the most dangerous Sioux alive. Happen ye hear more about Red Cloud and Sittin' Bull, but they can't touch Tashunka Witko. Sittin' Bull's great, so's Red Cloud, but when it comes to fightin', they both take orders from Tashunka Witko. I've lived with him and I know him. When he shows up, it means just one thing."

"What?" challenged Stacey bluntly.

"War."

"Now, see here, Perez." Colonel Fenton's patient voice was still disinterested. "It's plain you're dead serious, but I can't quite see what you're getting at. What's so disturbing to you about this Tashunka Witko? I don't believe I've ever heard the name."

"No, nor any of the rest of us," broke in Stacey belligerently.

13

"Maybe you'd like it better in English." The low-voiced interruption came from behind them. The officers turned to see Clanton standing in the lamp shadows, tall and dark as any Sioux.

"Damn you, Clanton!" Stacey's tones were angry. "I wish you'd knock when you come in. All you Indian-lovers sneak around like hostiles."

"I'm waitin' to translate Tashunka Witko for ye," the scout reminded them, grinning his enjoyment of the situation. "Get a good grip on yer hair, gentlemen." The officers waited while Clanton ran his hard eyes over them. "Crazy Horse!" He jumped the words at them deliberately.

"You might as well have said . . . 'Boo!' . . . for all the silly dramatics employed," growled Stacey. "What are we supposed to do now, wet our pants? Do you think you're funny, Clanton?"

"No." The white scout's reply slipped into the warm room like an icicle. "And I don't think ye are, either. Ye're supposed to be a competent officer on duty in the hottest hostile spot on the map and ye haven't got sense enough to add up Crazy Horse and five hundred Oglala fighting men moving across country in the guts of winter. It's like two and two, and the answer comes out to what Pawnee said . . . war."

Before Stacey's fury could find words, Colonel Fenton stepped in. "Clanton, I think you'd better apologize. After all, Major Stacey is a senior officer and certainly a gentleman. I won't have you. . . ."

14

"Sorry, Colonel," the scout interrupted, narrow-eyed. "I won't apologize and I won't serve under such an officer. I'm through."

Major Stacey's agreement churned with anger. "I'll say you're through, you impertinent, damn'. . . ."

"I'll not take yer cussin', Major." The big scout's hand slid down and back, its shadow hovering over the low-hanging butt of the Colt.

"Gentlemen! I'll remind both of you where you are." Colonel Fenton's indignant words filled the dangerous pause. "The discussion's ended. I want Clanton and Perez to remain. For the rest of you, good night." His final words followed the officers out the door. "And I don't want any talk of Crazy Horse spreading around the garrison. Is that clear? Major Stacey, I'll want you as soon as I'm through with the scouts."

With the officers gone, the colonel turned at once to Clanton. "Do you agree with Perez on the seriousness of his report?"

"Sure. Crazy Horse is the top Sioux war chief. He's *the* War Chief, with capital letters. He's not moving his village in wintertime jest fer the hell of it."

"It's a war village," said Perez. "Very few squaws along, no children, no old people."

"What do you propose doing?" Fenton asked of both of them, getting his answer from the half-breed.

"Somebody's got to keep tailin' that village. If

there's anythin' goin' on up there in the Wolves, Crazy Horse'll lead us to it. Clanton has got hisse'f a hunch there's a big war camp up in there somewheres. I'd listen to that hunch."

"How about it, Clanton? Do you want to go after that village? On up into the Wolves?" The colonel was decidedly lukewarm.

"I'm goin,', all right, but not up in the Wolves. I'm through workin' at Will Farney and I allow you know why."

"Don't be childish, Clanton. You're working for me. Just forget Stacey."

"I aim to. My outfit's packed and I'm pullin' out tonight."

"Well, I won't argue with you." Fenton was suddenly on his dignity. "I've been thinking you've been getting a little soft on the Indians lately. I'll have Sergeant Simpson draw your due pay. You can leave in twenty minutes." Clanton's face was as expressionless as a Cheyenne's. Turning, he left the room, ignoring the officer's charge. When the door had closed behind him, Colonel Fenton continued irritably: "Let's sleep on it, Perez. I think the whole thing's a whisper in a whirlwind. I've got four hundred regulars inside the best stockade on the frontier. Nothing could possibly happen."

"Somebody ought to go on up, tonight," reiterated the half-breed. "I would, but I been out sixty hours now."

"There's nobody else to go," Fenton informed

16

him. "Bailey and O'Connor went up the Virginia City Road this afternoon . . . two squads of cavalry and a big supply train for the mines."

"They'll never get through," Perez commented, then added quietly: "I'll go back out in the mornin'."

"Well, all right, but you don't have to go back out. You scouts have all been around Indians so long you can't see any color but red."

"Happen ye're right." Perez's final words managed to be ominous for all their softness. "I'm seein' red right now. I said months ago that they'd hit ye with the first big storm. That storm's comin'. I smelled it on the wind tonight. Mebbe twenty-four, forty-eight hours, but it's comin', and it's a big one."

"A red blizzard, eh, Perez?" Fenton laughed.

"A red blizzard," echoed Perez, and went out of the room.

The night Pawnee Perez returned to Fort Farney with the news of Crazy Horse's big war village was the nineteenth of December. The new day dawned clear and bright with no cloud bigger than a pipe puff in the sky. Fenton and Stacey were in fine spirits. In their respective ways, the one with ponderous humor, the other with caustic sarcasm, both had chided Perez about his "blizzard", but by late afternoon the horizon to the north lay piled high with lumpy shoulders of lead-gray cloud. The wind dropped to a sullen whisper and an uneasy quiet lay over Fort Farney. By late afternoon, as Sergeant Orin Duffy put it: "A ring-nosed sow with the snortin' sniffles could have smelled snow with her snoot in six inches of swill."

To begin the day, Fenton had ordered Perez to abandon his proposed continued tailing of Crazy Horse. A wood train had been scheduled to go out, and, with Clanton gone, Perez found himself saddled with the duty of guiding it. There was no trouble and the half-breed got the loaded wagons back to the fort about 4:00 p.m. Although he hadn't seen a moccasin track or a feather tip, hadn't heard an owl hoot or a fox bark, he was more certain than ever that the blizzard building to the north held disaster for Fort Will Farney in its dirty-gray gut.

When he reported to Colonel Fenton, he repeated his hunch and warning: "Colonel, I never heard so much quiet in my life, and I didn't see a single blamed pony track all day long."

"That's good." The officer nodded. "It's like I told you . . . nothing to worry about."

"If ye know Indians, there's plenty to worry about. Old Jim Bridger always told me . . . 'When ye don't see 'em and ye can't hear 'em, that's when they're there.' And old Jim knew about Indians. They're out there somewheres." A quick hand wave to the north. "I know they are."

"Well, you were right about the blizzard by the look of that north sky," the fort commander admitted uneasily. "Maybe you're right about the hostiles. I'll have Stacey mount a double guard on the stockade and change the outposts on Signal and Humpback Hills every two hours. Good enough?"

"Better than a buffler arrow in the butt," grunted the scout, "but, if I was ye, I'd. . . ." His words were broken off by Major Stacey's sudden entrance.

"Bailey and O'Connor are back!" Stacey's color was high. "Just came in the east gate. Black Shield and a big bunch of Minniconjou jumped them up north of Wolf Creek Crossing. They lost all the wagons, Lieutenant Wander and Sergeant Schofield killed, five troopers wounded. Bailey says the only reason they got away is that the Sioux stopped to fight over the wagons."

"Well, good God, send them in here!" shouted Fenton, for once aroused. "Let's hear the story."

"They're gone!" ejaculated Stacey. "Grabbed fresh horses and lit out, south. Said Clanton and the half-breed were right all along. Claimed they were getting out while the getting was half good."

"This is serious, Stacey." Fenton sank back in his desk chair. "For God's sake, what are we going to do for scouts? Perez is the only one left."

"What of it?" Stacey's question leaped with eagerness. "We don't need a scout to find those Indians. Let me take a column out and teach those red birds a lesson. Bailey said Black Shield followed them down, but caught up with them too close to the fort to jump them again. That means he's still hanging around out there. Let me go out in the morning and. . . ."

"How many troops did you want?"

"Two companies would be plenty, I'd say."

"Black Shield's a tolerably salty chief," announced Perez. "I wouldn't figure him to have less'n three hundred braves along."

"Well?" Stacey's inquiry was brusque.

"That yer idee of good odds . . . four to one?"

"I've said so!"

"We can't let this attack go by," interrupted Colonel Fenton. "If the storm is still holding off in the morning, we're going out. You can have your two companies, Stacey. It's time we took off our gloves."

Stacey thanked his superior and departed to brief his command. No sooner had he gone than Sergeant Simpson stepped in, saluting.

"Pardon me, Colonel. That scout, Clanton, just came back to the fort. Wants to see you, sir. Says it's real important. . . ."

"Ye kin relax," said Clanton, coming in at the door, bumping past the sergeant. "I changed my mind when I left here, Colonel. Couldn't let well enough alone. Had to run out that hunch of Perez's and mine about that war camp."

"Yes?"

"Well, I found it. Fifty miles up the Tongue.

About a thousand lodges. That means better'n two thousand warriors. Mostly Sioux, some Cheyennes. I snuck in there about an hour short of daylight. Crazy Horse had jest come into camp and they was havin' a whale of a powwow. It was still blacker'n the insides of a buck's gut, so I got in close enough to hear plenty. They're goin' to follow that storm down on the fort. Pawnee . . ."—a quick nod went to Perez—"ye was sure right about that."

"What do you suggest we do?" The fort commander's inherent mite of imagination was swelling rapidly under the apparent respect of both scouts for Crazy Horse and his war camp. Colonel Harry Fenton was a slow man to grasp a tactical danger—but he was not stupid.

"Get ready for a siege, that's all. What else can ye do?"

"Major Stacey wants to go out with a column in the morning."

"That's nice," drawled the white scout. "They'll butcher him, quick."

"I don't agree, Clanton!" The colonel's observation was sharp. "You scouts are all Indian-jumpy. I think Stacey could break up the attack before it gets started."

"Ye mean ye're actually goin' to let him go out?" The big frontiersman's words were disbelieving.

"It all depends on the weather. We'll see. The thing to do now is get the fort ready for repelling this attack of yours in case it materializes. You two

21

men go get some sleep. You're all the scouts I have, and, if Stacey goes out in the morning, one of you will have to go with him."

"It won't be me," stated Clanton succinctly, but the scout's words were drowned by the colonel's shouting for his sergeant.

"Simpson! Simpson! Get the Officer of the Day in here."

"Yes, sir! Anything else, sir?"

"Yes, you might as well get the rest of the officers, too. And tell them to hop it!"

"Yes, sir!"

Perez and Clanton squatted along the wall of Fenton's office, smoking. Around them the normal evening quiet of the post began to break up as Clanton's report of the coming Indian assault spread throughout the garrison. Groups of enlisted men gathered on the parade yard west of Fenton's office. In a few minutes the officers started filing in. Over the whole fort a subdued hum began to grow, at first faint and indefinite, quickly becoming positive and unmistakable—the whispering, lisping gibberish of hundreds of frightened human tongues muttering in the dark.

As yet no official confirmation of Clanton's report had gone out from Fenton, no orders had been issued, no alert given. But the fort *knew,* and the fear that hung over it was so heavy you could feel it pressing down like a thick, moist hand.

Quickly sucking their pipes in the shadows, watching the nervous officers approaching and entering the C.O.'s office, Perez and Clanton were discussing, of all things, the weather.

"When do ye figure she'll hit?" the big man wanted to know.

Perez, studying the sky to the north, which even in that black night seemed to have a dirty color independent of the surrounding darkness, took his time in answering. "Along about noon to dark, tomorrow."

"Closer to night, mebbe?"

"Yeah."

"Gonna be a big one."

"Big as a bull's bottom," grunted the half-breed.

"What do ye aim to do?"

"Stick around." Perez shrugged. "How about ye?"

"Yeah. I'll likely stick, too. Ye figure that damn' fool'll go out in the mornin'?"

"Sure. Don't ye?"

"Yeah, I reckon. Ye goin' out with him like Fenton asked ye?"

Perez considered this a minute, hunching down in his wolf coat as he answered. "What else?"

"Ye kin duck out like Bailey and O'Connor. Nobody'd blame ye. Everybody knows Stacey's rid yer hump raw."

"Well, he's rid ye, too."

"Yeah." The white scout's words were pointed. "But his ridin' me's been different."

"Yeah, I know. Ye're the only one that's treated me like I was white."

"Ye're white. Ye look white." Clanton's statement was simple, without guile.

"My father was white," said Perez, and the two fell silent.

After some minutes, Clanton knocked his pipe out. "Ye figure the hostiles'll get into the stockade?"

"Not if Stacey stays inside."

"They'll try and bait him out, ye figure?"

"Sure." Perez nodded. "Don't ye?"

"Yeah, I reckon. What time is it?"

"About twelve."

"Conference ought to be breakin' up any minute," surmised Clanton.

"Comin' out right now," grunted the black-bearded half-breed. "There's Bolen and Drummond."

"And Stacey," added his companion. "Lookit the grin on him, will ye? That means he got his way about tomorrow."

"It's a dead man's grin if he did."

"Reckon so," was all Clanton said.

II

The twenty-first dawned as sparkling clear as the day preceding it, but it was frost-bitter cold. The crouching cloud to the north seemed not to have shifted its ominous bulk an inch. There could be no doubt that *Wasiya* was squatting up there back of the Wolves. It was equally obvious that the lead-gutted old devil was waiting for something. But for what? Down at Fort Will Farney the weather was as bright as a fresh-minted penny—no wind, no clouds, no worry! It was cold, though—colder than the hubs of hell with the axles frozen.

Pawnee Perez stood outside Colonel Fenton's office, his hunched shoulders burrowing into the deep fur of the wolf-skin hunting coat. The jutting black beard was already ice-tipped with the condensed moisture of his breathing. As he waited, a similarly fur-clad figure came slouching across the parade yard.

" 'Mornin', Pawnee. Nice day."

"For caribou, mebbe." The half-breed's short answer was garnished with a flash of white teeth. "What're ye doin' around? I allowed ye cut yer string last night."

"Hell, that was last night. Today I got me an urge to see Injuns."

"Reckon ye won't be disappointed."

"Reckon not. What do ye make of the weather?"

"Same as I said yesterday. She'll hit along late this afternoon."

"Me, I don't think so, now," observed Clanton. "Cloud 'pears to have pulled back a mite."

"Gettin' set to jump," grunted Perez.

"Might be you're right." Clanton nodded toward Fenton's door. "Stacey in there now?"

"Nope. Hasn't showed yet."

"Speak of the devil. . . ." Clanton glanced across the parade yard.

Major Stacey hurried up, brushing past the scouts to enter the colonel's office without a word. Clanton and Perez grinned at each other.

"He's a cute one, he is," opined the tall scout. "What do ye think they'll do? Ye reckon Fenton'll still let him go out chasin' Black Shield?"

"Dunno," Perez muttered thoughtfully. "The colonel's usually right cautious. He's had hisse'f a night to sleep on it. I figure he may have switched his mind some."

"I allow ye're right," said Clanton dryly, as the door of Fenton's office opened. "Here comes God's gift to the cavalry now. And get yerse'f a travois-load of that face. The old boy's told him he can't go out and play this mornin', and junior's sore." As Stacey stomped past them, Clanton cooed: "Good mornin', little man."

"Go to hell," snapped the officer, red-faced, his quick stride continuing, unbroken.

"There's Simpson wavin' us to come in." Perez nodded to Clanton. "Let's go."

"Right behind ye." Grinning, the big scout followed the half-breed toward the office. "I do hope the colonel's hind end isn't as puckered as his friend's this mornin'."

As expected, Colonel Fenton informed them he had advised Stacey to hold off on the planned excursion outside the fort. "I anticipate no real trouble, mind you, but I respect your opinions. At the same time I've instructed Major Stacey to get his troops ready in case the picture should change. If any hostiles show up outside, we're going after them. I'll go along with you two on looking for trouble, but damn it all, if they come around here asking for it, they'll get it."

The scouts looked at one another, saying nothing.

"Stacey seems to think he can handle the situation with his cavalry," the colonel continued. "Of course, should he go out, I'll insist on some infantry support. About six squads, I think."

Again the scouts said nothing, and the post commander concluded, addressing Perez: "As to scouts, he won't have Clanton and doesn't want you. But it was agreed you would go in case of any action. How about it?'

"Sure, I'll go." Perez's hunched shoulders shrugged acceptance. "If he's brain struck enough to think he can whup two thousand Sioux with less'n a full troop of pony soldiers, I allow I'm just crazy enough to tag along and watch him try it."

"Good." Colonel Fenton stood up. "You stick around, too, Clanton. If anything breaks, I'll work you in on it some way."

"I imagine," grunted the big scout.

Outside, the tall man drew a deep breath, exhaling slowly. "Whew! Well, that's a relief. Now all we gotta worry about is the cussed Sioux sendin' in a bait party." A dozen scattered rifle shots from the north stockade wall punctuated his statement. Both scouts whipped around in their tracks to stand like startled elk, heads up and into the wind, eyes narrowed, ears straining. The dry crackling of the rifles continued atop the wall, the answering lead from outside the fort whanging and ricocheting off the stockade's top logs.

"Ye kin start worryin'," asserted the half-breed. "There's yer bait party."

The first shots were still echoing as Perez and Clanton raced for the north wall. Behind them, as they scrambled up the ladder to the catwalk atop the stockade, the fort was coming hard awake.

Brass-lunged non-coms were bellowing a confusion of orders, troopers were tumbling from barracks partly armed, half asleep, completely rattled. Down by the main gate Captain Howell, Stacey's second, was trying to marshal the detail the latter had ordered formed up. Colonel Fenton was coming from his office in a puffing run, behind him the chop-running figure of Major Phil Stacey.

"What do ye make of it?" Clanton asked Perez, the two of them peering through rifle slits.

"It's a bait, all right. Seems to be jest the ten of them."

"Yep, and look how they've split it up . . . two each of Oglala, Hunkpapa, Minniconjou, Cheyenne, and Arapahoe. That's no accident."

"No, they probably sat up half the night arguin' who would get the honor of the first coups."

"It for sure means the main bunch is laid up for an ambush."

"For sure," agreed the half-breed.

"Lookit the crazy devils ridin' around out there! They don't give a damn for all the lead what's bein' slung their way."

"They got more brass than a bronze monkey's butt when they're really up to somethin'." Perez's words were terse. "I hope to God Colonel Fenton ain't goin' to fall fer that come-on."

"Hey, Pawnee!" The half-breed's fellow watcher was excited. "Do ye see what I see? 'Way over there on Humpback Hill. Jest below that cedar clump that sticks up like a topknot." Perez's searching gaze followed his companion's. "That's him, ain't it?"

"It's him," the half-breed muttered. "I could tell that red ramrod ten miles off. Looks like he'd been starched stiff, then glued on to stay."

"Make out anybody with him? Must be four or five of them."

"Can't be sure about the riders from this distance, exceptin' Tashunka Witko, but from the hosses I'd say, let's see . . . that's Red Cloud's paint stuff . . . Dull Knife's Appaloosie . . . White Bull's sock-foot sorrel. I don't recollect that other pony, but I'd guess it was American Horse sittin' him. He usually rides a black like that and wears one of them seven-foot war bonnets."

"*Aii-eee!*" Clanton grimaced. "They sure got their heavy guns with 'em today!"

"Yeah." Perez nodded. "And here comes ours." His gesture indicated Colonel Fenton and Major Stacey coming toward them along the catwalk.

"Well, boys," the colonel's query was brisk, "what do you think of this?"

"Yes," Stacey echoed him, "what *do* you think of this? Where's your two thousand warriors, Clanton?"

"Waitin' fer ye to come prancin' and brayin' out with yer pony soldiers," the scout answered acidly.

"You think those are decoys out there?" Colonel Fenton, as usual, was patiently serious.

"We know they are," Perez answered for both scouts. "The main bunch is out there. We jest seen Crazy Horse and three, four other big chiefs over on Humpback Hill."

"I don't see anybody over there on Humpback." This from Stacey. "And besides, don't be ridiculous. That's our second signal station over on that hill."

"Well, now ye know why ye didn't get any signal from that station," grunted Clanton, searching the hillside again, seeing that the Indians had, indeed, disappeared.

"No, and ye never will," added Perez quietly. "How about the other station, Colonel? Signal Ridge?"

"Simpson brought me a hello from them just now. They flashed . . . 'Many Indians!' . . . five times, then quit."

"They're gone, too," said Clanton simply.

"The hell you say!" contradicted Stacey, the irrepressible. "They probably abandoned post. They'll show up any minute now."

"Well!" Colonel Fenton's interruption hit the scouts like a knife in the ribs. "In any event we've got that hay train out there, and. . . ."

"You what?" Perez literally shouted.

"A hay train, four wagons," Fenton countered stiffly, taken aback by the half-breed's vehemence. "Sergeant Duffy and sixteen men. Went out at four this morning. They should have been back by now. We needed that hay . . ."—the colonel spoke defensively now, knowing he'd erred tragically—"and Major Stacey figured we could get it in before the Sioux showed up. From Clanton's report, Stacey figured they couldn't get down here before noon at the earliest."

"What does he figure now?" Clanton threw the junior officer a hard scowl with the words.

"I figure I'm still right," Stacey snapped defiantly. "If the hay wagons have been jumped, it's by a band of scouts, or by that scoundrel, Black Shield. That main body Clanton reported couldn't possibly have got down here yet, providing they're coming at all."

"And I told ye they'd get down here before day-

31

light." The big white scout's tones were flat with anger. "That was *my* report, damn ye!"

"And I say not before noon, damn *you!*" Stacey was shouting. "We haven't heard a shot from up there. That hay meadow is only six miles out. We could hear any firing up there." As if to document the accuracy of his angry observation, a faint popping of musket fire carried down on the freshening north wind. In a momentary lull in the nearer firing of the hostile decoys, the more distant shots rode in clearly.

"We thank you, Sergeant Duffy," drawled Clanton sarcastically, tipping the fox-skin cap graciously in the direction of the musket fire.

"That's from over west of Peyo Creek," barked Perez, checking quickly. "Is that hay outfit working in Bay Horse Meadow?"

"Yes," Fenton answered nervously. "Isn't that right, Stacey?"

"Yes, sir, and with your permission I'll go out after them right now!"

"Naturally. We've got to bring them in, but you'd better take another six squads."

"We can't spare them from the fort." The major's statement crackled with fine decision. "And by the Lord, sir, I don't need them."

At this point Perez, racking his mind for some way to save the men who were about to be committed to this irresponsible command, glanced down to see Captain James Howell, sitting his horse at the head of the waiting troops below. Perez didn't know Howell, but he knew men. The captain looked as cool as a brook trout under a willow root. "Why not let Captain Howell go out with the relief party? Clanton can take them. I kin follow with Major Stacey and strong infantry reserves. That way we kin, at least, keep the relief from gettin' cut off."

Colonel Fenton opened his mouth to agree with the half-breed, but Stacey forestalled him. The red-bearded cavalryman's mind was as quick as it was quirky.

"A damn' good idea, Perez!" he exclaimed heartily. "But Howell's too good a man on defense. I'm not worth a cent on this cooped-up fort fighting. Had all my experience with open movements, cavalry stuff. But whatever the colonel says, of course. . . ." Too many years the regular Army man, Major Phil Stacey, not to know the optimum moment for the deft wafting of a posterior osculation, rankward.

"Stacey's right. I need Howell, here. Go ahead, Phil, but for God's sake be careful. Your orders are to go out and bring that hay train in. Nothing else. I agree with the scouts that those Indians outside there are decoys. Pay no attention to them and whatever happens, don't go past Eagle Point on the main trail. Under *no* circumstances, down Square Pine Ridge. Is that absolutely clear?"

"Yes, sir!" Stacey's eyes were snapping.

"Perez will go with you."

"All right, Perez." In the moment of Stacey's coming triumph, even the half-breed was eagerly accepted. "Let's go!"

Clanton had stood by wordlessly throughout this last exchange. Now his voice went sharply to Colonel Fenton. "Colonel, let me go with 'em. I can't do anythin' here. I'm a scout!" Stacey was already swinging to the ground below, but Perez caught the remark and stepped quickly back toward his fellow scout. The half-breed's eyes were burning like six-hour coals, his lean face darkly flushed. In Pawnee Perez "that feeling" was coming up. The wind of the hunt was in his nostrils, bringing the death stink of *Yunke-lo* with it. His words came in the barking gutturals of the Prairie Sioux.

"No!" His slit-eyed stare riveted the white scout. "This here is my war party. Ye stay here. That crazy fool . . ."—jerking a thumb toward Stacey— "is ridin' a dead man's pony. Somebody's got to stay here what kin bring a support party out to us, quick. That's ye!" His long, brown finger stabbed suddenly at Clanton.

Before either the colonel or Clanton could answer, Perez had dropped off the catwalk, twelve feet to the ground below, and was running, high-shouldered and unbelievably swift, toward his waiting dun gelding.

"I'll be damned if he isn't a queer duck," stammered the officer. "Never saw such a man."

"Duck? Man? Hell . . . ," murmured the big scout, his fascinated gaze following the hunched figure of the running half-breed. "Did ye catch that look he give me? The way his voice went to growlin'? And lookit the lopin' way he runs! Ever see a man run that way?"

"Can't say as I have," the colonel said.

"He's a wolf." Clanton's statement lost none of its force for its softness.

III

Fifty infantry, thirty horse, three officers, one civil scout—quickly they went, splashing across the ice-rimmed shallows of Spruce Creek, forging up the narrow Virginia City Road, the foot soldiers at a swinging double, the cavalry at a jingling trot. With the infantry group strode stolid Captain J. C. Bolen, thinking of his wife and three small children behind him in the precarious shelter of Fort Will Farney. With Bolen was youthful Second Lieutenant Barrett Drummond, remembering his pretty bride fluttering a gay kerchief after him from the north stockade gate. With the horse troop, square-faced Major Phil Stacey, thinking of nothing but teaching the bloody Sioux a lesson, remembering nothing but his own willful determination to be a hero.

Well, a lesson was taught that day and it was a bloody one: a hero was made, but he was a dead one.

Stacey was barely out of sight of the fort before he disobeyed his first order. Instead of ignoring the decoys who had retired up the trail as he advanced, he pressed hard after them. Perez at once reminded him of Fenton's expressly forbidding just this tactic, being thanked for his concern by a spleenful suggestion that he return to the fort, "as fast as your yellow-bellied horse can carry you!"

The half-breed's wide mouth had clamped into a thin slash above the sooty beard. His narrow face seemed frozen by more than the rising wind as he answered quietly: "If ye go down Squaw Pine Ridge, I quit."

"I know the orders, Perez." The officer was too excited to consider seriously the scout's warning. "You stick to scouting. I'll run the troops." The half-breed didn't answer, merely slouched lower in the saddle, hunching his narrow head, swinging his quick gaze more nervously than ever.

As the troops approached the forbidden Squaw Pine Ridge, the decoys became unaccountably bolder, riding back in crazy dashes at the leading group of pony soldiers, scarcely firing their own rifles, their purpose obviously to excite and draw out. Stacey played obediently to their lead, urging his mounted command forward, widening the gap between it and the following foot soldiers. Perez took sudden note of three things: all firing from Bay Horse Meadow had ceased; the sky overhead, blue when they had left the fort, had gone sullenly gray; the character of the trail was narrowing dangerously.

At this point the track of the Virginia City Road ran along the spine of a high, bare ridge, the sides of which pitched their ice-patched slopes downward at dizzy angles. Ahead, half a mile, lay Eagle Point, the beginning of the sharp downdrop of Squaw Pine Ridge. Perez, thinking now of the way Peyo Creek forked the bottom of that ridge, kneed his pony in alongside Stacey's.

"Squaw Pine is jest ahead . . . ," he began.

Stacey cut him short. "Let's worry about that when we get there." The officer's tones were as gay as a pheasant hunter's with a fat covey under his feet and plenty of shells in his pocket.

Perez disregarded the interruption. "The ridge pitches down, steep, to Peyo Creek Flats. There's heavy timber jest beyond. I figure the main bunch'll be in that timber and in the gullies runnin' up both flanks of the ridge."

"I don't give a damn what you figure, my boy!" Stacey was almost friendly in his exuberance. "I'm out here to remind your red brothers they can't knock over our supply trains and shoot up our work details. They've been giving us hell for six months and now, by God, they're going to get it back."

Again Perez ignored him. "Duffy's quit firin'. That means he's either wiped out or they've left him to come over and help Crazy Horse spring the *wickmunke* on ye. In the first case we can't help him, and in the second he's probably already on his way back to the fort. In either case, we ain't goin' to be of any help to him by goin' ahead now."

"You're not only an Indian, Perez . . ."—Stacey laughed—"you're getting to be a squaw!"

For the third time the scout disregarded the officer's remarks. "The blizzard is movin' in on us. An hour from now ye won't be able to see the trail, let alone the hostiles."

Major Stacey, in high spirits, conned the open sky that showed ahead in the trail, marking the downward plunge of Squaw Pine Ridge. Silhouetted against that patch of gray the hostiles checked their rearing horses, shaking their feathered lances, the half dozen who possessed them firing their muskets into the air, the whole pack of them screaming Sioux and Cheyenne invective into the buffeting wind. Obligingly that chill carrier whipped the savage insults back along the windswept ridge to the frozen ears of the following troops.

"There's your Eagle Point, Perez! Now what do you say? Still want to go home?" Stacey demanded of the scowling half-breed.

But Perez wasn't listening to the officer. Ahead, the decoys had turned and plunged off the skyline, down the pitching decline of Squaw Pine Ridge. One of their number, a huge Oglala brave riding a flashing bay-and-white pinto, hesitated, cupping his right hand to direct a last, hoarse challenge. The words came bucketing down on the wind, the deep Sioux gutturals carrying clearly. *"Ho! Sunke Wakan manitu, Hehaha akicita tela opawinga wance. H'g'un! H'g'un!"*

"What the hell did he say?" Stacey asked cheerfully.

"That was Sunka Sha, Red Dog, the Oglala. We're old friends. I shot his brother in a wagon scrape up the road last summer. 'Pears he remembers me," muttered Perez grimly. "He called me by their name for me, Little Pony Stealer. Said the medicine men had promised them a hundred dead white soldiers. Red Dog hoped Little Pony Stealer would be among the hundred, and that his heart was good."

Wheeling in his saddle, Major Stacey shouted back to his infantry. "Bolen! Drummond! Close up. Come on, hurry up!" By this time his own group had reached Eagle Point and he checked it, waiting for Bolen and Drummond to come up.

Squaw Pine Ridge ran in a thirty-degree decline a distance of perhaps 600 yards to the flats of Peyo Creek at its bottom. Riding those flats now, the Indian decoys raced and wheeled their ponies. Shortly Bolen and Drummond joined Stacey. The three officers, with Pawnee Perez, studied the scene below.

"Perez thinks there's two thousand hostiles hidden in that timber and the gullies flanking this ridge.

He thinks they're laying for us to come down there." There was thinly veiled contempt in Stacey's words. "Personally," he continued, "I think there's no more than three hundred in any event . . . probably the same band that jumped our supply train yesterday, Black Shield's outfit." The major looked at his juniors challengingly. "What do you think?"

Bolen's answer was fast and candid. "I don't know. I'm scared as hell for some reason."

Young Drummond was neither confused nor intimidated, being easily Stacey's equal for dash and snap decision. "I think you're right, Major! And if that *is* Black Shield's gang down there . . ." —here the youngster's voice went properly dramatic—"I want a crack at them. I went through the Academy with George Wander."

"Yes . . ."—Stacey got into the selfless act, too —"and Schofield was the best company sergeant a man ever had."

Perez's words dropped onto the end of Stacey's noble pronouncement like the slotted door of a box trap. "I won't go down with ye. I heard yer orders from Colonel Fenton. I'm in my rights to quit right here. And, mister, I'm quittin'."

"Why, you scum-bellied half-breed b. . . ." The commanding officer's bitterness was broken into by a thundering war shout from below. All eyes were immediately focused on Peyo Creek Flats.

Out of the timber flanking the level meadow charged 300 mounted braves, men and horses smeared with vermilion, ocher, cobalt, decked with eagle feathers, heron plumes, dyed-hair tassels, buffalo horns, bear claws, beads, quills, copper and silver ornaments, pennon lances, and gaudy blankets: the full, wild accoutrement of the paganly beautiful Sioux war dress.

At the banks of the creek the charge halted, the Indian horsemen pulling their mounts back to leave the figure of a lone chief standing out against their painted ranks.

On the ridge above, Perez cursed silently. The one thing he hadn't anticipated! Once again the fox-minded Crazy Horse had outsharped him. The identity of that chief below shot the last chance of stopping Stacey. His appearance at just that moment was a master stroke of red planning. The half-breed made silent obeisance to the fertile brain of Tashunka Witko, even as he tightened his knees on Sosi's ribs preparatory to wheeling him for Fort Will Farney.

The ensuing action went precisely as he knew it must.

"Who's that chief?" Stacey's barked question rapped out in the cold air.

"Black Shield," said Perez, heavy-voiced.

"Black Shield!" The commander's shout was triumphant. "You hear that, boys? Just what I said. There's the red son who got our train and there's our Indians with him, just three hundred of them. Let's go!"

Perez tried one last, desperate interruption. "Clanton and me seen Red Cloud and Crazy Horse this mornin'. Don't go down there. Fer God's sake, don't do it! They're waitin' fer ye, baitin' ye with Black Shield. Can't ye see that?"

"I can see Black Shield and three hundred braves. And I see that you're the same damn', treacherous 'breed I always thought you were. Now cut your stick, Perez, and cut it fast. We're going down there, and God help your dirty soul when I get back to Fort Will Farney!"

"God help yers," said Perez evenly. "Ye'll never get back." But Stacey was gone, shouting to his troops, starting them down the decline. Perez sat his gelding, watching the white-faced troopers go over the lip of the ridge. Some of them looked at him curiously, a few waved hesitantly, half smiling.

The scout returned the gestures without the smiles. These were brave, frightened men—fathers, husbands, sons—going unquestioningly out on the long trail. As they went, Perez honored them, and felt bitter sorrow for them. It was not the first nor would it be the last time the brave had died under the orders of the vainglorious.

Lieutenant Drummond, ranging the flank of his infantry group, the last one over the edge, urging them to greater speed, called out cheerily: "Come on, boys! Snap to it. We don't want them to get away."

"They won't," Perez muttered, half aloud.

"They'll wait fer ye." With the words he jerked Sosi hard around, pointing him back along the road. The little gelding jumped as the heels of the buffalo-hock boots hammered into his ribs. Seconds after the last of Drummond's men slid over the crest of Squaw Pine Ridge, the buckskin pony was belly-skimming the snow crust back toward Fort Will Farney.

Behind Perez, in the bottom gullies along both frozen flanks of Squaw Pine Ridge, the Sioux were living out the letter of the scout's last statement— waiting for Major Stacey and his 100 white soldiers. To the east crouched Makhpiya Luta, Red Cloud, with 700 mixed Cheyennes and Sioux; to the west, Tashunka Witko, with 800 Oglala and Hunkpapa Sioux; on the north, from creek flats, Black Shield and his Minniconjou fired back at the advancing pony soldiers and walk-a-heaps.

Presently the last group of infantry was past the halfway mark down the ridge. In the brush-choked gully on the west, Crazy Horse looked at High-Hump-Back and Man-Afraid-Of-His-Horses. They nodded back, hard-eyed. "*Hopo!*" said Crazy Horse. "Let's go!"

Stacey's eighty men heard the sudden drumming of 6,000 pony hoofs and drew back, bunched and crowding, huddling down on the bare, icy spine of the ridge, a pitiful handful of confused white sheep, the cry of the Sioux wolf echoing terrifyingly in their frightened ears.

● ● ●

Perez rode only a short way back along the Virginia City Road before putting Sosi down the steep sides of the hogback ridge. No use making it any easier for the Sioux than it had to be. Get down off the ridge and travel the gully bottoms, that was the only way.

He had not covered half the distance to the fort when a switch in the wind brought him the rhythm of galloping hoofs. He threw Sosi off the trail, forcing him into a heavy spruce growth. Wrapping the gelding's nose, he waited, black eyes scanning the gully southward, right hand balancing the long Colt lightly. Whoever it was riding this back trail rode alone. The half-breed grinned. Some Sioux or Cheyenne lodge would be mourning tonight.

The figure that shortly came galloping up the gully was no Indian, however. Perez kicked the little horse out on the trail, the other rider sliding his bay to a snow-showering stop.

"Howdy, Pawnee. What the hell's the shoutin' about?"

"Stacey's in a *wickmunke*, Hawk. I rode out on him when he went down Squaw Pine Ridge. Black Shield was teasin' him down by showin' hisse'f and three hundred braves on the flats. Stacey figured that's all the hostiles they was, and down he went. I hit out before the shootin' started, but I know Tashunka Witko and Makhpiya Luta got him boxed proper. Ye goin' on up?"

"Yep. Fenton heard the firin' and sent me out ahead of the relief. Captain Tendrake and fifty men are followin'."

"Ye'd best not go up there," Perez growled. "It's no use. They got Stacey and they'll get ye."

"I'm goin'," said the white scout, "but ye'd best stay away from the fort after leavin' yer troops like that."

"Ye ain't lookin' at no hero, Hawk. This here's jest a job to me."

"Hell, I know that!" snapped the other. "But Fenton'll jest figure ye deserted, mebbe even hang the blame of the ambush on ye. Swing around Farney and keep ridin'."

"Go on back." The black-bearded half-breed's warning was harsh. "I'm goin' to warn Tendrake back, too. Then I'm goin' on into the fort. Them fools has got to be warned and I aim to warn them if I get the Dry Tortugas fer it."

"So long." Clanton's eyes were suddenly carbon-hard. "I'm ridin' north."

"Ye're a fool," Perez said, and swung Sosi past his companion's mount, turning the little gelding southward and kicking him into a high lope. The white scout watched the half-breed for a moment, then turned his own mount to ride north. In five seconds his figure was just a shadow; in ten it had disappeared completely.

The white door the thickening snows shut behind John Clanton was never opened. His body was

45

never found, nor his horse. The official records of Fort Will Farney list him as an heroic casualty of the Stacey Massacre.

Fifteen minutes after leaving Clanton, Perez rode into the head of Tendrake's relief column. Repeating his story he got the expected reception.

"Good Lord, Perez! How could you leave them? That's desertion. Fenton will hang you!"

"Well, I aim to give him the chance." The half-breed's white teeth slashed at the words. "And if ye'd admire to watch my feet kickin', ye'd best take my advice. Don't go down Squaw Pine Ridge. Mebbe, if ye stay up on top, they won't come after ye. Leastways, it's yer only chance. Best take it!" The last the scout saw of Tendrake's command it was going at a dog-trot up the Virginia City Road, the men leaning into the whipping wind, their column ragged and broken by the stumbling and falling of the soldiers in the treacherous footing of the ridgeback.

When Perez hammered on the north stockade gates, it was 2:00 p.m. and as fish-belly gray as twilight, the snow already beginning to pile in low, driving waves against the bottom logs of the fortress walls. The noise of the building storm was such by this time that no sound of firing to the north could be heard—providing there was any to hear.

Colonel Fenton heard the half-breed's story in silence. When it was done, his statement was typically heavy. "I've tried hard to like you, Perez, but your report leaves no alternative other than to believe you are guilty of arrogant cowardice at the very least. And there will be more than one man in the fort who will question whether you might be actually involved in the ambush itself. If Major Stacey gets out all right, we'll leave it at simple desertion. If he doesn't, mister,"—the colonel's blue eyes went flat cold—"I'm going to hang you! Meantime you're under technical arrest. That's all."

"I allow ye'd better not worry about me, Colonel. This fort'll be under siege by nightfall. Little Wolf and Man-Afraid get together under Crazy Horse, it ain't no raid. Clanton's two thousand was accurate. Ye'd best believe that."

"I've lost all faith in you, man. When Clanton gets back, we'll see. But God help you if anything happens to Stacey."

"Don't worry about Stacey, nor Clanton neither. They're done fer." The scout spoke unfeelingly. "Ye jest buy my story and start yer dispatch riders for the Muleshoe Creek telegraph station while they can still get out. Come dark ye're goin' to have Sioux ringed around so tight ye can't spit for hittin' ten of them."

"We'll be all right as soon as Tendrake brings Stacey back in."

"Supposin' he don't?"

"I don't suppose things, Perez." The colonel's conclusion was brittle. "Now go get yourself

47

something to eat . . . and stay around barracks until I send for you. You'll find Missus Collins and the women serving hot food in the kitchens. Get along."

Shaking his lean head hopelessly, Perez slunk across the calf-deep snows on the parade yard. Beyond he could just make out the sick yellow windows of the company kitchens. The cold, intense all day, was deepening now. It bit into a man so hard it left tooth marks. *Zero, anyway,* thought Perez, *and dropping by the minute.* Ahead, the rough log door of the kitchens jumped at him through the white smother.

Inside he found Lura Collins and accepted the mug of bitter, black coffee she brought him with one of his rare, flashing smiles. While he drank, she sat on the bench across the table from him, her almond-green eyes regarding him steadily.

"I can't eat," said Perez, his black glance returning her stare. "My belly's knotted up like a colicky calf's gut."

"What's eating you, Perez? You look sort of strange, sort of frightened, maybe. I've never seen you frightened. You *are* afraid, aren't you, Pawnee?" Her voice was instantly low, going out to the swart half-breed like a soft, white hand.

"Yes, I'm afraid, ma'am."

"Why? Don't tell me the great Pawnee Perez is afraid of Indians!"

Her eyes needled him with the words, the amber

48

lights in them playing sharply against the green irises. There was something hard about this girl that fascinated Perez. She wasn't like the other women of the fort. To them Pawnee Perez was an evil half-breed, the sort of man one hurried the children past and heard their husbands call "that damn' black 'breed of the colonel's". But to Lura Collins, Perez felt he was something beyond his mixed blood and dark appearance. Not a pretty man, Pawnee Perez, not a nice man. Perhaps even, by white standards, a very inferior man. But to Lura Collins and her kind the world over, such as Perez would always be just one thing—a man.

Lura's life at the fort these six months following the hostile ambush death of her young lieutenant husband had been a strange one. No one knew why she stayed or why she was allowed to stay. The women all felt she had her "nasty green eyes on the colonel's eagles", and consequently gave her a very cold time of it. But the red-haired girl had set about making herself a place on the post. She petted the other women through their cramps, sat with their children, did their fancy sewing, all to such good effect she shortly had the officers' wives wrapped around her slender finger just as she had their husbands captivated by her equally slender figure. Within thirty days of her arrival— Lieutenant Collins having been ambushed by the Sioux while bringing her up from Laramie—she had progressed from the vinegar-tongued description of "that red-headed slut" to the syrupy safety of "that poor, dear Missus Collins".

Watching her now, Perez knew all the excitement of that months-gone day when he had headed the troops sent out to relieve her husband. The relief had come too late to save the young officer, but Perez's arrival *had* saved the lives of his new bride and the escort of eight troopers. Since that time the half-breed and the girl had seen little of each other, but when they did meet, their glances never failed to lock, and, being the kind of a man he was, each time they did, Perez knew he was looking at his kind of woman. Not once had her hot green eyes failed to receive his hard stares with interest.

"Ma'am," the bearded scout spoke at last, "I'll tell you somethin'. That Major Stacey and all the men with him is dead." At the girl's involuntary gasp his thin face twisted. "Shut up. I want ye to listen." She nodded, her slanting eyes wide, full mouth parted. "If Captain Tendrake gets back and brings in this report on Stacey gettin' wiped out, which he will, ma'am, Colonel Fenton's goin' to guardhouse me. I want ye to remember me if that happens."

"What do you mean?" She glanced nervously at the other women. "Please hurry, they're watching us. How can I do anything . . . ?"

"Ye kin do anything you want,"—he paused meaningfully, black eyes glittering as they trapped hers—"with any man on this post."

"Except Colonel Fenton." Lura Collins was returning his stare full measure.

"Except nobody," said Perez. "Jest remember what I said. This place is goin' to be in the middle of hell with the lights turned out . . . and damn' soon! When it is, ye remember Perez."

The girl flushed. "I've got to go. The mother hens are beginning to cluck. Can I get you some more coffee?"

"No. I'm goin' over and camp on Fenton's door stoop. It's four o'clock. If Tendrake's comin' back, it ought to be about now. I want to be there when he makes his talk." Coming up off the bench and around the corner of the plank table in one sinuous move, Perez grabbed the startled girl by the arm. His long fingers clamped into the soft flesh with fierceness. "Remember me!" he said, and was gone even before she knew he had hurt her arm.

IV

Perez had no more left the kitchens when a commotion sprang up along the north stockade. The scout could see nothing, but a lull in the wind brought the deadened reports of three or four shots fired from the top of the stockade. These were answered from outside the fort by a male bovine bellow that could have originated only in the hairy chest of a bull buffalo or the brass-lined lungs of a certain company sergeant. A haunting trace of

Celtic delicacy in the inhuman roar seemed to rule out the buffalo.

"Hold yer fire, you crazy apes! Since when has Crazy Horse been wearin' a sargint's stripes and sportin' hisself a head of short, red hair?"

A minute later Perez was helping force the gates ajar for Sergeant Orin Duffy and his survivors to stagger through. The scout had guessed right about Duffy's attackers leaving him to join the ambush on Stacey. The sergeant had abandoned his wagons, making it in on foot under cover of the storm. A blizzard can be a warm friend as well as a cold enemy, as ten lucky privates and one red-nosed Hibernian sergeant would testify for the rest of their lives.

The gates had scarcely closed on the hay-train survivors when they opened again to admit Captain Tendrake and his fifty infantry, frozen not alone from their twelve-mile march up and back the Virginia City Road. Their frost-rimmed eyes had beheld sights enough to chill every man in the company long past the memory of any storm. Five minutes after their return an exhausted, horrified Captain Tendrake was gritting out the details of his bloody find. Perez was present, as were Sergeants Simpson and Duffy, and Captain Howell.

"When I reached Eagle Point, the snow was only beginning. I could see Squaw Pine Ridge and Peyo Creek Flats. At least two thousand Indians were galloping their horses around on the flats. When they saw us, they set up a howl. We found out soon enough what they were howling about. Two hundred feet down the ridge we found the cavalry, a group of twenty. There were empty cartridge cases heaped around in drifts, and pools of blood, a lot of it apparently Indian blood.

"All the bodies were scalped and mutilated. At this time the hostiles started up the ridge toward us. Two main chiefs led the advance. One, a very big man wearing a scarlet blanket and riding a spotted stallion, the other, a small man, very straight on his horse and dressed in black furs. He was riding Major Stacey's sock-foot bay. I retreated at once. As soon as they saw me get to the ridge top, they split and went down both sides of the ridge, disappearing in the timber.

"I expected an ambush on the way back, but nothing happened. We didn't see an Indian. On the way up, I met Perez, here, who told me he had deserted Stacey before the fight began. He warned me back and told me Stacey would be dead before I reached him. God help you now, Perez!" the captain concluded, turning gray-faced on the scout. "Eighty white men shot and hacked to pieces out there. You left them when you knew what they were going into, when you still might have helped them. The white man doesn't live who could look you in the face after that. May God have mercy on your miserable soul. No man in this fort ever will!"

"Amen," said Perez flatly, the muscles of his jaw clamping shut.

"Glory to God," breathed Sergeant Duffy, "the whole splendid lot ave them byes dead and scalped in the snow."

Realization comes to a dull man slowly, but it comes hard at last. Fenton's question was laced with despair. "Tendrake. Howell. What in God's name are we going to do?"

Captain James Howell, cool and hard as Perez had guessed him, took over. "Put every man on the stockades. Free the prisoners. Arm every man. Packers, clerks, storekeepers. Wire the powder magazine and put the women and children in it. If the hostiles get over the stockade . . . blow the magazine."

"How about this man?" Tendrake's query indicated Perez.

"Him, too!" snapped Howell. "We can worry about his damn' morals later, if we live to do it."

"All right, Howell, let's go." Fenton was getting into his coat. "But Perez is under arrest and that's final. Clear out the guardhouse if you will, but leave him in it."

"Don't be a fool." There are fighting men to whom rank means nothing when the lead starts flying. Howell was one of them. "This man is the best shot in the stockade."

"I won't have him loose in this fort!" shouted Fenton, already at the door. "Lock him up!"

Perez said: "I'd like to fight fer ye, Colonel, and I'd sure hate to be locked up if Crazy Horse gets over the stockade."

"Yes, that's pretty raw even for a half-breed." Howell's sharp agreement sided with the scout.

"Half-breed, whole-breed, what's the difference? This is a treacherous man and I won't trust him again. Lock him up, Howell."

"I'll take him over," Tendrake offered. "Let Howell look to the stockade. I'll get the prisoners out and put Perez away."

"Good. Come on, Howell. Let's go." Fenton's voice crawled higher with tension. Hurrying out the door, however, his eagles banged once more against the captain's bars.

"You get the women and children in the magazine," Howell directed. "I'll see to the walls."

Tendrake turned to Duffy wearily. "Come on, Sergeant, let's take the prisoner over."

Perez had no intention of going into that cell-block. The scout had a normal aversion to dying in any form, but to be cooped up, weaponless, in a six-by-eight cell in a fortress that was liable to be hip-deep in hostiles before the sun got up wasn't his idea of the way to make the big jump. Even as the captain spoke to Duffy, his quick glance darted around the room. But other heads, older in the business of handling harder men than Captain Tendrake's, were in the colonel's office. As Perez's muscles tensed for the lunge at the captain, standing unwarily in the still-open doorway, the scout felt the Colt jam into his back.

"Let's not do it, now, Perez, lad. Go along gentle-like, eh? Shure, I feel sorry fer yez, but orders is orders." The half-breed had some working knowledge of Sergeant Orin Duffy's abilities in a fight; at the same time the tail of his eye caught Sergeant Simpson sliding around Colonel Fenton's desk and picking a Spencer out of the wall rack.

"Let's go." He shrugged resignedly.

"Shure now and that's the way to talk," clucked Duffy. "Yez'll just walk along easy-like and none ave yer Injun tricks, eh, lad?" The sergeant gave the Colt in the scout's back just the nuance of a 200-pound shove. "One little move and yez'll find me finger as light on this trigger as the kiss ave a feather on a virgin's sweet lips!"

"Ye talk a lot, Duffy," grunted Perez, and started moving toward the door. Outside, the scout thought, in the choke of that wind and snow much could happen. It was 100 yards across the parade yard. Many a man's fortune had twisted in ten.

But Perez was wrong. Sergeant Orin Duffy had as heavy a hand as he did a light trigger finger. He kept shoving the Colt so hard into the scout's kidney that Perez feared to make the slightest move other than to keep walking steadily ahead. Inside the prison building, Duffy prodded the scout into the nearest empty cell, refusing even to turn him over to the corporal of the guard.

"Yez just help the captain to release the other prisoners, dearie," he cooed to the corporal. "I'll incarcyrate this little man meself."

Within the cell Perez sighed with relief. "Look, Duffy. One more jab in the kidney with that outsize howitzer of yers and ye'll have me injured inside fer life. Ease off now, eh, friend?"

"Shure, lad." The sergeant's accents were apologetic. "'Tis none ave me doin'. I don't believe yez're the durty slob yez profess to be, but I'm only a sargint."

"Sure, Sergeant. We're friends. Now, ye jest say a couple of Hail Marys fer me."

"Faith now, Mister Perez, yez don't really think the red scuts'll get over, do yez?"

"They kin if they want to."

"The saints pertect us. . . ." Duffy's supplication was rudely interrupted.

"Come on, Sergeant!" Captain Tendrake's irritation was compounded by fatigue. "Let's get these other men out of here. The old man wants them all armed and on the stockade in ten minutes. You and your Sioux friend can continue your love story later."

Perez watched, emotionless, as the two sergeants herded the prisoners out into the snow. Tendrake took even the guard corporal along, leaving the scout with nothing but a forest of iron bars and a sputtering stove fire for company. One look around Fenton's guardhouse was enough to let the prisoner know that Lura Collins was his one hope. It would take a drunken grizzly with a hard hangover and six crowbars the best part of a long winter to crack that cell-block. The half-breed was something of an authority on frontier detention homes, having studied a good many from the inside out. A greased rat couldn't have got out of this one unless he had somebody to give him a shove.

To the frozen watchers on the stockade, it seemed God had forgotten Fort Will Farney. Numbed by the ferocious cold and the crawling memory of Stacey's massacre, the men manned the catwalks and lower rifle slits like cattle awaiting the approach of the slaughterer. The cold itself was an enemy to match any red foe. The instant a man stepped into it, his nostrils were driven flat together and sealed, his mouth literally gasping to get the air in, and then, deprived of any warming progress through the nose passages, the inhalation struck his lungs, frost-cold. Fifty breaths and a man's chest ached so he could hardly draw the fifty-first. Within ten minutes of leaving shelter, his hands were numb to the wrists and his feet were frozen stumps upon which his best progress could be a lurching, blind stumble. In twenty, the frost had gone to his shoulders and knees, leaving him to clump along the icy catwalks like an armless stilt walker.

No soldier could stand more than thirty minutes of such exposure and control his actions. In such temperatures a man could barely hold onto a rifle, let alone operate one. And there was a tragic joker in this cold deck—Fenton's fuel supply was dangerously low. The Sioux had caught him with barely half his winter's wood hauled in. He had plenty to keep the kitchens and main barracks going for a week. After that, providing they hadn't found a quicker way meantime, the hostiles only had to wait for their ice-bellied ally, *Wasiya*, to reduce the garrison for them.

This and other pleasant prospects gamboled lightly through the colonel's mind as he and his officers huddled in the watch hut at the north gates.

"What time is it, now?" Fenton directed the question aimlessly.

"Two a.m.," answered Captain Howell.

"Eight hours since Tendrake got back. No sign of the Sioux yet!" The colonel did his best to find a little fun in the fact. The others failed to take fire.

"And none of your missing scout, either. I guess the half-breed was right about him, anyway." This was from Howell.

"He was right about Stacey, too." Tendrake's interpretation was bitter.

"He's been right about most things he's anteed up on since I've been on this post," said Howell bluntly.

"Yes, he has," agreed Fenton seriously. "But you can't trust him apparently."

"Appearances have hanged many an innocent man." Howell was passing rank again. "He's half Indian and doesn't see things our way. That doesn't make him wrong. Personally I think he sees them a lot better. I still think he ought to be out here with a gun in his hand."

"If I let him out, he'd be just as apt to go over the stockade and join the hostiles. We can't chance that. He knows the fort by heart."

"Oh, hell," Howell said vehemently. "You've let Stacey poison you on the man. I trust I don't belittle the major's memory when I remind you he conducted himself like a fool today. It's clear he bolted his orders and bears full responsibility for the loss of his command. No thinking man could seriously suspect Perez had anything to do with that ambush. He certainly didn't ask to go along! No, sir. The 'breed was just too smart to go down the ridge with Stacey. If it's a crime not to be a damn' fool, Perez is guilty."

Fenton was too confused to rise to this challenge of his opinion. He barged ahead with his own lead-footed line of thought. "Perez thought we should get dispatch riders off for Muleshoe Creek before the Sioux got into position around the fort. But, damn it, we haven't even seen an Indian. I can't be calling up relief from Fort Loring for a siege that hasn't even started. They'd laugh me out of the service." As he went along, the fort commander began to listen to his own arguments. "Why, I'll wager the Sioux have already retired, gone north, or wherever Clanton said their damn' camp was."

"I'll go with you on that." Tendrake's support was more hopeful than reasonable. "This whole thing will blow over with the storm."

"Sorry, gentlemen." Howell was a taciturn, bitter man, an extremely competent officer who had been on the frontier longer than either Tendrake or Fenton. "Your conclusions are dead wrong. It's already too late to get a rider out."

"What the devil are you talking about, Howell? You haven't given up, have you?"

"Not quite, Colonel," replied the young officer grimly. "But half an hour ago, when I came on watch, God hauled off and gave me a look at something."

"Such as?" Tendrake crowded him tersely.

"One of those freak clear spots broke a hole in the storm. For a minute or two I could see black sky and stars for about two-thirds of the compass, southeast, south, southwest."

"Well, what of it?" Colonel Fenton was cracking a bit.

"Well, black sky and stars wasn't all I saw. Smoke, too, gentlemen. Lots of it. As far as I saw, thin spirals and wisps of it. Blue-gray. Wood smoke. The kind that crawls up out of Sioux lodge

61

smoke holes on just such a fine winter's evening. We're surrounded."

"Oh, my God!" exploded Tendrake. "That finishes us."

"There's a chance for outside help!" Fenton's surprising statement jumped with hope.

"How so?" Howell queried.

"I just remembered Bailey and O'Connor. They're sure to stop at Muleshoe Creek and telegraph Colonel Boynton at Fort Loring. Surely they'd think of that. Don't you agree, Howell? Why, Boynton may just have started a column up on a hunch!"

"It won't wash, Colonel." Howell was curt. "Providing Boynton thought anything of it when he got it, he'd still be awaiting a confirmation of it. Don't forget the dear old Army, sir. Three copies of everything and a brigadier's signature before a corporal can go to the latrine."

"It's our only chance," muttered Fenton peevishly.

"Our only chance," Howell contradicted him, "is still that chance to get a rider out. We can hang on here for a week likely. Maybe a day longer. If a rider could get through, we'd have a chance. It's a hell of a chance, I'll admit."

"I won't order any man on that ride, Howell, and, if I did, how would you propose to make him go? Any man in his right mind would rather be shot than fall into the hands of the hostiles. And beyond the Indians, what about that blizzard out there? It's a hundred and ninety miles to Muleshoe Creek Station. In this weather any order to try and ride there would be a death sentence. Have you looked at a thermometer in the last hour?"

"Thirty below when I came in. But if it was ninety below, somebody's got to make that ride. If you won't order a man, we'll have to ask for volunteers. There's a lot of men in this stockade, Colonel, with wives and children sitting in the magazine. You'll get your volunteer."

Fenton was silent a moment before announcing wearily: "All right. Call a muster of the sergeants for ten minutes. In the kitchens. I'll see you there."

With the older man gone, Captain Tendrake turned to his companion. "You won't get your volunteer, Jim. Every man in this fort is scared blue clear down to his frozen toenails. And that goes for me, too."

"Come on." Howell's order was abrupt. "Let's get those sergeants in to the old man. You got the east wall. I'll take the west."

"Right," snapped Tendrake. "See you inside."

Colonel Fenton and his two captains waited impatiently in the kitchens. The sergeants had been briefed and sent out, Duffy being detailed to bring back their report. The minutes stretched from ten to fifteen to twenty, and still no Duffy. In half an hour he stomped in, hoarfrost and caked snow encrusting every inch of his figure. "Faith and bejabbers if that thermometer on the north gate ain't standin' at forty below! Holy Mither, what a fine night fer a massacree."

"Faith, and you weren't sent out to check the temperature," Captain Howell mimicked.

Duffy stood irresolute, head bowed, fur cap in hand. "Sure, now, yez can't blame the lads. 'Tis a-howlin' awful. . . ."

"No takers, is that it, Sergeant?"

"That's it, sir. There ain't an enlisted man in the fort to do yer ridin' fer you. We checked them all . . . twice."

"Well!" The captain's laugh was short. "That leaves us."

"It leaves you," said Tendrake unhesitatingly. "I wouldn't leave this fort for all the wives and children in Wyoming."

"And I can't," added Fenton dully.

"Well I can, and I will." Howell's reaction carried no heroics. "How about it, Colonel?"

"No. You know better than that. I don't even appreciate the offer. I can't spare you."

"Then there's no one to go and we can sit and wait for Crazy Horse to come and get us."

"That's it, Captain. We sit and wait. There's no one to go and. . . ."

The interruption came in the low voice of Lura Collins. The girl had refused to share the shelter of the powder magazine with the other women, prevailing on Colonel Fenton with the claim her presence in the kitchens would serve to keep more than the coffee warm. Now, unnoticed, she had come up to stand behind the officers. "You're forgetting someone, Colonel."

Fenton looked up, annoyed. "Oh, hello, Missus Collins. No coffee, thank you. We. . . ."

"What did you say, ma'am?" Captain Howell ignored his superior, shooting his question directly to the girl.

"You've forgotten the best man on the post, Captain." The slanting, green eyes were wide, the petulant mouth parted with excitement.

"You mean Perez?"

"Naturally. He's just a half-breed, of course,"— Lura Collins let the words fall with scalding deliberation—"but he's a man. He'll make your ride for you. Unless, of course, the competition is limited to pure breds."

No one answered the girl, the silence following her caustic outburst serving only to highlight the mutterings of the fire at the far end of the room and the howl of the blizzard outside.

∨

That blizzard of 1866 carried many a two-legged destiny in its frozen belly—and one four-legged one. In his deep-strawed box stall, Kentucky Boy stirred restlessly. The big stallion was used to the royal treatment that went with being the C.O.'s personal mount, and now he wasn't getting it. Kentucky Boy was a bluegrass Thoroughbred, a tall, flashy, blood bay, sixteen hands at the withers, deep through the heart, big-barreled, long-ribbed, short-backed. A hot-blooded horse, Kentucky Boy, 1,300 pounds of line-bred bone, muscle, satin skin, clean limbs, powerful body, a violent-tempered brute, nervous, taut, willful, withal a man's horse, iron-jawed, velvet-mouthed, with lungs as big as a fierce, vain, six-year-old stud horse, with a twenty-foot stride and the bred-in bottom to hold on it till heart broke or arteries burst.

The big bay stud had not been ridden in three days, or fed in the past twenty-four hours. He missed his groom, his rolled oats, bran, currycomb, workouts. His normal bad temper was inflamed to the point of fury. He slammed the thin bar plates on his rear heels repeatedly into the sides of the stall, lashed out at the stable door with angry forehoofs, bit savagely at the wood of his manger, kicked his water bucket three times around the stall, stomped it flat with jabbing, forehoof blows. After that, he just stood there, spraddle-legged, ears back, eyes rolling, blasting the quiet of the stable building with a series of whistling stallion neighs.

He whistled in vain, for outside the storm whistled louder. His challenge went unheard. Outside, every human ear was bent to receive another, fiercer challenge—the war cry of the High Plains Sioux.

Kentucky Boy stopped neighing and listened. A half dozen answering whinnies echoed down the line of coarse-headed cavalry geldings, and then nothing. The stallion snorted, then fell to pacing his stall, whickering nervously. Beyond his split-log stable, a two-legged animal was putting her white shoulder to the course of destiny, turning its path aside, twisting it straight around for the stall door of Fort Will Farney's final and four-legged chance.

Lura Collins came into the guardhouse quickly, the sucking force of the following wind slamming the door behind her with bar-rattling force. "*Hohahe!*" Perez greeted her in Sioux, grinning. "Welcome to my teepee! What time is it?"

"About three a.m. I brought you some coffee."

"Meat, too, I see. Put it on the table there, and get me out of here. Keys are in the guard desk, top drawer. Hurry up."

"I didn't come to get you out, Pawnee. I. . . ."

"Get those keys, girl." The half-breed's eyes were slitted. "Ye're not goin' to let Perez die in here."

"No, I know that." The admission was helpless, the long-lashed eyes lingering on the scout. "And so do you, Pawnee."

"Ye bet I do. Get those keys."

Shrugging off her heavy wrap, the girl searched the desk. "They aren't here, Perez!"

"Grab that carbine outen the guard rack. Pass it in here." The three shots reverberated dully in the empty building. Perez stepped through the gunsmoke, grabbed the food, began wolfing it. Sailing the lid of the coffee pot across the room, he gulped directly from the steaming container. "Now, listen," he grunted between smacking mouthfuls, "and listen good."

The girl nodded, breathless.

"Ye get outen here, right now. Get me gloves and grub, fur gloves and about four pounds of jerky. Some hardtack, too. I want some of Fenton's coats. There's two or three hanging in his office. I want a garrison hat like he wears. That's the winter blue, with the earflaps. Fenton don't drink, but ye've got to get me whiskey. Try Howell's quarters. He 'pears man enough to handle a bottle. Put it in a canteen, all ye kin get. One other thing. I want a bucket of hot water. Ye got all that?"

"Gloves, coat, hat, hot water, jerky . . . ," gasped the girl.

"And whiskey!" snapped Perez. "Fer God's sake, don't ferget the whiskey!" Barking his words, the scout gave her the layout of the stables. "There's two rows of single stalls, tack room, a big box fer the colonel's hoss, that big Thoroughbred. Ye got that, now?"

"You mean Kentucky Boy?" The girl's eyes were dark with excitement.

"That's the hoss. Kin ye get down there with all that gear in ten minutes?"

"I'll do it." The pretty face was suddenly hard. "I'll do it, Perez!"

"Ye better"—the scout flashed her a grimace— "or the next hand on that white bustle of yours is liable to be a red one."

Lura Collins blanched. "Why, you dirty, foul-mouthed half-br. . . ."

"Don't say it," rasped Perez. "Call me a half-breed and I'll smash yer pale face up ag'in' that wall." The scout's thin jaw was writhing, his eyes glittering. "I can't take that from ye, girl!" He had her, then, his long hands clamping her arms close up to the shoulders, cruel thumbs and fingers meeting and locking in the warm prisons of her armpits.

"Perez! Don't!" The cry was one of real fear. "You're tearing my skin. Please!"

He stood back, the breath whistling in his nostrils, head bowed, face dark-flushed. A second fled, then another. He didn't look up until he heard the first sob. When he did look, he saw the bare whiteness of her arm where his grasp had shredded the cheap linen blouse, the blue of the bruising finger marks already darkening. He saw, too, the mouth-parted expression of fear, the shadow of pain darkening the green eyes, the bright glitter of a tear as it hesitated under the curling lash.

"Ma'am . . . God help me, I love ye."

"Perez!"

69

"I know. Ye don't need to tell me. But I'm glad ye never said it. Ye jest ferget what I said. A man gets crazy around a girl like ye, that's all. Good bye, ma'am. I'm goin' out of this fort fer keeps. Ye needn't mind gettin' the things. I'll get them."

The girl's voice was defiant. "You said ten minutes. I'll be there. I owe you my life and I'm paying off. I'll be there and I'll have the things. But I'm sorry I said what I did about you to Colonel Fenton and the officers."

"What do ye mean, ma'am?" The question came with the old, purring quietness.

"I mean I told them there was one man in the fort with guts enough to ride this blizzard. To get to Muleshoe Creek Station and telegraph Fort Loring for help. There wasn't a man in the fort who would volunteer to do it. I told them you would. I shamed them with you." The lash of the girl's voice curled back on herself. "I thought I knew men!" She paused, all the anger gone out of her. When she spoke again, her voice was toneless. "God forgive me, Perez, I thought I knew you."

The half-breed looked at her a long three seconds. "I thought ye did, too, ma'am," he said, and turned quickly from the door.

The girl's shoulders straightened, her head swinging up, startle-faced, the soft-thrown stone of his statement beginning to widen the green pools of her eyes with the spreading rings of its implications. "Pawnee. Oh, Pawnee, I'm sorry!"

70

But the half-breed's expression had gone dead. Shouldering the guardhouse door open against the blast of the wind, he murmured: "Don't ferget the hot water, ma'am. It's fer the hoss."

Perez had never had his hands on Kentucky Boy, but the horse had yet to be foaled that the Pawnee half-breed couldn't make a kitten of in five minutes. When Lura entered the stall, the stud was nuzzling the scout as though the latter had bottle-broken him away from his dam's milk.

"I thought this was a bad hoss." The half-breed grinned as Lura came in. "The damn' fool's actin' like I'd had him since he quit shovin' his mammy's bag."

"He's a man's horse," said the girl, dumping her burdens in the straw. "You can't fool a horse about a man. They know a man even if some people don't." Her last words were humble. Perez didn't miss their meaning.

"Don't worry about that, ma'am. I reckon we don't know yet who's right, the hoss or the people."

"I know, Perez." Her eyes were on him again. "And this time I'll never forget it."

"Ye didn't bring the water." The man ignored her statement and the sweeping look that went with it.

"Right here," she said, ducking out the stall door to return with the water. "I had to put it down to get in."

The half-breed talked fast, his words as lean as

the jaw which housed them. "Dump that bran in the water and mix it up. Start bucket-feedin' him while I get the saddle on. He'll eat better with somebody holdin' the bucket. He's rotten-spoiled."

The girl fed the horse the steaming bran while Perez cinched the saddle tight. When he had the girth up where he wanted it, he dived under the manger to reappear with two Indian parfleches, a Winchester, two Colts, a long Sioux skinning knife. "My fixin's," he told the girl shortly. "Had to get them out of scout quarters. Run into Duffy on the way out."

"What?" Lura asked apprehensively.

"We'll have to jump it. Duffy was jest goin' up onto the north gate and that changes things. I've got to go out that gate. Duffy won't set still fer havin' any whizzer like the colonel's coat run on him."

"Perez! What are you going to do?"

By this time the scout had laced the parfleches behind the saddle, rammed the Winchester into the scabbard, buckled on the Colts. "Can't do anything but run a cold bluff. Put the jerky and hardtack in that left parfleche. Got any whiskey in that canteen?"

"Yes."

"How much bran left?"

"He's eaten about half of it."

"Pour a big jolt of whiskey into what's left."

Lura followed his instructions while Perez dived under the manger once again, slipping back out with his wolf-skin coat and a heavy canvas bag. As he emptied the bag into the right parfleche, the girl noted the flashing stream of the copper-jacketed contents. "Courtesy of the Sixteenth U.S. Infantry, Colonel Harry J. Fenton, commanding." The grin was wide. "Ye got that whiskey-bran down that hoss?"

Lura nodded, upending the empty bucket to show him. The scout nodded back, slid around under Kentucky Boy's neck, a braided Indian hackamore in his hand. The girl's eyes widened.

"You're not going to ride him with a hackamore!"

"Ma'am, he's got a mouth as soft as a baby goat's nose. He could be rode with nothin', but this is jest to let him think he's got a bridle on. I don't want any kind of a bit in his mouth when he starts breathin' rough."

"Perez, how far is it to Muleshoe Creek?"

"Hundred and ninety mile. Why?"

"Do you think he can make it?"

"I reckon. If he don't die, meantime. He's the most hoss ever I see."

"Oh, Pawnee. He's so beautiful. I. . . ."

"Don't worry about the hoss, ma'am. He'll go the distance."

"How about you, Pawnee?"

"Me, too." The scout nodded succinctly. "If I kin keep my hair on."

"You will . . . oh, Perez, you will!"

73

"Yeah, I allow I will. Wouldn't be tryin' it otherwise. All right, Boy," he soothed the horse, making the last slide-knot adjustment on the check braid, "now ye got plenty of mouth. Let's make long tracks away from here. Get the door, girl."

Turning with the words, the scout bumped into Lura Collins standing close behind him, arms half reaching, mouth parted curvingly. "I said, get the door, ma'am. Time's runnin' out on me." The girl stood, motionless, her long, green eyes sweeping his dark face, her body so close to his the warmth of it came to him even through the deep wolf skin.

"It's running out on both of us, Pawnee." Her voice was lower than a wind whisper in a willow grove, her eyes burning up at him in the stable gloom. With the words the perfume of her came clouding around the bearded half-breed, a dizzying, sudden, female fragrance. It was in his nose. He was tasting it on his lips.

"We'll see if we can't stop it fer five minutes." The phrase came guttural as a bear's growl, the reaching arms with it cording into her soft back with paralyzing force.

"Ah, no, Pawnee . . . Pawnee, don't. Please . . . please. . . ." The lips that crushed off the words were as hard as the hands which held her. . . .

Sergeant Orin Duffy sat hunched in the guard hut at the north gate, contemplating the manly rigors of stockade life. His watch companion, Corporal

74

Sam Boone, had just departed kitchenward for another pot of hot coffee. Alone for the moment, the sergeant, for lack of better company, was talking to himself.

"Faith, now, Duffy, me lad, yez had best be composin' yer talk with the Lord. With Father Flannagan down to Fort Lorin' fer the winter there's no one but yerself to do it. And with them haythin Sioux squattin' around yez like buffler wolves waitin' fer a sick cow to freeze to death, who else is goin' to axminster Extreme Unction? No one, Orin, me lad. Yez had best be thinkin' ave yer sins. Now, let me see. There wuz that Comanche girl down in Fort Riley last summer, but shure the Lord don't count them haythin conquests. Then there was Kelly's colleen. But then, faith, I wuz that drunk I didn't recognize the girl till Dennis lowered the boom. Ah! Macushla Machree! 'Tis somethin' awful fer yez to be sittin' here. Orin, me bye, with no prayst within two hundred miles. . . ."

"Shall we pray now, Duffy?" The cynical question jumped the sergeant's nerves.

"Damn yer black soul, Perez! Comin' sneakin' in on a man like that. Why didn't you knock?"

"Indians never do," grunted the scout. "Come on. Help me get this gate open. I'm goin' out."

"The hell yez are! Whut fer?"

"Colonel Fenton's sendin' me to try and get through to Muleshoe Creek."

"God in hivvin, yez don't mean it?"

"Sure. What the hell do ye think he let me outen the pokey fer? Good behavior?"

"I dunno. Last I heard, he wuz goin' to keep yez in there till Satan shook hands with Saint Peter."

"Well, he changed his mind. It's an old woman's privilege. I'm ridin' out. Come on."

"Did the colonel give yez a pass, now?"

Perez sensed the crafty change in the voice, tensed accordingly. "Duffy, ye've slipped your head hobbles. Do I usually get passed out fer to go on a scout?"

"This is different. Captain Howell sez nobody cracks them gates to so much as spit out ave without a pass from Colonel Fenton."

"All right, Sergeant," the scout bluffed, "ye wait right here while I amble back and have the old man scribble ye out a nice long set of instructions. I'm sure he'll be delighted havin' his dispatch held up while yer touchin' devotion to Howell's orders is satisfied. If I know Fenton, he'll be tickled to know Captain Howell has taken over the command. I'll be back. . . ."

"Ah, well, now, Perez, lad. Hold up there. On second thought maybe yez have a point. The ould man ain't in the mood to. . . ."

"Ye bet he ain't. Let's go."

"Yes, sir." Duffy was heading for the hut door. "Don't let me detain yez."

Outside Duffy put his shoulder to the stockade

76

gate. Glancing around, seeing no mount, he queried: "Ye're not goin' afoot, are yez, man?"

"I got my hoss back of the hut here. Give me about four foot of openin' there."

"God rest yer soul, bye!" Duffy shouted as the wind boomed in through the crack in the opening barrier. "Yez'll never make Muleshoe Crick in this weather."

"Not if ye intend standin' there wobblin' yer big Irish jaw all night!" the scout shouted back, bringing Kentucky Boy out from behind the watch hut. "Get the hell outen that gate, Duffy. We're comin' through." As the scout spoke, the sergeant turned from the opened gate, noticing the horse for the first time.

"Wait up, lad." His brogue went soft. "Ain't that Kentucky Bye yez're leadin'?"

"Colonel Fenton. . . ."

"Colonel Fenton never lets anybody ride that horse. Yez'll have to get a pass, Perez."

"I've got it right here, Duffy." The scout moved easily toward the soldier, reaching inside the wolf-skin coat as he went.

"Kape yer hand out ave that coat." Duffy clubbed his carbine threateningly.

"Whatever ye say, Sergeant." The hand came up and away from the coat with looping speed. Duffy threw up his arms protectively, but a man doesn't move fast when he has been on watch half an hour with the temperature standing at forty degrees below. The Colt barrel flashed into the side of his head with a ringing crack, and Perez stepped back to let the non-com's body slide forward into the snow. "Easy, Boy, easy," the half-breed soothed the plunging Thoroughbred. "Like as not ye'll see other bodies in the snow this side of Muleshoe."

Swiftly retrieving the sergeant's carbine, slinging it over his own shoulder, Perez wondered what he was going to do about the unconscious Duffy. Left as he was, he would freeze to death in ten minutes. At the same time Perez couldn't risk taking him back to quarters. As he hesitated, a looming figure bulked up out of the storm.

"Hey, is that you, Duffy?"

"Who's there?" The scout parroted the Irish sergeant's thick tongue.

"Sam Boone. Whar's the damn' gate? Ah've lost ye ag'in."

"This way, Sam."

"Say, Sarge, you ain't seen that half-breed, have you?" The corporal talked as he came along. "He done busted out and stole the colonel's hoss. Thet gal he'ped him. Stable sergeant caught her comin' outen Kentucky Boy's stall. He jest herded her into the kitchens as Ah was comin' away with the cawfee."

"Faith, now, Sam. Jest kape comin' with that cawfee. I feel real faint. In fact, me bye"—the scout's dark face lit up—"yez'll find me ignarunt body a-lyin' in the snow where Perez knocked me thick head in. And please close the blasted door after him. The haythin scut haz done left it wide open behind him."

By the time he called the last words, Perez had the horse out the gate. Throwing a last glance back through the narrow opening, he saw Corporal Boone stumble over the prostrate form of Sergeant Duffy, heard him curse as he discovered its identity, waited only long enough to see the tall hill man come running toward the open gate.

Seconds before Corporal Sam Boone reached the stockade opening, the swirling snows closed behind the rump of Kentucky Boy. The puzzled soldier peered strainingly out into white nothingness. Even as his quick eye picked them up, the double line of tracks, man's and horse's, leading away from the gates, faded under the shifting drive of the piling snows.

Fifty yards out Perez began circling the stockade from the north gates around to the south wall. Here he turned due south, still leading Kentucky Boy, still stepping each step as cautiously as though it had been high noon of a clear autumn day. He did not expect to encounter any hostiles abroad. It was somewhere between 4:00 a.m. and 5:00 a.m., the temperature hovering near fifty degrees below. The wind that had been screaming crazily for twelve hours had suddenly fallen away to a ghost's whisper. The snow fell straight down.

Perez picked his way, cat-footed, through the

whiteness. Every feathery bush and loaded tree branch, the unwary jarring of which might unloose a telltale downslide of piled snow, was fastidiously avoided. Behind the scout, blowing softly, enjoying the bite of the keen air in his belling nostrils, Kentucky Boy stepped as gingerly as a buck deer with wolf smell in his nose. This was a new game, very fascinating. Keep your neck stretched out, follow the man. That was apparently the idea.

Perez figured that, next to women, horses were the nosiest creatures in the world. And he knew that the surest way to arouse the curiosity of either was to ignore them. The furtive actions of the man ahead of him excited Kentucky Boy's inquisitiveness. His reaching nose hung on the tail of the scout's wolf coat like a Walker or Blue Tick hound following a fox-drag. Horse-wise, the half-breed never looked back, only clucking softly now and again when the big stud walked up too close on him.

When he had counted a thousand steps south, Perez nose-wrapped the tall Thoroughbred, gentling and whispering to him the while. Then they went forward again, caution redoubled.

The half gloom of coming daylight was beginning to penetrate the blackness of the blizzard and they were getting into a belt of timber at about that distance from the fort where the scout calculated to find the Sioux lodges, if indeed he found them at all. He had no knowledge of Captain Howell's spotting of the lodge smokes, but had unknowingly placed the location of the teepees almost exactly. "If we kin get another mile without walkin' into somebody's teepee flap," he whispered to the curious Thoroughbred, "we kin mount up and make our run fer it."

But the half-breed knew he faced a greater danger than stumbling into the hostile lodges, a danger made vastly more imminent by virtue of Kentucky Boy's being a stud—the Indian pony herd! The red men always placed themselves between their enemies and their own precious horse herd, hence Perez's certain knowledge that once he got past the lodges his biggest danger lay still ahead. Walking into a harebrained covey of half-wild Indian mounts in company with an eye-rolling studhorse of Kentucky Boy's evil virility would be about as entertaining as leading a cross-bred collie into a cavvy of house cats. The half-breed had no illusions about what would happen should any such equine symptom develop. Trying to hang onto 1,300 pounds of hot-blooded Kentucky stud, while he was simultaneously trying to cover every broomtail mare and kill every scrabby stallion in sight, would add up to a very short ride for Pawnee Perez.

The scout grinned mirthlessly at the thought. Oh, well. With any kind of luck, they'd get over the next mile without bumping into either lodge line or pony herd. As it happened, luck was looking the other way—and so was Perez.

The first warning was an explosive snort from Kentucky Boy, the kind of nose-cleaning blast that always follows a horse's getting his first whiff of something he doesn't like. Perez was under the stallion's neck in an instant, holding his head hard down. But the damage was done. Off to the right came an answering snort, followed by two or three inquiring whickers. The next moment a single file of mounted warriors shadowed up through the slanting snows. The braves had apparently not heard Kentucky Boy's snort, but were nevertheless on the alert because of the nervousness of their own mounts. They passed so close to Perez he could hear the grunting and breathing of the ponies, the muted jingle of the frozen harness, the guttural conversation of the riders.

"I heard something."

"So did I."

"Aye. Me, too. It was over this way."

"It sounded like a horse."

"It was a buck deer. I know their snort. It was a buck, that's all."

"Wi Sapa is a wise mare. She doesn't whinny at bucks."

"Ha! That mare is stud crazy. She would neigh at a mouse if she thought he could service her."

"Shut up!" The warning came hissing from the last rider in line, a handsome, dark chief whose black horse now came bulking up out of the snow mists. "Nothing could be heard with you *heyokas* yammering like curs over a string of buffalo guts. Sit still and listen."

The line halted abreast of and about ten yards out from Perez's hiding place. The scout held his own breath, Kentucky Boy's nose, Duffy's carbine. Had he had a third, spare hand, he would have been holding something else just for luck. If Perez had a God, he was talking to him just then. Very earnestly. Those ponies out there were warm. As they stood, the smoke curled off their gaunt flanks and steamed from their nostrils in spurting plumes. This would mean they had been out on patrol, were returning, that the lodges lay somewhere close at hand. As if this weren't enough, the snowfall slacked momentarily, letting still more daylight down through the storm, allowing the scout to see the whole line of waiting warriors. For the first time he got a good look at the chief on the black horse, a look which clamped his hard-held breathing yet tighter: Nakpa Kesela, American Horse, the number-three war chief.

The shock of this revelation for Perez lay not in the chief's reputation, but in the fact his identity let the scout know what kind of a horse he sat. Usually the Indians favored geldings for war-party work. Mares, if very well trained and not horsing, were sometimes employed, stallions almost never. The latter's eagerness to challenge or court, as the sex of the enemy's mount might dictate, was too much of a hazard for any but a very great warrior.

American Horse was unquestionably a great warrior, and the nervous black brute he bestrode was unquestionably a stallion.

Luck, an iron hand, and the fact that none of the mares in the hostile patrol were horsing had allowed Perez to keep Kentucky Boy quiet up to this point. But if the Thoroughbred winded that black stud, the fat was not only in the fire, but burned till hell wouldn't have it. The half-breed tightened his hold on his luck. He didn't tighten it quite enough.

American Horse sat his mount for a long twenty seconds. During the silence it seemed to the scout the blizzard itself stopped breathing. Finally the chief put his heels into the black, sending him up the line of standing ponies on Perez's side.

Just before the chief drew even with the half-breed's cover, his deep voice grunted. "*Hopo. Hookahey.* Let's go!" Never was command so enthusiastically obeyed. Everything—Indians, mares, geldings, stallions, scout, and chief—went at once.

Kentucky Boy bombarded out of the spruce clump that had shielded him and Perez, showering snow all over the six nearest Indians. As he went, Perez with him, fists knotted in the waving mane, legs catapulting him onto the charging bay's back. He made no attempt to head the crazy animal, letting him career full-tilt into the war chief's black. Nearly three-quarters of a ton of grain-fed

Thoroughbred hit 800 pounds of winter-thin Indian pony, massive shoulder to scrawny rump, and the result was inevitable. The squealing black went jughead over flailing heels into the snow, American Horse somewhere in the leg-threshing mess with him. Kentucky Boy, instead of tarrying to make a fight of it, kept right on going—for a notably sharp reason.

As he had swung up on the plunging stud, Perez had flashed the long skinning knife from beneath his wolf-skin coat. As Kentucky Boy slammed into the Indian pony, the scout had slammed the knife into Kentucky Boy: not once, but three, four, five times, the driving blade whipping into the startled bay's rump. The impetus of the stinging slashes carried the big horse squarely over his fallen foe and right on through the scattering line of the hostile patrol.

Pawnee Perez was not the boy to linger, monkey-a-horseback, in the middle of a studhorse fight when a keen knife and a hard arm could get him elsewhere, especially when he had 190 miles to ride with such a charming farewell committee to speed him on the first lap of it. Turning in the saddle, Perez threw back his head and let out the long-drawn, wolf-howl victory call of the Pony Stealer People. Behind him, as the bay stallion flattened into his stride, he could hear the sounds of the gathering pursuit, sounds that were the least of his immediate worries. The Indian pony hadn't been dropped which could catch this big horse under him. After the first thirty jumps the scout pulled the bay down to a hard gallop.

Definite light was coming now, gray and sick through the blizzard's shroud. This light, moments later, guided him through the sleeping lodges of the Oglala siege lines. A few early-rising oldsters, toting in wood for the morning's cooking fires, were the only witnesses to the half-breed's dash through the camp. These scattered wildly for the shelter of the nearest lodge, and, as the bay cleared the last of the teepees, Perez threw another derisive wolf howl at them.

VI

The short break in the weather the early morning of the twenty-second closed like a trap behind the half-breed as he left the Indian village. All that day and the following night he rode south in a freezing blackness that scarcely varied with coming dawn or departing daylight. Twice he stopped to dry-feed the blowing stallion, carefully rationing him with the rolled oats which mingled with his own hardtack and jerky in the left parfleche. The second day and night went as the first, and after them the third day.

That ride of Pawnee Perez, south from Fort Will Farney through the blind gut of a north-plains blizzard, must remain at once a pride and mystery to the West. Horses and men will circle in a blizzard, but Kentucky Boy and the half-breed rode a line as straight as a surveyor's chain. Seventy-two hours, one hundred and ninety miles, one horse, one man, no fires built, hardtack, jerky, dry oats, and snow— that was the way of it.

Senses are lost in a blizzard and instincts smothered in the careening darkness. Nostrils are riveted shut, eyes, mouth, and nose jammed and plugged with frozen snow. And always the incessant yelping and bawling of the wind, screaming at a man, slashing at a horse, buffeting, hammering, pushing, twisting, till the rider's brain is reeling from the sheer force of its constant driving. No wonder the West still marvels at that ride, at the sheer guts of one man and one horse, a sullen man of uncertain pedigree, a blue-blood Kentucky racer, strange companions, indeed, to ride one of the greatest of frontier history's forgotten trails. Had Pawnee Perez been a white man, you would know his name as you do Custer's or Kit Carson's, but history has no use for half-breeds. . . .

It was the third day. Perez, feeling the dropping bite of the temperature, knew the sun was gone, another night crowding in on him. Suddenly, through an uplifting swirl of snow, Muleshoe Creek loomed ahead. The scout knew that ford where the Virginia City Road crossed the stream as you would your back yard. Beyond it, still invisible behind the sheeting snow, would lie the log hut and huddled corral of the telegraph station.

Now was the time for a man to get off his horse and walk softly. If there was any place on the Virginia Road better suited for a Sioux ambush, Perez didn't know of it. The Indians would probably have that station covered like a blanket. Still, with the snow as heavy as it was, a man ought to be able to sneak in all right. Biggest danger would be getting shot by the jumpy troopers manning the tiny post.

Perez eased down off Kentucky Boy. They had made it! The thought leaped through him with electrifying warmth. They had broken through Crazy Horse's hostiles. They had lasted out the cold. They had beaten both the Indians and the blizzard.

Perez was not a pleasant man, but the grin that cracked the frost-bitten face at the sight of the Muleshoe Crossing was one of rare happiness. Beyond that ford lay fire and food and a warm bed for him, hot bran and a cozy stall for the great horse that trembled so violently beside him. More important: beyond that ford lay the wireless that would flash the news of Fort Farney's disaster to the waiting troops in Fort Loring, the troops already alerted no doubt by the earlier message that Bailey and O'Connor must have sent, the troops that would come snow-plowing up the Virginia City Road to reach Colonel Fenton's besieged garrison just before life and death to the strange red-haired girl whose passionate promises he had carried away with him.

Perez thought only of Lura Collins as he went stumbling down toward the ford. She had made him know a happiness that made the frozen stump of his left foot a mere inconvenience, the frost-dull hands and face simple injuries to be borne with a short grin and a shrug. She had been his woman and she was going to be his woman. That had been her promise to him when he'd left her. That was all that mattered now—that and the unbearable fact that she was a white woman!

Behind the scout, Kentucky Boy staggered, half blind with fatigue. Once he stumbled to his knees and would have gone down, but the man was instantly there, holding his head up, clucking to him in an outlandish tongue. *"H'g'un. H'g'un.* Come on, Boy. *Hopo. Hookahey. Owamyeke waste.* We're there, sweetheart. Co-o-o, Boy. Get up. *Hun-hun-he!* Easy, easy. . . ." The big stud was up then, lurching along, head literally on the man's shoulder, eyes glazing, protruding tongue lolling between yellow teeth.

They were across the creek, going up the far bank. They had made it, man and horse. Perez had the wolf grin working overtime. Kentucky Boy sensed the triumph working in the man, perked his halting footsteps in response.

A low hummock of snow appeared in the trail ahead. In wearily avoiding it, the scout stumbled,

went sprawling, face down, over a second hummock hidden behind the first. With tired curiosity,
Kentucky Boy reached down to sniff at the
obstacle that had tripped up his rider. His black
muzzle, idly pushing aside the crusted snow,
became still. The thin nostrils flared as the scent
got into them. Uprearing, the stallion lunged back
and away from the still, white mound, eyes rolling,
ears pinned.

Perez, coming up out of the snow in time to
observe the horse's spookiness, reached over to
brush the snow from the spot the animal had been
nuzzling. The scout's narrow eyes widened
slightly. "Dirty Charley" Bailey had never been the
half-breed's idea of a pretty man. Even so,
observing him thoughtfully at the moment, Perez
decided he had looked much better with his hair
on.

There was no need to question that first mound
now, but the scout did so perfunctorily. Beaver
O'Connor didn't look any better than Bailey,
having even a cruder haircut. That job was done
either in the dark or in a hurry, mused Perez, for a
considerable patch of the scout's sandy scalp lock
had survived the lifting, to dangle rakishly over his
wide-open left eye.

"Sloppy work," commented the half-breed, his
professional disgust aroused. "Probably a
Cheyenne," he grunted, going toward Kentucky
Boy. "They don't seem to understand ye have to

cut them loose before ye kin pull them off. Whoa, Boy. *Was-te, was-te.* Easy, easy."

The scout now knew what he would find ahead of him in the snow. And a few moments later he stood surveying the fire-gutted ruins of Muleshoe Station. The burned bodies of four troopers lay twisted among the embers, all but one stripped, scalped, mutilated. The left arms of three of them were severed below the elbow, identifying the raiders as the Cheyennes Perez had suspected them to be. "Little Wolf and his boys, unless I miss my guess," the scout said aloud. "I wonder why they didn't chop the fourth one?"

Turning the body of the unmarked trooper with the toe of his boot, he had his answer. Suspended around the dead man's neck, its thin chain glinting dully in the fading light, hung a silver cross. "*Aii-eee!*" the half-breed exclaimed. "Little Wolf, all right."

The chopping off of the left hand or arm was the Cheyennes' tribal trademark, not to be confused with the equally quaint custom of their Sioux cousins—slitting the throat from mastoid to mastoid. By its presence here among the Muleshoe Creek dead, Perez knew the identity of the killers as surely as though he had witnessed the murders. By the same token he could guess the identity of their leader by the respect shown the Catholic soldier. All Plains Indians feared the man who wore a cross, but none of them practiced this regard with the fervor of Little Wolf. He was probably the most ruthless butcher among the Cut Arm People, but his personal medicine was the cross and he never took the war trail without donning the famous, foot-long silver cross that was his favorite charm.

"I hope ye boys had quit kickin' before ye lost yer fingers," said Perez, turning quickly away from the cabin. As he did, he noted Kentucky Boy gazing curiously at the still forms. "I told ye ye'd get used to lookin' at bodies in the snow, ye prick-eared crow-bait. Come on. Let's us evaporate outen here before them Cheyennes nominate us with a war axe to run on the same ticket as these boys."

Perez put five miles between them and the station before halting. He hand-led Kentucky Boy every step of the way, disregarding the danger of Indian surprise and the gale force of the blizzard. The half-breed didn't have an ounce of the lard of sentiment on his lean frame. He used his own feet because he knew the horse's only chance of getting back his wind was a five-mile walk-out. And he knew that the horse was his only chance of covering the remaining thirty-five miles to Fort Loring. Without Kentucky Boy to carry him, Perez would become just the third, white mound on the trail north of Loring.

The walk took an hour of precious time, but at the end of it the bay stud's breath had quit sobbing and the scout's frozen left leg had got feeling back into it as far as the ankle. He fed the horse the last of the hardtack, pouring half the remaining whiskey down the beast's throat after the biscuit. Finishing the canteen himself, he unsaddled the stud, abandoning saddle, ammunition, parfleches, Duffy's carbine, his own Colts. All were quickly cached, Perez marking the spot for an early return.

Carrying only his Winchester and the shells in it, he swung up on the bay, putting him down the trail at the best gait the lead-legged stallion could furnish. Kentucky Boy responded with all the breeding in his deep body, but, even as he started, he was running rough. Feeling the off-rhythm pounding of the great heart and the ragged fluttering of the lungs beneath his clamping legs, Perez knew he was riding a dead horse.

A rider in a blizzard casts no shadow, but as he began those last miles Perez had thirty-one shadows trailing him down the Virginia City Road. Five miles back, at Muleshoe Station, Little Wolf, the Cheyenne, stood with his war party looking down at the fresh tracks of a man and horse. The still-standing north wall of the stable sheltered the tracks from the covering snows. They led out south, down the Virginia City Road, before they disappeared in the open snow.

Squatting over them, fingering and smelling their depressions, squinting at them intently, a wizened warrior crouched. He was a dwarf of a man, no taller than a short pony's withers; he was

Tonkasha—Red Mouse—best of the Cheyenne trackers.

"*Akicita*?" Little Wolf barked the question.

"No. No soldier." The little man shrugged. "White scout."

"How long?"

Again the withered brave shrugged. "Who can say? It is a cold trail."

"Any smell?"

"A little."

"Tonight, then? He passed this way tonight?"

"Oh, tonight sure."

"If his horse is tired, we might catch him?"

"Why not?"

"Tonkasha says . . . 'Why not?' " echoed Little Wolf to the waiting braves. "Let's go. Let's go after him." Within seconds the stark walls of Muleshoe Station stood alone.

The Junior Officers' Winter Ball was the highlight of Fort Loring's social season—a trite expression admittedly, but then it was a trite ball. Fort Loring had grown up. No longer the dangerous frontier outpost, no longer the sanctuary for the handful of hard-bitten troops fending off the hostile thousands swarming down on the early traffic of the Medicine Road. To be sure, Red Cloud, Crazy Horse, and Sitting Bull were familiar names. To be sure, emigrant trains trying to run the forbidden rapids of the Powder River still went aground the red rocks guarding its disputed channels. But that wasn't Fort Loring. That was days and days away, somewhere up that crazy north trail. The Virginia City Road they called it, didn't they? Some such name. No matter, anyway. It was outside Fort Loring's world by a million miles—well, anyway, two hundred and twenty-six miles. What was the difference?

At the moment, 11:30 p.m., December 24, the big thing was the Junior Officers' Ball. Everything was going splendidly. Lights, laughter, champagne, dancing; handsome, uniformed men, beautiful, perfumed women. The whole gay panoply of a Christmas Eve military ball shone and echoed through the gleaming windows. What matter that the worst blizzard in a decade was howling down the scratchy efforts of the post musicians? It was Christmas Eve!

Two hundred and thirty-six miles north, Christmas Eve was coming to another garrison. There were lights there, too, but only the flicker of the lone stove in the deserted company kitchens. There were women there, but they weren't beautiful and they weren't dancing. They were huddling like clay-faced dolls in the bowel of the powder magazine awaiting the war whoops that would mean the Indians were over the stockade and signal the explosion that would flash the magazine logs to flying splinters.

There were uniformed men there, but they

weren't handsome and they weren't laughing. They were shoveling. Shoveling to keep the monstrous drift of the snow from piling to the top logs, shoveling to keep the crouching Sioux from walking over the very top of the stockade on the crest of the rising snow pack. Shoveling and cursing and praying. Cursing that none of them had had the courage to ride for help to Fort Loring, that the damned Collins slut had freed her black-bearded lover, that of all men fit to live the only one who might do so would be the sneaking half-breed who had led Major Stacey into the massacre and precipitated their whole hopeless situation. Praying that God, on this His only begotten Son's birthright, might deliver them from the red evil that hovered, waiting beyond the blizzard.

And six miles north of Fort Loring, the man they cursed, and the delivery they prayed for, rode a dying horse down the ice-sheathed North Platte River. Five miles. Four. Three. Two. One. And so, finally, faintly through a wind-driven hole in the storm came the lights of Fort Loring.

Midnight. Intermission. Colonel Gerald Boynton had just danced a Virginia reel with Captain Swinnerton's captivating wife. The entire ballroom was applauding them delightedly. Into the lights, the warmth, the applause, tottered a figure from another world.

Two protesting non-coms put their hands on him as he entered the door. He flung them away from

96

him, like an angry bear. Out onto the deserted floor he advanced, lurching, stumbling, a monstrous, bareheaded figure in a great wolf-skin coat: a frozen, blizzard-borne ghost. From the matted ice on his beard to the caked snow on his buffalo-hide boots, an inhuman, unreal apparition. The women drew back, gasping; the men hesitated, wondering.

The figure in the center of the dance floor stood swaying, arms groping aimlessly like great, stiff clubs, lean face turning like a death mask, now here, now there, frost-black lips moving soundlessly.

"My God!" A single voice broke the silence. "The poor devil's blind. He can't see!"

The men surged forward then, surrounding Perez. "Good Lord!" breathed a young lieutenant, bringing his hands away from the scout's coat, "his clothes are frozen on him."

"Leave his clothes on. Get some blankets and bring him over here on this settee by the stove." Colonel Boynton's orders were terse. A grim-faced captain shoved a flask into the commander's hand.

"For God's sake, get some whiskey down him, sir. That man's dying. Where the hell's Major Johnston?" The post surgeon pushed forward.

"Here," he responded, bending quickly over the fallen man. "Leave him right where he is. Don't get him near that stove. If he thaws too fast, he'll lose his whole face. Give me that flask." The group watched, wordless. "Coffee. Hot and black. Hurry it up!" The surgeon barked his instructions as he pulled the spilling flask away from the blackened face.

With the whiskey and, close-following, scalding coffee, Perez rallied. His eyes flicked open. The cracked lips moved. "Somebody look after that hoss . . . outside. . . ."

"Give me that flask again," Major Johnston ordered quietly. One of the non-coms who had followed Perez in spoke slowly as the surgeon forced more whiskey down the scout. "The horse is dead, mister. He's down right where you left him, just outside the door there."

The half-breed grimaced, spitting whiskey and blood on the floor. "Get away, let me alone. I'm all right. Now, listen. . . ." Harshly he told them, the words coming haltingly through lips blue-twisted with cold. "Fort Farney's surrounded. Two thousand hostiles. Sioux. Cheyennes. Crazy Horse. They killed Stacey and eighty men. Ambush. Squaw Pine Ridge."

"My God, man!" Boynton was incredulous. "When?"

"Three days ago."

"Three days! You rode here from Farney in three days? In this blizzard?"

"I'm here," said Perez grimly.

"They got the wireless at Muleshoe?" This from the captain with the flask.

"Little Wolf got it. Killed everybody."

"Flask!" snapped Major Johnston. "He's going out again."

"I'm not goin' any place," gritted Perez, "but ye'd best be goin' some place, Colonel. They got wood up there for mebbe a week. When that's gone and the storm lets up, the Sioux'll get them. Mebbe meantime ye kin beat Tashunka Witko to yer friend, Fenton."

"Great Scott, man! I can't get a column up to Farney in a week!"

"Ye'd best try," the scout gasped, fighting back the shadows that seemed determined to get between him and his listeners. "They'll hang on fer ye. The old man'll fight and that How . . . that Howell,"—the half-breed shook his head, forcing the words to come—"he's tougher'n a half-boiled boot."

"He's out again, Colonel." The surgeon spoke flatly, as the exhausted man's head sagged. "Let's leave him alone."

"Can't you get him around again?" The commander's query echoed the confusion of all. "We don't even know his name or who he is."

The surgeon glared at his questioner, started to say something, decided better, then seized the scout's shoulders. "Come on, man," he urged gently, "come around. Who are you? Can you hear me? Who are you?"

The half-breed's lips moved painfully. "John Perez . . . white scout . . . Sixteenth Infantry."

"All right." Major Johnston stood up. "That's all. Get this man into a bed right here. Wrap him in blankets. No other heat. Send someone for my bag. And clear out. All of you. I think this man's earned the right to die in peace."

The two non-coms picked the unconscious scout up as tenderly as a child. "Bring him along," ordered the surgeon, pushing through the lingering onlookers.

A nervous young woman stepped back to let the soldiers by with their pathetic burden. "What a horrible-looking person!" she whispered excitedly to her lieutenant husband. "You'd never believe he was a white man!"

"Looks like a damn' 'breed to me," the young officer remarked disinterestedly.

Like Fenton, Boynton, if nothing else, was competent. He got his relief column out of Fort Loring at 2:00 a.m. and up the Virginia City Road to Fort Will Farney in a really remarkable five days. Fenton had been out of wood twenty-four hours, the blizzard had abated, and the Sioux, not dreaming other troops were within two hundred and thirty-six miles, were leisurely moving up to begin the pleasant work of burning Fenton's masterpiece to the ground. They had not, however, got much farther than lobbing a few incendiary long shots down into the enclosure when a scout from Little Wolf rode in with the news of Boynton's approach.

"The Eagle Chief from Fort Loring. Plenty pony soldiers. A sun's journey away. Plenty walk-a-heaps, too. How many soldiers? Oh, just plenty. Really plenty. No need to worry about there being plenty of soldiers. Let's go. Let's get out of here."

On the racing hoofs of this messenger's fagged pony an Oglala had lathered in from American Horse. The only difference in the Sioux's report and that of Little Wolf's Cheyenne was the natural one between a Cut Arm dullard and a Throat Slitter poet.

"The Eagle Chief is coming. The pony soldiers are as many as tick birds around a green-scum buffalo wallow. The walk-a-heaps swarm like maggots in a dead dog's belly. There are inestimably more than plenty of both horse and foot. The Cheyenne's eyes were bad. His tongue was weak. *Hopo. Hookahey.* Let's go. Right now!"

Red Cloud knew the rules of war-party poker too well not to see a busted flush when it was staring him in the face. He pulled his Sioux out, heading back for the Tongue an hour after the word came from American Horse. Black Shield and his Minniconjou followed suit. White Bull and his Hunkpapas threw it in. Dull Knife had already ordered his Cheyennes to the trail on the strength of Little Wolf's earlier message.

Tashunka Witko and his 600 Oglala Bad Faces hung on alone, departing only when the morning sun of the thirtieth began flashing off the carbine barrels of Boynton's cavalry six miles down the Virginia City Road. Fort Will Farney was saved, but the strange, dark-skinned man who had saved it lay quietly on a hospital cot in Fort Loring, face pallid, eyes closed, lips still. If he breathed, the covering sheet gave no sign of it.

The bulk of the report was a foot long, and to a man with mental gut enough to grind up such terms as "total pedal atrophy" and "desiccation, left manual, partial," no doubt very digestible. But any man, even a half-breed scout, could chew up that last line without any trouble: "Discharged. Partial Disability. Limited Service." Perez, sitting fully dressed on the side of his hospital cot, handed the paper back to Major Johnston with a wry smile and no comment.

"How do you feel, Perez?"

"All right. I couldn't fight a bear."

"You'll improve."

"Mebbe. What'd Fenton say about my job?"

"Well, I had to tell him about the disabilities."

"Yeah, I reckon. Anythin' else?"

"Sergeant Duffy's downstairs with your horse and outfit."

Perez stood up, wincing as his withered foot touched the floor. The surgeon stepped forward. "Here, let me help you. . . ."

"Not quite," the scout gritted, pulling away.

"Reckon I kin stump it. Got to start learnin' sometime."

"You should have let me take it off," said Major Johnston as he eyed the twisted limb resentfully. "The damned hand, too. They're no good to you."

"Ye talk like a white man, Doc." Perez grinned. "Ye ferget an Indian gets on his pony from the right side. All I need of this left leg is jest to peg me on oncet I get aboard. As fer the hand, I'm savin' it fer a friend who collects them."

"A friend who collects desiccated left hands?"

"Yep. Desyccated or otherwise. Jest so they're left ones."

"Now, who in the hell," the surgeon asked curiously, "would go around collecting left hands?"

"Oh, any Cheyenne, Doc, but I'm savin' this one fer Little Wolf. I allow he'd admire the way she's shriveled up and curlicued. He's a connysewer."

Outside the building, Duffy greeted him effusively. "Perez, me bye! It's good to see yez. Though, faith, I wouldn't have known yez, but fer them Satan's whiskers. What's happened to yez, lad?"

"What's happened to ye, Duffy?" The half-breed eyed him steadily. "I've been in that meat house close onto a month and nobody's been near me."

"Ah well, now, Perez man. . . ." The soldier looked at the ground, shifting his heavy boots uneasily. "Lots ave things have happened. Colonel Fenton's been relieved of his command. I've taken meself a widdy woman. . . ."

"Congratulations," said the scout, his voice falling to quiet seriousness. "What about Missus Collins, Duffy?"

"The gurl? Shure now, she's fine. Everybody pattin' her on her pretty back fer gettin' yez to make that ride. . . ."

"Does she say that? That she got me to do it?"

Duffy glanced up in time to catch the spark shooting in the dark eyes. "Not just exactly that, lad. I. . . ."

"Quit stallin', Duffy." The half-breed's wide mouth tightened. "What're ye coverin' up? About the girl, I mean?"

"Shure, 'tis nothin', now. I wouldn't give it another thought."

"Well, *give* it another one." The voice was flat as a trigger's cock. "Right now."

"Aye, lad." Duffy's tones were miserable. " 'Tis jest that she's been shinin' them green eyes of hers at the C.O. here, and. . . ."

"Boynton?"

"The colonel, yes."

"Well?"

"Father Flannagan is marryin' them right after the review this mornin'. I'm sorry, bye. Yez would have me tell you."

"It's all right, Duffy." The scout's voice was soft again. "Anythin' else?"

"Hivvins, yes. I almost fergot. Missus Collins gave me this note fer yez."

Perez took the envelope, shoving it, unopened, into his hunting shirt. "Thanks, Duffy." The half-breed turned away, taking the reins of the eagerly whickering Sosi. "I'll give yer regards to Red Cloud."

The sergeant stood looking after the scout, presently remembering something else he'd forgotten. He panted up to the limping Perez, his blue eyes wide with importance. "Yez ain't leavin' the fort, Perez lad?"

"Not any sooner than it takes me to. Why?"

"The saints fergive me. I fergot all about what Colonel Fenton sent me to tell yez in the first place!"

"Well?"

"Well, yez can't leave yet, lad. Yez have to wait fer the review!"

"The hell ye say! So Colonel Fenton's a busted hero and they're goin' to wave him a touchin' farewell. Ye kin tell the old man to take his damn' review and. . . ."

"It ain't his review, bye." The Irish sergeant spoke with all his soft mother brogue. "It's yerz." Perez stood motionless, the meaning of the old soldier's statement flooding through him. Duffy's voice continued gently. "You're the hero, lad, and there's not a man ave us who stood to them top logs and shoveled, or kneeled in front ave them rifle slits and prayed, whut don't know it."

When Perez looked at the sergeant, his black

eyes were charcoal-dry. "I'm no hero, Duffy. I made that ride jest to show Fenton and the rest of ye lyin' on your damn' bellies and pukin'." The scout's voice was tired, no longer bitter. "I'm goin' back to my people, Duffy, if they'll take me. I've tried for ten years to be 'Perez' . . . now I'm goin' to be 'Pawnee'."

"Perez, lad. Colonel Fenton writ to Washington about yer ride. The guv'ment has sent you a citation and voted yez a generous reward ave money, to boot. We'd all take consid'rable pride in seein' yez get what's comin' to yez. Yez shouldn't ride out on us, bye."

Perez gave in to the humble sincerity of the appeal. "All right, Duffy. What time is the review?"

"Ten-thirty. That's jest half an hour."

"I'll be there. Ye kin tell Fenton."

"Thank yez, lad. We're all that proud of yez!"

The scout limped around the corner of the hospital barracks, Sosi trailing after him. Presently he found what he sought, a deserted place along the west fort wall where he could have the morning sun warming his stiff body. Squatting awkwardly down, one knee first, like an old squaw, he eased his back against the logs, reached inside his shirt, sat looking at the small, white envelope. When at last he opened it, he studied the writing with a deep frown and the occasional aid of an underlining finger. His lips moved slowly, framing each difficult word.

Dear Perez,

I'm asking you to forget everything that went between us. In return, I promise I sha'n't forget any of it. Colonel Boynton and I are going to be married today after your review. Oh, Pawnee, we're all so proud of you! I'll be there today and I want you to look at me. I want to know that "your heart is good for me". You'll always be remembered by your "girl".

Lura Evalynn Collins

The scout reread the letter three times, each time turning it to the blank side as though to discover some overlooked postscript. Finally he replaced the paper in the envelope, folding and refolding it carefully.

An inquisitive snow bunting hopped perkily toward him over the frozen ground. The half-breed eyed the bird, measured the range, decided it was too long, waited patiently for it to shorten. The quid of light-leaf burley shifted speculatively from one angular cheek to the other. When wind, light, range, and target were just so, Perez spat. The thin stream's trajectory was flat as a war arrow's flight. Splat! Dead on. Not a drop wasted.

The little bird cheeped shrilly, shook its insulted head, hopped indignantly away.

"Let that be a lesson to ye," admonished the scout, laboriously hunching himself erect. "Never trust a woman . . . or a half-breed."

· · ·

Infantry, cavalry, band, and color guard wheeled, and turned in the muddy slush of the parade ground. Behind Perez and Fenton, Captains Howell and Tendrake sat their horses. Behind them stood the silent ranks of the heroes of Fort Farney. On the far side of the parade yard stood another silent group: the women and children who had spent that terrible week in Fort Farney's powder magazine. Fronting this group, red hair gleaming in the morning sun, Lura Collins waited, poised and breathless.

Still another gathering watched the wheeling troops. Rank on blanket-wrapped rank they squatted; the stony-eyed Agency Sioux, allowed to witness this flexing of the white man's military muscles as a reward for their adherence to the miserable terms of their slavery.

The final, smallest group on the parade yard impressed even the Sioux. Ten paces in front of Colonel Fenton and Pawnee Perez, Sergeant Orin Duffy rigidly presented the colors of the Sixteenth U.S. Infantry and the Fourth Cavalry. Behind Duffy, their empty saddles black-draped, stood three borrowed cavalry horses. The saddles might be empty, but the names that went with them would be long remembered. *Major Phil Stacey, Captain J. C. Bolen, Second Lieutenant Barrett Drummond.*

Perez, looking at all this, was seeing only the girl across the field, her red hair loose in the wind, her curving figure graceful as a doe's.

Fenton's speech was concise. He praised the heroism of the men and women at Fort Will Farney, lauded the courage of Major Stacey, Perez, and, in the same breath with his reference to the latter, included a eulogy on the heart and breeding of Kentucky Boy, together with his sincere thanks to Colonel Boynton for the use of the field.

After that, he called Perez forward, quickly handing him the long, yellow envelope.

In a quiet that was thick enough to slice with a spade, the half-breed took it, holding it uncertainly for a moment. The envelope bore no seals, no address, but it carried within it the official commemoration of his ride, actually *voted* to him by the government in Washington! No wonder that Pawnee Perez hesitated to open it.

Watching him, Colonel Fenton had more stomach for this moment than did the confused half-breed. And where Perez was uneasy because he *didn't* know what was in the envelope, Fenton was upset because he *did*.

"Go ahead, man." The smile wobbled awkwardly. "It's yours."

The scout, withered left hand hanging uselessly, fumbled at the unsealed packet with his right, finally getting it clumsily open. In it were three $100 bills. And nothing else.

"Congratulations, Perez. And good luck. Now, about that money, man, I know it. . . ."

"Sure. I know. Don't ye worry none about it,

Colonel." Somehow the grin had the old, quick flash. "It's better than a poke in the eye with a sharp stick." In the silence that trod the heels of his remark, Perez turned his horse across the field.

"The poor devil!" Captain Howell's suppressed curse went to Tendrake. "It's a damned shame."

"There was three hundred dollars in that envelope." The other shrugged unfeelingly. "Probably more money than he ever saw. He'll go on a half-breed high lonesome and wake up thinking he's had a hell of a time."

Howell's sneer was scathing. "Three hundred dollars for a man's hand and foot for saving two hundred and fifty white lives? For robbing the Sioux and Cheyenne of the biggest victory they ever dreamed of?"

"I can add to your 'righteous indignation'," Tendrake troweled on the mortar of his sarcasm. "Two hundred dollars of that money is back pay he had coming. I drew the voucher myself. The government authorization was for one hundred dollars." Howell's answer was to raise his right hand in a stiff salute after the departing scout.

"Now, what the hell was that for?" queried Tendrake irritably.

"That," his companion muttered slowly, "was for the bravest man I ever saw . . . white or half-white."

VII

Pawnee Perez had ridden into the short history of Fort Farney alone. He rode out of it the same way. His departure from Fort Loring was as unattended as had been his arrival. Even the weather, conspiring to set the stage of similarity, sent a lead-gray snow front crawling suddenly over the Big Horns to pile up ominously behind the low flanks of the Laramies, quickly blotting out the bright sun of the parade yard.

Corporal Sam Boone stood on the low stoop of Mrs. Lura Collins's quarters, hunching his shoulders to the building wind, stomping his feet against the cold.

"Beg pardon, ma'am. Ah'm Sam . . . uh, Corporal Boone, that is. Friend of Pawnee's, ma'am. He give me this envelope to bring to you."

"Please come in, Sam." The girl took the envelope, standing aside for the soldier. "Is Mister Perez going to leave the fort soon?"

"He has left, ma'am."

"Oh, no! In this storm?"

"It ain't much of a storm, ma'am. Not to him. He's rid worse ones." The lanky corporal looked at the girl directly.

"Yes"—the green eyes dropped—"I know."

"Ah guess you do, ma'am."

"I wanted to see him." Her words were as soft as

111

the mouth that framed them. "He left the parade yard so suddenly. I tried to get his attention, but he wouldn't look at me. He wouldn't look at anyone, Sam. What was the matter with him?"

"Ah don't know, ma'am. Them half-breeds is funny."

"You say you were his friend, Sam. Didn't he say anything to you?"

"Well, ma'am, he didn't have no real friends, exceptin' that other scout, Mister Clanton, who was kilt by Crazy Horse. Otherwise, I guess it was jest me and Duffy knew him at all."

"But he didn't say anything, Sam?"

"No, ma'am. He give me and Duffy each a hundred-dollar bill. Then he ast me to bring that envelope over to you. That's all. Maybe you better look at it, ma'am."

Lura Collins nodded, her manner abstract. "He was such a strange man, so bitter." The long fingers opened the envelope. "He always made me feel so uncomfortable. . . ."

"He made a lot of us feel like that, ma'am. It was his way."

"No . . ."—the tall mountaineer thought the girl's words fell as softly as snowflakes on a pony's winter coat—"that wasn't his way, Sam. I didn't know until today what his real way was . . . how he really makes you feel." She paused and the quick eye of the hill-man caught the flash of the tear as it fell. "Oh, Sam! He makes you feel *ashamed!*"

"Ah've got to go, ma'am. Ah shouldn't be here anyway. Ah. . . ."

"Sam, wait." The envelope was open wide now, then the girl's voice suddenly questioned: "Why, there's nothing in it at all. Just a blank piece of paper. Not a word of writing on it. I don't understand."

"Ah do, ma'am. About the writin', Ah mean." The big Southerner's drawl was apologetic. "Pawnee, he couldn't write. Didn't know how."

Perez rode the out trail five miles, then turned north across country. There was a short cut away from the treeless valley of the Platte that cut ten miles off the regular route to Muleshoe Station. If he was going to get up there, where he'd cached his outfit ahead of nightfall, he'd have to hump it. As he hit the cut-off, the rolling grayness from the Big Horns shut in on him, and the first big flakes slanted into his squinting face.

All afternoon he rode north, the snow setting in heavier all the while, the temperature dropping steadily. By 4:00 p.m., nearing the cache, the weather had come down hard, and Perez, slumped and shaking in the saddle, was a sick man.

Twice along the trail he had stopped and vomited, the second sickness bringing nothing but thin, yellow bile flecked with scarlet. For an hour now, he had been coughing, deep, lobar barks that left his chest aching, his body wringing wet. Wiping his mouth after the first paroxysm twenty minutes before on the trail, the back of his hand had come away smeared with bright crimson mucus.

Nor was it the scout's wasted body alone that was sick. The past two hours his nerves had been going. Every normal trail sight had had his reflexes jumping crazily. Now it was a snow-draped juniper looming around a turn, sending him spasmodically kicking Sosi off the trail and into the underbrush, now a brown cottontail snow-bombing out of a hummock of bunch grass, starting him in a wild dive for the Winchester under his knee. Since leaving the Platte Trail outside Fort Loring, he'd been unable to shake off the feeling he was being followed. Again and again he'd doubled back to look along his own trail. Nothing had come. Not a twig crack, not an owl hoot, not a pony whicker. Finally, he knew there was nothing there. Only wind and snow and loneliness—and nerves.

That had been hours ago, before the coughing and vomiting. He hadn't been sick then. Now he knew he *was* sick. Knew the things he thought he heard were only shadow sounds jumped up by the twisting sickness within him.

For the first time in his life Perez fought fear, the empty, frantic dread that comes up in a strong man when the ferrous vein runs out of nerve ore that has always graded pure iron. That snuffle off there to the right wasn't a pony. That queasing creak wasn't a frozen saddle squeaking. That changing form up ahead wasn't a mounted brave waiting, motionless, back of the shifting snow screen.

The half-breed gritted his teeth, forcing his hand to stay away from the Winchester, and kneed Sosi on forward into the clearing across which his cache lay. He was out in the open then. In the clearing. And that changing form up ahead *was* a mounted brave waiting behind the snow!

Sosi stopped, nostrils flaring, ears flicking. Perez sat him quietly, head sunk forward, shoulders hunched. The dark eyes, dull with fever, were still bright enough to recognize an old friend.

"*Hohahe*," said American Horse. "Welcome to our teepee. We've been waiting for you."

Around him now, the scout could see the others, ghost warriors sitting phantom ponies, gray and unreal in the uncertain twilight: Elk Nation, Short Bear, Crazy Lodge, High-Hump-Back, Bob-Tail-Bull—old friends, all. He did not need the darting glance over the hunched shoulder to tell him of the others waiting there behind him. The dull glow of the silver cross hung its image a moment in the tail of his eye: Little Wolf, the Cheyenne, was back there, with Tonkasha, the little Red Mouse, grinning at his side, and the shadowy backing of a dozen others looming on their flanks.

"*Woyuonihan*," Perez returned American Horse's greeting, touching his withered left hand to his brow. "*Wolakota*. Peace. *Hun-hun-he*. I have come home to my people."

"*Hohahe*! Welcome!" barked Little Wolf, and shot him in the back.

The scout stiffened, half-turning in his saddle to face the Cheyenne. A dozen mushrooms of black-edged orange bloomed around the clearing's border. The sound of the lead whacking into the half-breed's body shaded the flat reports of the rifles by a scant half second. Perez's right hand slid into his coat front, hesitated, fell away, tight-clenched.

Sosi, unconcerned with the shooting, began walking interestedly toward American Horse's whickering stallion. Perez's body lurched twice to the shifting withers, slid off the right side of the horse, dragged a few feet in the stirrup, broke loose, flopped over to lie still, half covered in a snowbank.

The Indians were around him then, dismounted. Little Wolf seized the half-breed's left arm, partially pulling his body out of the snow, the broad hunting knife flashing upward. A tall shadow fell between him and the scout. Little Wolf turned angrily as the restraining hand closed on his arm.

"Tashunka Witko has said no." American Horse nodded soberly. "Tashunka Witko says it was a great ride. He said . . . leave him his hands to guide his pony on the long trail."

"The hair, too?" demanded the Cheyenne defiantly.

"He didn't say about the hair." And the Sioux shrugged.

Little Wolf's knife whipped downward almost before American Horse had spoken. With a snapping jerk the Cheyenne chief flung the scalpless body from him, kicking it backward with a propelling shove of his knee. The limp figure went into the bank with enough force to bring a showering cover of snow down from an overhanging spruce, and, when the fall ceased, only the slack right arm of the scout remained visible.

"The hand was no good, anyway. All curled up!" snapped Little Wolf. "*Hopo*, let's go."

"*Hookahey*," agreed American Horse. "Let's go. It's getting cold!"

The wind moved in on the heels of the departing ponies. The piling snows were beginning their merciful work of covering the last sign of the body under the spruce. A whirling ground gust, smoking across the surface of the snowbank, spun around the exposed hand, tugging peevishly at the crumpled bit of paper in the stiffening fingers. A second or two and it was almost free. Another second and it was rolling across the frozen ground of the clearing, a skittering, walnut-sized ball of crinkly green. Against the waiting root tangle of sagebrush it caught and lodged securely.

The last snowy breath of the thieving gust followed it quickly, burying the hundred-dollar bill almost before it stopped rolling.

TALES OF THE TEXAS RANGERS

I

"THE FOUR HORSEMEN OF THE WEST"

To understand the grim and violent nature of the Texas Ranger's work, one must first understand the grim and violent nature of the enemy against whom he fought. To do that, one must be able to command his imagination to march back across more than a hundred years of history to the time when Texas was young. There was no law whatever then in all her quarter-million square miles of raw wilderness—until the Rangers came. The Rangers were always outnumbered by the enemy. The odds were frequently four to one, five to one, and even ten to one. Yet time and again these fearless men answered their captain's cheery call of—"Follow me, men!"—straight into the face of certain death. And, somehow, time and again, when the last bark of Colt or Winchester had growled off across the silent prairie, it was not the Texas Rangers who were bewailing the loss of comrades dear or bemoaning the departure of brave brothers suddenly called away. It was the enemy.

Who was this enemy? He was of three types. First, he was the High Plains horseback Indian, raiding and burning deeply into the peaceful settlements. He murdered the luckless white man wherever he might find him—by his lonely campfire, standing guard over his livestock, or in the peaceful slumber of his cabin bed. Second, the enemy was the crafty Mexican border bandit, the vengeful *vaquero* of old Mexico. Stalking in the dead of night across the Río Grande, he seized and drove off the horses and cattle herds upon which his American neighbor depended for his very life. Third, he was the brutal American badman—the cold-eyed gunman, the killer, those who flooded into Texas following the Civil War. The badman preyed mercilessly upon friend and foe alike and knew no law but that of the deadly Colt revolver.

These, then, were the enemies of Texas. To fight them—to hunt them down and kill them like the outlaw animals they were—became the dangerous job of the Texas Rangers. The Rangers were thus, in the very beginning, a product of grim circumstances and violent times. A Ranger never killed a man he did not have to kill, but he had to kill many men. He swore, in the oath he took, never to surrender himself or his arms, never to desert a comrade, never to retreat. Yet he was commanded, always, to give the enemy the first shot! He brought the only law to a vast and desolate land—a land so big that one famous captain actually rode a far-flung, circling patrol of 1,600 miles in thirty days without once coming near its borders.

The Ranger had no regular uniform, no badge, no battle flag, no insignia of rank, no company doctor, no medical care, no military benefits whatever. He had to furnish his own arms and his own horse—a good one, at that, worth at least $100. And with his meager pay, he had to provide all expenses of both his mount and himself. For the magnificent reward of $37.50 a month (which as often as not was never paid) he was privileged to risk his life in the name of frontier law and order.

The great wonder remains that he would accept such terrible odds of Indian, bandit, and badman for this miserable pay. The proud answer to that is that the Ranger never fought for money. He fought for a land—Texas—and he fought for a cause—freedom from fear and oppression. As he fought, so he was—a man made up of equal parts of the three dangerous forces which had created him. He could trail with the savage cunning of a Comanche brave. He could ride with the furious skill of the Mexican *vaquero*. He could shoot with the quiet-eyed deadliness of a Tennessee mountaineer. He was the finest individual fighting man the West ever produced. He faced the greatest odds, with the least possible chance of success, of any law officer in frontier history.

This is his story. Turn back the clock of time a century and more! Spring to saddle and ride with the Texas wind through blind-black river thickets, over blazing sunlit prairies, across burning desert, and snow-swept mountain passes. Take the dark and desperate trail of the Four Horsemen of the Far West: the Comanche brave, the Mexican bandit, the American badman, and the Texas Ranger. Follow it with the last, the deadliest rider of them all. Share with him his lonely outpost camp. Eat with him beside his cheery mesquite fire. Sleep with him beneath the wheeling southwest stars. Fight with him inside the screaming circle of the Indian ambush. Laugh with him against the hopeless odds of the closing Mexican cavalry trap. Stand beside him as he meets the thunder of American outlaw guns. Come meet his famous captains and his fearless men. Peer back into their wondrous times through the gunsmoke of a hundred years. Ride again with the Texas Rangers!

II

"THE WAR CLOUDS GATHER"

The Americans first came into the Spanish province of Texas with Moses Austin in 1820. They settled the rich and beautiful bottom lands between the Colorado and the Trinity Rivers. The following year, Mexico revolted against Spain. As a result, Texas became a member province of the new Republic of Mexico. Shortly thereafter, the leadership of the American colony passed to its founder's talented son, Stephen Austin.

Young Austin wisely made his peace with Mexico. But for several years the little colony hovered between success and failure. To aid it in its brave struggle, Mexico passed a generous law encouraging more Americans to settle in Texas. Hungry and greedy people in the United States took sudden notice of the rich new lands to be had for nothing. They came in a wave. By 1830, this flood of American fortune-hunters had gotten out of hand. The Mexican government could no longer control them. They would not pay taxes or obey the laws. So Mexico abruptly closed the borders of Texas to further emigration from the United States. But the action came too late.

In 1835, the belligerent Texans revolted. For a full year they fought like savages against the Mexican Army. Finally the Mexican dictator, General Santa Anna, was defeated disastrously on the field of San Jacinto. Texas had won her independence. She was now a sovereign nation, responsible to no one but herself. The saga of her famous Rangers followed swiftly.

The actual ordinance that created the first official corps of Texas Rangers provided for three companies of fifty-six men each. Each company was officered by a captain and a first and second lieutenant. A major commanded the entire corps, subject to the orders of the commander-in-chief of the army. The latter, of course, was fiery old Sam Houston, first president of the Republic of Texas.

Privates were enlisted for one year. They were paid $1.25 a day for all expenses of themselves and their horses. Officers were paid the same as officers of equal rank in the United States service forces. Each Ranger was ordered always to be ready with a good horse, saddle, bridle and blanket, and a hundred rounds of powder and ball. Then came the disturbing part of the ordinance. The Rangers were named a "special body of irregular troops." As such, they were entirely set apart from the regular army of Texas, as well as from her volunteer militia.

This seemed like an innocent distinction at first, but it was not. It went deeply into the heart of an uneasy frontier tradition and distrust of vigilante forces. The Texans were suddenly very worried. Many good citizens of the young nation shook their heads uncertainly at this delegation of "special powers" to an irregular force.

"We have created a raging monster!" warned one of the founding fathers. "This rough band of cutthroat horsemen may very well decide to make their own laws as they ride along!"

This was no idle nightmare. The thoughtful citizens realized that at once. Frontier history was full of dark chapters written by such night-riding bands of hard-eyed volunteers. "Stranglers" they were called, after their vicious habit of first hanging their captives to the nearest gallows tree, and only then inquiring into their real guilt or innocence. So the grim warning struck its chill into many a heart and mind throughout the settlements. Where vigilante groups had done as much before, what was to keep the Texas Rangers from turning into a lawless band of midnight stranglers? What was to hinder them from becoming as much of a menace to peaceful citizens as to the savage enemy? The unhappy settlers did not know. They could only hope.

Actually the special force had been created for one reason alone. That was to defend the isolated western frontier against Indian raids while Texas was fighting her war of independence with Mexico. But the Rangers had had little chance to prove themselves. The Indians had been wisely quiet during the war. And why not? argued the crafty warriors. Why bother killing the hated *Tejanos* when their Mexican brothers were doing such a good job of it for them?

So the fierce braves had stayed home. As a result, the frustrated Rangers had been made to look worse than useless. With little or nothing to do, they had taken to quarreling among themselves and to making considerable trouble in the various frontier settlements where they were quartered. But what would happen now?

The war was over and the Indians were raiding again with all their old-time, savage fury. Would the Rangers do anything now? That was the somber question over which the worried settlement fathers exchanged uncertain looks. For the answer to it they turned their anxious glances westward toward the Comanches' lands. The Rangers did not keep them waiting.

III

"FIRST BLOOD FOR PRIVATE SMITHWICK"

It was early January, 1836. The night was freezing cold in the Ranger camp at Hornsby's station, ten miles below Austin on the Colorado River. A sleety rain was driving in from the north, chilling the thinly clad riders, hunching the nervous rumps of their mounts on the picket line. The cook fires went out repeatedly. The water for the coffee could not be brought to a boil. The howl of the wind rose higher. The men gathered here belonged to Captain Tumlinson's company. This was one of the three original companies of Texas Rangers created only a few months before.

The men were new to one another and to their commander. They had been on the Indian frontier seven weeks, yet none of them had seen an Indian nor heard a war whoop. Their nerves were worn thin with the waiting. Their strength was sapped by the constant day-and-night riding after an enemy who had seemingly disappeared. And yet, wherever the Rangers were not to be seen, there the red men would spring up to kill and burn. Then they would disappear again before their pursuers could catch them.

In the settlements ugly talk sprang up. The Rangers were a quarrelsome, trouble-making lot, some said. Others claimed that the Rangers made no real effort to find and punish the Indians; they only sat in camp, drew their pay, and looked the other way when a ranch was burned or a lonely settler was scalped in his cornfield. Disband them, urged these critics. The sooner they were done away with, the better it would be for the Texas taxpayer. So went the talk.

Meanwhile, Private Noah Smithwick of Tumlinson's company was nodding over the miserable smoke of his sentry fire. Beyond him, his few companions were struggling with the balky flames of their supper fires, trying to achieve a sodden meal of moldy bacon and rain-soaked cornbread. Suddenly Ranger Smithwick's weary eyes were staring at a ghostly apparition, staggering toward him from the dripping blackness of the river timber. No words could ever improve upon Smithwick's own account of what followed.

"Suddenly," the startled young Ranger related, "a white woman, an entire stranger, her clothes hanging in shreds about her torn and bleeding body, dragged herself into camp and sank exhausted to the ground. When at length she recovered, she told us that her name was Hibbons. That, in company with her husband, brother, and two small children, she was journeying overland up to their little home on the Guadalupe, when they were attacked by a band of Comanches. The two men were killed, the wagon plundered, herself and the children made prisoners. She was bound onto one of the mules and her little three-year-old boy on the other.

"The second child was a young babe. The poor little creature, whose sufferings the mother could not allay, cried continuously. At once, one of the redskins snatched it from her and dashed its brains out against a tree. The cunning redskins knew there was little risk of their outrage being discovered quickly. When a cold, rainy Norther met them at the crossing of the Colorado, they sought the shelter of a cedar brake and lay by to wait for it to subside. Wrapping themselves in their buffalo robes, they were soon sound asleep. But there was no sleep for Missus Hibbons.

"The brave woman knew that there was no time to lose. Another day's travel would take her so far beyond the reach of the settlements that it would be impossible for her to escape and procure help before the savages reached their stronghold. She waited only until assured by their breathing that her captors were asleep. Then, summoning all her courage, she carefully tucked a robe about her sleeping child and stole away, forced to leave him to the mercies of the brutal barbarians.

"She felt sure the river they had crossed was the

Colorado. She knew there were settlements below. She made straight for the river, hiding her tracks in its icy waters. Fearful of pursuit and discovery by the Indians, she had spent nearly twenty-four hours traveling the distance of but ten miles to Hornsby's station. Fortunate, beyond hope, in finding the Rangers there, she implored us to save her child. She described the mule he rode, the band of Indians, and the direction they were traveling.

"Hastily dispatching our supper," Ranger Smithwick continued his report, "we were soon in the saddle. With our trusty guide, Reuben Hornsby, we traveled on until we judged that we must be near the trail. Fearful of crossing it in the darkness, we halted and waited for daylight.

"As soon as it was light enough, our scouts were out and presently found the trail. It was fresh and well-defined. The marauders did not seem to be at all alarmed as to the consequences of their prisoner's escape. It was about ten o'clock in the morning when we came upon them just preparing to break camp.

"Taken completely by surprise, they broke for the shelter of a cedar brake, leaving everything save their weapons. I was riding a fleet horse which, becoming excited, carried me right in among the fleeing savages. One of them jumped behind a tree and fired on me with his musket. Unable to control my horse, I jumped off him and gave chase to my assailant on foot, knowing his gun was empty. I fired on him and had the satisfaction of seeing him fall. Leaving him for dead, I ran on, hoping to bring down another. But the brave I had shot lay flat on the ground and loaded his gun. He discharged it at Captain Tumlinson, narrowly missing him and killing his horse. Ranger Conrad Rohrer ran up and, snatching the gun from the Indian's hand, dealt him a blow on the head, crushing his skull. We then achieved the main object of the expedition, the rescue of the little Hibbons boy. The Indians, careful of the preservation of their small captive . . . they intended to make a good Comanche of him . . . had wrapped him warmly in their finest buffalo robe. When we rushed upon them, they had no chance to remove him.

"The other Indians," Private Smithwick concluded, with that rare sense of understatement that was to become the trademark of the Rangers, "made good their escape into the cedar brake. The scene of the rescue was on Walnut Creek, about ten miles northwest of Austin. There was a suspicious moisture in many an eye long since a stranger to tears, when the overjoyed mother clasped her only remaining treasure to her heart. . . ."

The aftermath of Captain Tumlinson's bold night ride after the Comanche killers brought more than a few manly tears to a lonely handful of tough young Rangers on the Indian frontier. It brought to the Texas settlers the happy realization that the

Texas Rangers, for all their poor pay and thread-bare garb, meant deadly business. Overnight, the feeling changed. The frightened pioneers had found a champion at last. From this time forward, any Indian who came into the settlements to burn and kill would do so only with the certain knowledge that within the day, perhaps the hour, of his evil deed, the Texas Rangers would be riding his bloody trail.

It was, indeed, but a small beginning in the Rangers' promised war against the fierce Comanches—only one Indian killed and one white child recovered. Yet it was a beginning. And it stopped the settlement talk of disbanding the force. The "rough band of cut-throat horsemen" had proved itself. No one in Texas could know when or where the Indian fire would next burst into flames, but everyone now knew that whenever or wherever it did, the "rag-tag" Rangers would be there to put it out.

IV

"LIEUTENANT RICE AND THE CHEROKEE UPRISING"

It was May 18, 1839. Lieutenant Jim Rice was worried, and for a very good reason. Things were entirely too quiet that late spring morning along the San Gabriel Fork of the Little River, and he did not like at all the Indian sign he was staring at in the damp sand of the riverbank. He halted his small patrol of Captain Andrews's company of Texas Rangers on the east shore of the lonely stream. Low-voiced, he consulted his lean, gray-eyed sergeant, Innes Simms.

There was disturbing cause for hesitation. For three years now the Rangers had roamed the frontier in ceaseless pursuit and punishment of the raiding red men. The battle had been fierce and constant. There had been no respite for the handful of hard-riding volunteers who had sworn never to surrender to the enemy. All during those three restless years the Indians had struck almost daily against the white settlements. Now—suddenly—for the past three weeks not a single painted warrior had been seen. It was as though the silent prairie had opened wide and swallowed up the wild red horsemen.

Why? What were they up to? It was a big part of Lieutenant Jim Rice's job to find the answer to that grim question. He had one dark clue. For months Texas had been hearing rumors of a sinister plot. The Mexicans, eager to retrieve the loss of Texas to the hated *Tejanos*, were at work on a devilish scheme to win it back. The plan was chillingly simple—to incite all the Indian tribes in Texas and stir them into uniting with the Mexicans and rising up to massacre every white *Tejano* between the Red River on the north and the Río Grande on the south. The rumor further hinted that the revolt of the red men was to start with the most powerful tribe in the east—the Cherokees. Then it was to spread with the speed of prairie fire to the Indian warlords of the west—the Comanches.

Yet, the closest watch and most diligent patrols of the army and militia had failed to reveal a single positive proof of the existence of such a plot on the part of the Indians and Mexicans. In fact, there was every evidence to the contrary. The Comanches were still raiding. As long as they continued to do so, the Texans could know they were not uniting with anybody. They were still doing their bloody business in the same old way—every roving band for itself. That was the situation up to three weeks ago. Now it was entirely different.

In the three weeks since young Lieutenant Jim Rice had reached the frontier, there had been no Indian raids whatever. His orders had been to lead his Rangers in pursuit of the rumor the army and militia had been unable to track down. He and his little company were to do everything in their power to seek out some proof of the threatened uprising. Yet in the whole three weeks they had not seen a single Indian pony track until this hushed moment. There was not the slightest doubt about what the lieutenant was staring at now. The sign which had halted his tiny command on the banks of the San Gabriel was a deep-pressed trail of unshod Indian war-pony hoof prints. They were only hours old. And they angled straight across the silent stream toward Mexico.

Nor was that all. In the lead of the unshod hoof marks lay a single line of alien pony tracks—a set of sharp-cut prints such as were left only by the iron-shod hoofs of a white man's mount. Or a Mexican's.

"What do you think, Innes?" said the youthful officer at last in a husky voice.

"Same as you, Jim," grunted his weather-beaten sergeant. "That there shod horse ain't got no good business in among them barefoot Indian ponies."

"Could be a Mexican. Is that it?"

"That's it," said Sergeant Innes Simms.

"Only one way to find out for sure, I reckon," murmured Lieutenant Jim Rice.

"I reckon," said the grizzled sergeant, nodding in agreement.

Jim Rice turned to his waiting Rangers. "Follow me, men," he said quietly. And he spurred his bright bay gelding across the shallow stream toward old Mexico.

The Rangers rode hard. The trail was broad and easy to read. It told of a big band, perhaps as many as thirty braves, with more than a hundred stolen horses. Lieutenant Rice had seventeen men, including himself and a friendly Lipan Apache tracker. He did not hesitate. Two-to-one were far better odds than the Texas Rangers were accustomed to getting. They rode on.

At six o'clock in the evening, the Lipan tracker halted his pony. He held up a warning hand, motioning the young officer forward. The Indians were just ahead, in the heavy timber along the small stream beyond the next rise.

Lieutenant Rice hesitated now. That "small stream" was the San Gabriel, the same body of water the Rangers had left that morning. In twelve hours of trailing, the Indians had swung completely about and come back to it. Did that mean they knew they were being followed? Would they be waiting in ambush for the outnumbered Rangers?

Lieutenant Rice did not know. Nor could he wait to find out. The sun was already low. The prairie twilight would follow swiftly. In the succeeding darkness the treacherous red horsemen could easily slip away to safety across the Mexican border.

"Follow me, men," said the white-faced youth for the second time that day.

"You heard the lieutenant, boys!" Sergeant Innes Simms grinned. "Let's go!"

And go the Rangers did. Up and over the river rise and swooping down upon the startled Indians beyond it. The red men were just putting their ponies out to graze, after having watered them in the stream. They had no chance to mount them. They ran for the trees at the riverbank, firing back at the charging Rangers.

Three of the Indians were shot down in the first rush. The others succeeded in reaching the river timber. From this shelter, they fired back so desperately that the Rangers were forced to fall back. They took what cover they could and continued to pour a hot fire into the tangled brush that hid the Indians.

Darkness ended the attack. Under its cover, the remaining red men stole away. They left the huge herd of Texas horses and the bodies of their three dead comrades. Young Lieutenant Rice advanced to claim the spoils of his first Indian fight. What he found there in the lonely darkness made the brief encounter with the enemy one of the most important Indian battles in Texas history. For only two of the dead men were Indians. *The third was a Mexican.* Upon the bullet-riddled body of Manual Flores, the dead Mexican, Lieutenant Jim Rice found the evidence he was seeking. It was all there in the bloodstained document that Jim Rice took from a secret pocket in the Mexican leader's jacket.

According to that document, the Indians were to gather north of San Antonio as soon as the new grass came in 1839. A Mexican force of 5,000 cavalry and infantry was to cross the border and join up with them west of the white men's settlements. All Texans were to be killed or driven out of the country. The land was to be returned to the Indians and to be divided equally among the tribes taking part in the uprising. Meanwhile, the Indians were to cease all raids on the settlements, lulling the Texans into a sense of security. The ordinarily peaceful Cherokees of east Texas were named as the principal tribe involved in the first act of the great massacre.

That was enough for Lieutenant Rice. He did not linger on the banks of the San Gabriel. For this was 1839. The new grass was already well up. The Indian raids had ceased three weeks earlier. Did that mean the eastern tribes were already gathered? Did it mean that the Mexican invasion force was even now poised and waiting to strike across the border? Again, Lieutenant Rice could not know, and again he could not wait to find out.

Within the hour his weary men were riding once more, pressing homeward with the mysterious document that could mean the difference between life and death for the young Republic of Texas. As he spurred his bay gelding onward through the night, Lieutenant Rice was sure of but one thing. Thinking of it, his heart swelled with pride, his tired body straightened in the saddle. In that long-gone moment of prairie darkness, twenty-five miles from the capital city of Austin, Lieutenant James O. Rice sat very tall on his little bay pony. He had the fate of Texas sealed safely in his breast pocket. And the Texas Rangers had put it there!

"THE DAY THE RANGERS STAYED AWAY"

The proud annals of the Texas Rangers are as full of things they did not do as of things they did. Having uncovered the Mexican-Indian plot in time to render it harmless, they had done their dangerous duty in full. They took no official part in the brutal expulsion of the Cherokees from Texas that followed. But since that expulsion set the stage for their first great era—their no-quarter war with the western Comanches—it must be briefly considered.

When the Manuel Flores papers captured by Rice's Rangers were made public, the panicky citizens demanded action. They got it. Old Sam Houston, that tall and towering friend of the red man, was no longer in office. The new president, Mirabeau Buonaparte Lamar, hated all Indians with deep passion. Under his orders, the army of Texas was at once dispatched to drive the Cherokees from their highly cultivated lands in the eastern settlements. This, despite the fact that there was no proof at all that their chiefs had agreed to the treacherous proposals of the Mexican war agents.

The fact that the Cherokees had made no preparation to take part in the vicious plot did not save them. They were Indians. They were taking up some of the best farmland in Texas. They had to go or be driven out. A party of four "peace commissioners" was sent to parley with the head chief, Bowles. Their real purpose was to make sure the Cherokees did not leave before the army troops got into position to "help them go". The brave Bowles, although he knew his cause was already lost, could not bow down to the bandit demands of the greedy Texans. Although they wore no masks, they were simply robbing him and his people, and the old chief knew it. But he was unafraid. His people, he announced with pathetic dignity, would fight.

It was what the Texans had wanted to hear. And it was all they wanted to hear. The hopeless encounter lasted less than forty-eight hours. It was brought to its shameful close when Chief Bowles was captured and shot down in cold blood.

Leaderless, stunned by this turn of events after twenty years of faithful friendship with the white man in Texas, the sorrowful survivors of the most civilized Indian tribe in American history fled northward into the wilderness of Arkansas. But even this wasn't enough for the Texans. Caught up in the fever of their long-standing fear of the red warriors, the white troops decided to make a clean sweep of it. They fell upon the remaining east Texas tribes and drove them after the Cherokees. To this outbreak of "pure piracy upon the plains", the Delawares, Shawnees, Caddos, Kickapoos,

Creeks, and Seminoles were shocked and unbelieving victims. Yet they had no chance. They knew that. They were being punished for the scalpings and cabin-burnings of their ancestors. Against such a charge there was no safety but to follow the panic-stricken example of the Cherokees.

From the loblolly pine forests of the Sabine to the inner prairies of the Brazos, the Indians of eastern Texas gathered up their loved ones and fled for their lives. Within short weeks a great silence fell over the settlements. For the first time in nineteen years the throb of the dance drum and the thrill of the war whoop were heard no more. The cook fires no longer smoked. The council houses stood deserted. Only the restless wind prowled the village streets. The Indians were gone. The last pitiful remnant of their former power—a small band of Cherokees lost from the main group and trying to reach the safety of Mexico—were surrounded and destroyed on the west bank of the Colorado. Among the dead was John Bowles, beloved son of the old chief. The so-called Cherokee Uprising was over. The despised "redskin" had been driven forever from the settled eastern part of Texas.

The good citizens of the new Republic of Texas looked on and nodded "well done" at the sinful work. But they nodded too soon. For the Great Spirit had not forgotten his red children. Out of the trackless western plains, Lone Wolf listened in slant-eyed silence to the news of the Cherokee disaster. Lone Wolf was the war chief of all the Comanches. He was a wise and crafty leader. He knew the white man well. When he heard what had befallen Bowles and his gentle people, he knew he must act fast. Within the hour, he had gathered his dark-skinned sub-chiefs into high council. He had one frightening question for them. If the pale-faced *Tejanos* could do this monstrous thing to Indians who were their faithful friends, what might they do to red men who were their bitter enemies?

Lone Wolf did not know the answer to his own question. But one thing was certain. He had to find that answer, and find it fast! The old chief stood up. He put away his pipe and reached for his war shield. The council was at an end.

"Paint your faces and tell your women good bye," he told his scowling listeners. "Take your best ponies and make your strongest medicine. We are going to the white man's big village where the Mexican black robes used to live. We are going to San Antonio!"

VI

"COLONEL KARNES AND THE COUNCIL HOUSE FIGHT"

The new year of 1840 was nine days old. The January sun was warm and bright in the plaza of old San Antonio. The two guards on duty in front of the Bexar County Rangers headquarters were in understandably excellent humor.

"I allow," drawled Private Pettus Tucker, "that you and me had best be lookin' for a new job, Bates. I ain't seen a Comanche for so long I forgot what one looks like."

Corporal Bates Isbell, on the point of agreeing with his friend, took another look down the dusty street. His eyes narrowed suddenly. "Take a good squint yonder," he said softly. "Mebbe it'll freshen your memory!"

Ranger Tucker peered hard. His good-natured grin faded. Riding slowly across the plaza, the sparkling winter sun flashing off their tasseled lances and gaudily painted buffalo-hide shields, were three Comanche war chiefs.

"Reckon I'd better run in and tell the colonel," muttered Private Pettus Tucker.

"Reckon you better had," agreed Corporal Bates Isbell, easing his big horse pistol in its worn holster.

142

Inside the headquarters building Colonel Henry W. Karnes, San Antonio's famous red-haired Indian fighter, put down his turkey-feather pen. He laid aside the peaceful report he had been writing to General Albert Sidney Johnson, Texas Secretary of War. He reached, instead, for his long Sharps rifle.

"All right, Tucker," he said quickly. "Bring them in. Let's see what the red scoundrels want this time. I'll bet they've had enough of the Texas Rangers and want to quit."

Colonel Karnes was right. Lone Wolf's first words told him that.

"My people are tired of war," the old chief began nervously.

Lone Wolf did not like standing inside the little houses of the white men. The thick walls and the narrow, rifle-slit windows made him feel as though he were standing in a trap. He got on quickly with what he had come to say.

"We are ready to put aside our shields and lay down our lances. We want to ask the Rangers for peace."

Colonel Karnes looked at him and the two sub-chiefs with him. A grim smile of deep pride and satisfaction lit his lean face. The Comanches wanted to ask *the Rangers* for peace! After four years of fierce warfare against the whole army of the new Republic, the wild men of the plains had come to beg for peace from a tiny company of twenty-five Texas Rangers! No wonder Colonel

Karnes felt proud. But his smile was gone as swiftly as it had appeared. No peace treaty was possible, he told the three chiefs, not until the Comanches agreed to bring in all the white captives in their possession.

Lone Wolf and his companions muttered angrily among themselves. Colonel Karnes warned them they had but five minutes to make up their minds. Their ugly scowls grew darker.

Colonel Karnes took out his gold watch. He propped it on his desk, against the heavy barrel of his rifle. The Indians took the silent hint.

It was agreed, they nodded sullenly. They would return in twenty days with all the prisoners.

Colonel Karnes went back to his report. His quill pen scratched across the rough paper with urgent speed. He had no faith in the Comanche promise, he wrote General Johnson, and his Rangers would not take part in any further talks with them. The treacherous red men had lied too many times. The government had better send a strong body of regular troops to San Antonio at once. The Rangers' job was done. They had fought the savage foe for four bloody years. Now he was beaten and wanted to surrender. The war was over. Making peace was for politicians. Colonel Henry W. Karnes respectfully excused himself. He and his Texas Rangers wanted no part in the foolish business of "trying to bring sweetness and light to the murdering Comanches."

Two months later, on March 19, a trio of dark-skinned runners appeared suddenly from the west. When the citizens of San Antonio heard their news, they began putting up their heavy, wooden shutters. The Indians were coming! Like the Rangers, the frontier townsfolk had no use for any kind of an Indian but a "good" one. In Ranger language, this meant one with a Texan bullet hole between his eyes.

Lieutenant Colonel William S. Fisher, in command of the army troops stationed around the Council House, had no such prejudices. He prepared to receive the Indian delegation in good faith. But when its sullen chiefs stood before him, the officer perceived at once that he had been tricked. There were plenty of Comanches present, *but only one white captive.* Fisher knew that no less than half a hundred white women and children had been seized and carried off by the Comanches during the preceding four years.

"What is the meaning of this?" he demanded angrily. "Where are all the prisoners you promised to bring in to this talk?"

Lone Wolf was not present. Like Colonel Karnes, he was not a man of peace. Instead, he had sent his crafty medicine man, Muk-War-Rah.

Muk-War-Rah was an evil-looking man. He was shaved completely bald. His skull-like face and copper chest were smeared with ochre and vermilion war paint.

"We have brought in the only one we had," he said, grinning wolfishly. "The others are with other tribes." Then, striking his breast and leering fully into the white officer's face, he challenged insolently: "How do you like the answer?"

Lieutenant Colonel Fisher did not like the answer at all. The Rangers had been right, as usual. There was no reasonable hope whatever of making a treaty with these arrogant killers. They understood only one kind of talk—the harsh language that a loaded rifle and a naked cavalry saber spoke.

"Bar the door!" Fisher snapped to the soldiers outside. Then: "You are prisoners," he told Muk-War-Rah and the warriors inside the room with him. "We will hold you until every one of the captives is brought in!"

Fisher knew that the Indians understood what he was talking about. The lone captive, a little girl named Matilda Lockhart, had told him that there were many other white children and several women still in the Comanche camp. The Indians planned to bring them in one at a time in hopes of forcing the treaty to be made on their own terms. But the foolish white officer had made a grave mistake. He did not know that the fierce Plains warriors preferred death to capture.

"I will not stay here! I am going home!" cried Muk-War-Rah. He flashed a hidden knife from his buckskin hunting leggings, and sprang at the soldiers by the door. One of them barred his rifle, blocking the medicine man's escape. The desperate Comanche plunged his knife into him. Instantly the whole room was in an uproar.

Soldiers' guns crashed point-blank into the crowded braves. The room was filled with choking sounds of powder smoke. The few Indians who reached the door were shot down by the troopers stationed around the Council House. Outside the building, their comrades, braves and squaws alike, ran for their ponies. Again and again, the soldiers' rifles thundered into them.

When the last round was fired, the pall of gunsmoke drifted away. A terrible stillness lay over the dusty plaza of old San Antonio. Huddled against the bullet-riddled walls of the Council House, twenty-seven red warriors waited. All the rest, including three unarmed women and two small children, lay where they had fallen. Not a solitary Comanche had escaped that deadly ring of rifle steel. Thirty-five Indians had died in less than fifteen minutes.

An unwounded squaw was selected from among the terrified prisoners. She was provided with a swift pony and told to go home and tell her people what had happened. She was also to warn them that all the rest of the white captives must be brought in at once. The alternative would be war to the last Comanche. The squaw understood. She said that she would do as she had been told, and that she would return in four days.

She was never seen again. But her fellow Comanches were. The time was six months later, August 8, 1840. The place, Linnville, a sleepy little Gulf port town on the Texas coast. The players, 700 enraged red warriors. Their purpose, merciless, no-quarter revenge for the murder of their chiefs in the Council House massacre. The password was "*Pei-da Ta'kae-kih!*" Translated, this meant: "Death to the White Man!"

VII

"COMANCHE VENGEANCE"

It was hot that peaceful August morning in Linnville. In front of his dry goods store, old Avery Hudspeth mopped his brow and listened to the big-eyed ranch boy who had just ridden his lathered pony into town. Young Tobin Rhodes was beside himself with excitement. On his way home he had seen, far out on the western plain, a tremendous caravan of Mexican traders bound for Linnville. Their column stretched for half a mile. There were hundreds of them, maybe a thousand. Maybe more. Tobin Rhodes had not stopped to count them, or to wait for them to draw near. It was not every day a boy of twelve got to wake up the town with such wonderful news.

But old Avery Hudspeth had lived a long time in Texas. A thousand Mexicans coming to trade with

300 dirt-poor whites? It did not make sense to the old man. He would have to have a closer look before he believed that.

He hurried into the store and got out his ancient brassbound telescope. It was the one he used every day to watch hopefully for new ships entering Linnville's little bay from the Gulf of Mexico. It was a mighty stout and trusty glass. It would surely let a man see what was really under that big dust cloud, now clearly visible two miles to the west.

Thirty seconds later Avery Hudspeth had the venerable spyglass focused on the prairie. And five seconds after that his squinting eye popped wider than the three-inch lens through which it was staring. He saw an unbelievable cavalcade of savage horsemen. There were hundreds and hundreds of painted braves. Not only that, there were blanketed squaws, with tiny babes on cradleboards strapped to their mothers' dark-skinned backs. The whole war strength of the Comanche nation! They were hundreds of miles inside the western frontier, and coming at a breakneck gallop straight down upon the sleeping town of Linnville.

"Injuns!" Avery gasped to the startled boy. "A whole ring-tailed passel of 'em!"

He dropped the glass, and wheeled upon the frightened youth. "Boy!" he shouted. "You git back on that pony of yours and ride fer your life! Down the street! Git to Major Watts at the custom house. Yell your lungs out on the way. Them's

Comanches comin' out yonder, young 'un! And they're comin' fer us!"

Young Tobin Rhodes leaped on his pony. He knew it was not only his own life he rode for, but the life of every one of Linnville's innocent citizens.

Nobody remembers Tobin Rhodes today. They should. In the ten minutes it took the ungainly Comanche column to cover the two miles to town, he spread the alarm swiftly and well. Almost the entire population was able to flee to the safety of the bay. There, they were taken aboard the cargo lighter of a trading schooner lying offshore at anchor. From the dangerously crowded decks of the leaky barge, they watched in speechless horror as the Indians engulfed the town. They saw with their own eyes the death of gallant Major Watts, who had lingered too long in seeing that every woman and child was safely out of the settlement. Then, throughout the endless hours of the blazing August sun, they watched in helpless agony as the savages looted their homes, stores, and warehouses.

When nightfall came at last, no structure in sight had been spared. Everything of value that could be carried off on horseback had been removed and piled aboard the Comanche pack animals. Nor was that all. Between the dusk of August 8 and dawn of the ninth, the Comanche horde fired and burned to the ground every building in Linnville, Texas.

Stern proud men wept aboard the darkened barge. Their womenfolk prayed aloud and their little children cried piteously in the summer blackness.

When the next morning's sun rose, sick and smoke-gray, through the pall of wood ash, the Indians were gone. In less than twenty-four hours they had blotted out forever an entire city from the map of Texas. Legend has it that the Comanches killed thirty-five white people on their way to Linnville—exactly the number of their chiefs and headmen slain in the Council House massacre. The legend goes on to say that they took captive no more nor less than twenty-seven Texans—precisely the same number the soldiers had seized in San Antonio. Hard fact places the dead at twenty-five, the prisoners at thirteen. But frontier history is never too reliable. The fable is frequently as accurate as the fact.

In the case of the bloody Linnville raid, the legend holds one dark advantage. For it was the way a merciless Comanche mind would have conceived and executed such a violent crime: an eye for an eye, a tooth for a tooth, one white man's scalp for every Indian man, woman, and child who died in the soldiers' trap at San Antonio. In the end, only two singular and important historical facts stand out about Linnville. It was the first mass Indian raid ever conducted so deep into the white settlements of Texas. And it was the last. The Texas Rangers saw to that.

VIII

"PLUM CREEK AND BEN MCCULLOCH'S RIDE"

One reason alone had allowed the vast Comanche column to strike hundreds of miles inside the western frontier without challenge—and very nearly without discovery. Their scouts and outriders, coursing swiftly in advance of the motley horde, surprised and shot down every living soul in its way. Thus the Indian leaders were satisfied that not a single white Texan had escaped ahead of them to warn the settlements. They were right. None had. But what about the white Texan behind them? Indian-like, they had never thought of that. It was their first great mistake.

On August 5, a lone mail carrier, riding from Austin to Gonzales, crossed the Comanches' broad trail near Plum Creek. He took one scalp-tingling look at the thousands of unshod pony tracks and spurred on to Gonzales. As luck would have it, Ben McCulloch of the Rangers was in Gonzales that day. He waited only long enough to hear the mail carrier's wide-eyed report. Within the hour he was riding. Yet, already, he was too late.

When he and his twenty-four volunteers reached Plum Creek, the Comanche campfires were long cold. Grimly the Texans struck southward along the trampled course of the great Indian cavalcade.

Meanwhile, Linnville was burning and the red raiders were making their second mistake. Instead of scattering to gallop for home in small bands and by a dozen different trails—they set out in a body to return by the same route they had come.

By this time the whole of settled Texas was aflame with the ghastly news of the Linnville tragedy. Yet the all-important question went unanswered. *Where were the Indians?* No one knew. They seemed to have disappeared. If they were not found—and found soon—they would escape unpunished.

As usual, where no one else was able to do so, a Texas Ranger arose to supply the answer. Ben McCulloch and his men had lost the inbound Indian trail during a night of torrential rain. They picked it up again, near Victoria, only hours after the sack of Linnville.

At once, the tireless McCulloch, with three trusted scouts, rode on. Within six hours he was back, bearing electrifying news that spread northward from Victoria. The Comanches were coming! And they were coming as Ben McCulloch had suspected they would do. Straight back along the same bloody trail they had blazed in their death march to the sea! And more news. They would be nearing Victoria by sundown! There was time enough for the desperate Texans to make a stand.

In instant response to the bold Ranger's warning, the hard-faced horsemen raced toward the little settlement. By late afternoon 125 men were assembled on the prairie south and east of town. Shortly before sunset, the great Comanche host appeared.

The waiting Texans were stunned. Until that shocked moment, none of them had actually believed Ben McCulloch's report about the tremendous size of the Indian force. The oldest Indian fighter among them—Captain John J. Tumlinson of DeWitt County—had never seen so many red warriors gathered together in one company. The glittering line of their painted war ponies and flashing lances continued on out of sight beyond the distant curve of the treeless plain. The immense cloud of dust thrown up by their mounts and by the vast herd of 1,000 stolen horses they were driving before them towered a hundred feet into the wind-still summer sky.

Captain Tumlinson hesitated. He was in command of his and McCulloch's combined forces. The decision to fight, or to fall back and let the Indian horde pass unchallenged, was his alone. The Comanches had by now sighted the little white party. A detail of red scouts dashed forward to make sure of the Texans' apparent weakness. Ben McCulloch, guessing their intent, tried to forestall it. Calmly taking aim, he knocked their leader out of his saddle at 100 yards. It was an unbelievable shot, but the damage was done. The scouts had seen what they wanted to see.

Wheeling their ponies, they raced back to the main column with the gleeful word. There were only a handful of the hated *Tejanos* waiting up there! They could be driven under in minutes by the favorite Plains Indian tactic of stampeding the horse herd through them. The warriors, slashing in on the heels of the maddened horses, could shoot down the scattered Texans like crippled buffalo.

"Gather the great horse herd?"

"String the war bows!"

"*Pei-da Ta'kae-kih*! Death to the White Man!"

Seeing the Indian preparation and sensing at once its deadly purpose, Captain Tumlinson lost heart. Despairingly he gave the order to withdraw and let the Comanche column pass.

"McCulloch," he told his youthful second-in-command, "we have got to get out of here. They are too many for us. We will fall back toward San Antonio. Captain Matt Caldwell is up there with his army boys. We can join up with them and make a final stand together."

Ben McCulloch was a Texas Ranger. He had taken the oath never to retreat. "You can't do that, Captain!" he cried. "We must charge them now, or we shall never see them again!"

"We will retreat," repeated Tumlinson. "We have no other choice."

"But you will never get to Caldwell in time," objected the young Ranger heatedly. "The Indians will slip away and we shall lose them."

"You have my orders!" growled the older man, angry himself now. "Tell your men to retreat!"

"I will never tell them that!" snapped young McCulloch.

And he never did. Calling his three best men to him—Alsey Miller, Arch Gibson, and little Barney Randall, all of whom had scouted the Comanche trail with him—he told them what he meant to do.

"Boys," he said quietly, "we have got to ride far and fast. Captain Tumlinson is going to let the Indians go past. We have got to see they don't get away."

"What kin we do, Ben?" asked Alsey Miller anxiously. "I know you Rangers are six-toed wildcats in a Injun fight. But, shucks! Me and Arch and Barney are only just ordinary two-legged humans. What kin the three of us possibly do toward helpin' you halt a thousand fired-up Comanches?"

"Follow me and I'll show you." Ben McCulloch laughed. "And on the way I'll show you how to be Texas Rangers to boot. Either that, or show you how to die almighty quick, tryin'."

"Let's go," said Arch Gibson with a grin. "I allow I always wanted to be a Ranger anyhow."

"Me, too," said Barney Randall, and shrugged his shoulders. "I ain't signed no long-term lease on life recently. What you got in mind, Ben?"

What Ben McCulloch had in mind was chillingly simple. It was to ride around the retreating Comanche column during the night, pass the Indians in the darkness, find Captain Matt Caldwell and the army troops before dawn, and tell them where and how to set a trap for the murderers of Linnville before they could slip past San Antonio.

McCulloch's three companions nodded silently. They did not have to be told what might happen if the Indians got past San Antonio. Once beyond that point, there would be no heading them short of the frontier. They would be safely back in the trackless prairies of their buffalo-pasture homeland to the west. No pursuit could hope to find them there, and they would have gotten cleanly away with their great raid. When the other war-like tribes heard of that, there was no telling what terrible bloodshed could result. The Kiowas, Apaches, Cheyennes—all the violent High Plains tribes—might flare up and start on a war trail that would wipe out every settlement in Texas. It was no idle nightmare. The Indians could do it. The Comanches had shown them how at Linnville.

"All right, Ben," said Alsey Miller, tight-lipped. "What are we waitin' for? Let's ride."

That night Ranger Ben McCulloch and his three brave scouts made one of the most daring rides in frontier history. Today it is all but forgotten. Yet when it was made that sultry summer night of long ago, its failure could well have changed the map of our nation as we know it today. If Ben McCulloch had not refused to retreat with Tumlinson—if he had not decided to make his horse-killing ride to warn Captain Caldwell—if he had not succeeded in reaching the army troops in time—if he had not. . . . McCulloch did make his great ride and he did reach Captain Caldwell in time.

Just at daybreak of August 10, 1840, he and his exhausted comrades dashed into the army camp at Seguin, Texas. Caldwell, after a hurried conference with the youthful Ranger, decided to follow McCulloch's hunch and attempt to intercept the Indians at Plum Creek below San Antonio.

Camp was broken and the march begun at once. That night the army troops camped at the San Antonio crossing of the San Marcos River. Next morning the forced advance resumed. The way now led along the desolate trail the Comanches had left coming into the settlements. All day long the march continued across a prairie still burning with the fires set by the raiders. Flying ash, dense clouds of drifting smoke, and the stifling heat of the smoldering flames choked and blinded the weary men and horses. Yet that night they reached their objective. Camp was made on Plum Creek.

It was 10:00 p.m., August 11. Only one terse question remained in the minds of the bone-tired men. Again, it was Ben McCulloch and his sleepless scouts who rode out to seek the answer.

Then, in the smoke-filled dawn of the twelfth, they rode their staggering mounts back into the army camp. The wildest excitement ensued. Captain Caldwell had his answer. His troops were in time. Ben McCulloch's ride had not been in vain.

The Indians were less than three miles away. They appeared to have no inkling of the trap into which they were riding. The battle would be on—the issue won or lost—within the next thirty minutes.

The white troops were now in command of General Felix Huston, who had ridden in during the night with a large body of Texas militia. Caldwell was a far more experienced Indian fighter. He watched the nervous general closely. So did Ranger Ben McCulloch.

As the Indian force rode suddenly into view, one thought occupied the minds of Caldwell and McCulloch. Would Huston fail to charge at Plum Creek as Tumlinson had at Victoria? Ben McCulloch decided he dared not wait to find out. When the leading Comanche war chief spurred forward to incite his screaming warriors to attack, McCulloch's rifle jumped to his shoulder. A single shot echoed across the prairie. The war chief threw up his arms, pitched off his pony, and lay still, a neat blue bullet hole between his glazing eyes.

Ben McCulloch lowered his gun. He turned quickly to Captain Caldwell. "Well, Captain, there's their Big Noise quieted down. Reckon you know what to tell the general to do now."

Captain Matt Caldwell did, indeed, know what to tell his uncertain commander. Instantly he wheeled his horse. "Now, General," he shouted hoarsely, "is your time to charge them. They are whipped!"

Carried beyond himself by McCulloch's cool

marksmanship and Caldwell's high excitement, Huston ordered the charge. His command came in the nick of time. The Indians were about to stampede their huge horse herd into the troops. Instead, the unexpected suddenness of the attack by the white men caused the crazed animals to break backwards—squarely into the startled ranks of their own red masters. The result was an Indian shambles.

The cursing white riflemen shot down the hopelessly entangled Comanches like helpless, blind-running cattle. No quarter was considered. The merciless pursuit and point-blank firing continued until there was no living red man left within bullet range or horseback reach of the Plum Creek trap.

When the last shot had died away and the summer morning stillness settled again over the sunlit prairie, seventy-eight Comanche braves had ridden their last war trail. In his official report General Huston stated that their huddled, sightless bodies were found "concealed in thickets, sunk in the river, or on the outer prairie as high up as the San Antonio Road."

It was the Texans' greatest victory over the savage barbarians of the plains. The once-mighty war lords of the outer prairie were never the same thereafter. For another eighteen years they would continue to be a serious threat to the western frontier, but there would never be another Linnville, nor a raid of any kind into east Texas.

Ben McCulloch never claimed any personal credit for the victory. Ben knew better than that. He would have been the first to have doffed his battered hat and proudly saluted the real heroes. They were that ill-paid, little appreciated, often vilified "band of rascals" with whom he rode to frontier glory for a dollar and twenty-five cents a day—the Texas Rangers.

IX

"JOHN C. HAYS, SAVIOR OF SAN ANTONIO"

There was no rest for the Rangers. No sooner was the red foe driven back across the western frontier than a new enemy suddenly appeared along the southern border. It would be more accurate to say that an old enemy suddenly reappeared along that border. For the defeated *vaqueros* of old Mexico had never accepted the loss of Texas to Sam Houston's hard-pressed little army of rebellious *Tejanos*. In March, 1842, General Rafael Vasquez struck without warning. His troops slashed across the border at the heart of the still-shaky young nation— San Antonio. He seized the city within twenty-four hours and occupied it without resistance for two days. Then, just as suddenly and mysteriously, he withdrew his forces and returned to Mexico.

Texas paid dangerously little heed to the strange maneuver. It had been a bloodless affair, typically

Mexican. Forget it, was the Texans' attitude. It meant nothing. Texas had far more serious affairs to fret about. But did she? Vasquez would not have thought so! His seventy-two-hour expedition had been a deliberate trick, a bold adventure to establish the possibility of a real invasion. Today it would have been called a commando raid. Modern military men would have known what to fear next. Perhaps the Texas fathers did, too. For it is significant that they sent a little company of Texas Rangers to guard the threatened town, instead of the regular army troops. Just as significant was their choice of a commander for this tiny force.

For the first important time in Ranger history, we hear the name of Captain John Coffee Hays. "Jack" Hays was a fighting man from a fighting family. His father and grandfather had served valiantly with Andrew Jackson in the Creek and Seminole wars. He was named after General John Coffee, Jackson's most able and belligerent lieutenant. Young Jack came to Texas in 1838, looking for a fight. He found it at San Antonio. He was still only twenty-five years old at the time, but he had ridden four full years with the Rangers of red-haired Henry Karnes and fabled old Deaf Smith. He was ready for the test which history had in store for him along the Salado River. Nor did he fear that test in the least. And why should he? Did he not have Henry McCulloch for his lieutenant, and young Ben for one of his sergeants?

The McCulloch brothers were fighting Tennesseans like himself. They had come west with Davy Crockett. They had missed that doughty hero's death at the Alamo only because they had delayed three days to visit in the settlements. With men like these, what Ranger captain worth his $1.25 a day would worry about a few thousand Mexicans threatening to take back Texas? Certainly not Jack Hays. At least not until September 10, 1842. On that day he heard that General Adrian Woll of the Mexican Army had advanced across the border with a full-strength field command of cavalry, infantry, and artillery.

No one knows how many men Hays had at the time. Beyond doubt they were fewer than a hundred. The only official record lists them unglowingly as "the few Ranger spies under Captain John C. Hays at post San Antonio." Nevertheless, hearing of Woll's approach to the city, Hays set out with only five scouts to reconnoiter the Mexican column. His main objective was to ascertain the exact location of the enemy.

Woll, a professional soldier with European training, was not to be so easily found out. Under cover of darkness he divided his command, leaving the main road and advancing northward in four columns. It was not until daylight that Hays found the invasion force—drawn up in siege position, completely surrounding San Antonio. The resourceful Ranger did what he could.

Waiting for darkness of the eleventh, he stole deeply inside the Mexican lines. He had to know the enemy's true strength before carrying out the bold plans already forming in his restless mind. Had he been caught he would have been shot without military honors as a common spy. The prospect brought only a wry smile to the daring Texan's handsome face, and the smile faded swiftly when he had completed his dangerous count of the foe. Unless his Ranger arithmetic was wrong—and he had just risked his life to make sure that it was not—Woll had upwards of 1,300 men in the lines he had thrown around San Antonio. The city was doomed. Jack Hays knew that. He knew, as well, what next he had to do.

With his five scouts he rode northward through the autumn night, spreading the dread alarm. "San Antonio has fallen! Rally, Texans! Raise the old-time war whoop! Gather at Bexar! We shall fight them at the Salado!"

"CAPTAIN JACK SETS A TRAP AT SALADO"

In Texas of that time, the night-riding war cry never echoed in vain. The usual ragged volunteer army of settler-soldiers sprang up and came in from outside Bexar County. Nor, in that dark hour, did the embattled ranchers rally alone. That old war horse, Captain Matt Caldwell, brought down a force of eighty-five seasoned militia men from "up country". As senior officer of those present, Caldwell was at once elected commander of the 225 Texans who had gathered at Bexar. In swift agreement with Jack Hays's plan to "gamble all" on stopping the invaders at the Salado River, he ordered the march to that stream to begin within the hour of his arrival.

General Woll, leaving a garrison of 500 troops in San Antonio, advanced on the waiting Texans with 200 cavalrymen, 600 infantrymen, and a company of artillery. The two armies clashed across the Salado in the early dawn of September 17, 1842. The bloody struggle raged until merciful darkness brought a truce to allow both sides to retrieve and bury their dead. The Mexicans had asked for the truce, but it was the Texans who needed it. Their little force had suffered an irreparable loss late in the afternoon. Captain Dawson and his company of fifty-three men from La Grange had been cut off while trying to unite with Caldwell. Under point-blank range of Woll's artillery, Dawson had been forced to raise the white flag of surrender. The Mexicans had replied by pounding his position to bits with their cannon. Of Dawson's "fearless fifty-three", only fifteen men escaped to bring the sad word to the Texan lines. In turn, the Mexicans had lost a greater number: sixty dead. But they had had

1,300 to start with. The Texans had had scarcely 200.

Sleepless at his campfire that night, Captain Caldwell wrote in brave desperation to the government at Austin: *The enemy are all around me on every side; but I fear them not. I will hold my position until I hear from reinforcements. Come and help me . . . !*

But there was no time to send help to Caldwell's men. And no need to do so. Captain Jack Hays and his Texas Rangers made sure of that.

"They can't take the kind of casualties our boys heaped up on them out there today, Captain," he comforted Caldwell. "You wait and see. Come daylight tomorrow, there won't be a single *soldado* left in that river brush yonder."

Caldwell was not so sure. But Jack Hays knew his Mexicans. They were brave enough—brave as any man—but they were just like the Indians. Once they had had a good fight and killed a few of the enemy, they wanted to go home.

Two hours before dawn, Ben McCulloch rode back from a scouting trip with big news. "They're pullin' out, boys! Lock, stock, and cannon barrel! If we don't step spry, they'll make it clean away!"

But the Rangers were never famous for dragging their feet. And, besides, Jack Hays had a plan. He wanted to draw out, trap, and take the Mexican artillery.

"Get their popguns away from them, boys," he

told his men, "and Caldwell will have the rest of them chased back to Chihuahua by sundown."

All the Rangers had to do was push Woll's rear so hard he would have to drop the artillery back to cover his retreat. A forgotten member of Hays's company, who sprang for his pony in response to his captain's call, has left us this picture of Hays at that moment: *Captain Jack Hays, our intrepid leader, five feet, ten inches high, weighing one hundred and sixty pounds, his black eyes flashing decision of character, from beneath a full forehead crowned with beautiful jet black hair, was soon mounted on his dark bay war horse and on the warpath.*

Hays's strategy with the cannon worked perfectly. His men harassed and taunted Woll's flank so hotly that later the Mexican general is reputed to have offered $500 for the head of the "wild, black-haired youth upon whom he placed entire blame for his defeat." More importantly, the constant Ranger pressure forced Woll to drop his artillery back exactly as Hays had anticipated.

What happened then is best told in the words of another of Hays's devoted men: *At length the shrill, clear voice of our captain sounded down the line . . . "Charge!" Away went the company up a gradual ascent in quick time. In a moment the cannon roared, but, according to Mexican custom, overshot us. The Texas yell followed the cannon's thunder and so excited the Mexican infantry, placed in position to pour a fire down our lines, that they, too, overshot us. By the time the artillery hurled its canister the second time, shotguns and pistols were freely used by the Texans. Every man at the cannon was killed.*

With the capture of his artillery, Woll's retreat became a route. His "homesick" troops fled so swiftly that Caldwell's command completely lost contact with them. San Antonio was evacuated and abandoned as abruptly. By the time Jack Hays and his powder-grimed Rangers rode back into its peaceful plaza, the only Mexican soldiers left in Texas were those who would sleep forever on the lonely banks of the Salado River.

XI

"BIGFOOT WALLACE AND THE BLACK BEAN"

The story of Bigfoot Wallace and the black bean has become a Texas legend, and it is herein given as such without apology. Shortly after the Battle of Salado, Sam Houston had an idea. Since Hays and Caldwell had "so handily whipped the arrogant Woll," why not return the enemy favor and invade Mexico? Houston was now in his second term as president of the Republic of Texas. He was undoubtedly a remarkable man, maybe even a great one. But he made many a wild and wonderful blunder in his time. He never made a better one than the so-called Mier Expedition, the story of which follows.

In November, 1842, General Somervell, acting under Houston's orders, led the Texas troops out of San Antonio. With him, as "scouts and spies", went Jack Hays's company of trusted Rangers. The makeshift force moved across the Río Grande into Mexico, and seized the town of Guerrero. With the easy victory, Somervell's raging troops got out of hand. Shortly, looting and rioting through the streets of Guerrero, they were completely beyond Somervell's command.

The general got scared; Jack Hays became disgusted. Both men quit the expedition and went home. Hays headed for San Antonio, taking his Rangers with him. But the story of the black bean was only getting started.

Colonel William S. Fisher, the same officer who had ordered the Comanche massacre at Council House, took command of the troops who refused to follow Hays and Somervell back to Texas. He loudly announced that he would lead them on to undying glory.

Well, he led plenty of them to glory, all right. But it was scarcely of the "undying" variety. Among the 300 "unprincipled rascals" who decided to accompany him farther into Mexico were four later-to-become-famous Rangers. These were Ewan Cameron, William Eastland, Sam Walker, and the good-natured giant who was to build a deathless legend out of an ordinary bean—Bigfoot Wallace. We are told that Bigfoot was "the better part of seven feet tall" and that he "weighed twenty pounds less than a grizzly b'ar." "A size-fourteen shoe," we are asked to believe, "would not begin to encase his monstrous pedal extremities." The legend goes on to claim that he "spent twenty years killing Indians to find one with feet big enough so that he could wear his moccasins."

It was just as well that Bigfoot was a sizable man. History had a sizable job cut out for him. When Fisher's rebellious army reached Mier, which was no more than a miserable huddle of adobe shacks set in a desert of hot sun and little water, disaster struck. A Mexican cavalry regiment ambushed the Texans. Fisher was sorely wounded and forced to surrender. Every one of his men was captured.

They were marched 200 miles on foot, due south, to Saltillo, then another 200 miles west to Hacienda Salado. There they were imprisoned in an old military barracks. Their suffering was intense. Some of the weaker among them did not survive the blistering heat and thirst of the terrible trek. Those who did were in little better luck, for no prisoner had ever escaped from Hacienda Salado. But the Mexicans had never had anybody like Bigfoot Wallace penned up there. Bigfoot was determined to show them that, and "purty durn sudden" according to his own account.

At sunrise, February 11, 1843, he and his three fellow Rangers led the prison break. The war-whooping Texans overwhelmed the Mexican cavalry guard and set out across the desert for the Río Grande. But even Bigfoot could not lead them across that barren waste. Crazed with thirst, many of them blinded by the merciless glare of the sun, the fugitives were recaptured by the pursuing cavalry and returned to Hacienda Salado in irons. Here, Santa Anna, the cruel Mexican dictator, ordered that every tenth man among them was to be led out and executed. The manner in which those who were to die would be chosen was entirely heartless. There were 176 survivors. Into a pottery cooking vessel with a small neck were placed 159 white beans and seventeen black ones. The men who drew the black beans would be shot.

The drawing began. When its agony was over, seventeen of Fisher's troops had the black beans. The four Rangers found themselves with white beans. It was in that amount of chill silence that the legend of Bigfoot and the black bean was born. No amount of historical evidence, not even Bigfoot's own honorable denial, has been able to destroy it since.

"Boys," the legend quotes the drawling giant, "I got here a perfectly good white bean. Now, I never did cotton to pale-faced *frijoles*, and I will gladly trade it to any of you who have got a black one."

There was a proud moment, then, for generations

of Texans yet to come. Not a single one of the seventeen doomed men would surrender his black bean. To a man, they kept them and marched out to meet their deaths "grim-faced but unafraid." Bigfoot and the other white-bean holders were marched deeper into Mexico. There they were manacled and thrown into the deepest dungeons of Perote Prison. For many months they lay there, "rotting away with disease and kept in conditions of the most unspeakable filth." Eventually all who survived were liberated and made their various ways back to Texas. Later, many of them, Bigfoot and Sam Walker in particular, returned and wreaked a terrible vengeance in the Mexican War. But for the purposes of this story, their adventure ended with the drawing of the beans at Hacienda Salado. That drawing, and the events which led up to it, were important because they re-established two Ranger fundamentals that were, henceforth, to become the *living* heart of the Texas Ranger tradition:

(1) Like Bigfoot Wallace, a Ranger must always be ready to offer his life for a comrade's.

(2) Unlike Colonel Fisher, a Ranger must never again surrender to the enemy.

Fact or fable, the legend of Bigfoot Wallace and the black bean gave the famous captains of the Rangers who were yet to come something against which to compare their own courage and unselfish loyalty.

XII

"THE RANGERS 'WIN' THE MEXICAN WAR"

For the next four years the Rangers, spearheaded by Jack Hays's San Antonio company, ruled the border with "fleet pony and ever-ready pistol." In this hard-riding time Hays rose to be a colonel, the reward for his distinguished service in the defense of Texas lives and property against the continually raiding *vaqueros* of old Mexico. His methods in dealing with the border bandits, merciless by present-day methods, must be judged in the war-like light of his own times. It has been estimated that in that one four-year period alone, no less than a hundred Mexican nationals were "done in" by the border patrol. And this against the loss of "scarcely a single Ranger."

Hays had his grim reason for these summary executions. If his Rangers gained a feared name for never bringing in a live prisoner, hard necessity molded their lack of mercy. One successful theft of Texas livestock that was unpursued, or a single cabin-burning or ranch attack that went unpunished, was simply an open invitation to the next border violation. Jack Hays left very few such invitations lying around his part of Texas.

Then, in 1846, the service of the Rangers to Texas was interrupted by their enthusiastic tour of duty with Zachary Taylor's United States troops in the invasion of Mexico. Texas was a member of the Union now, and Uncle Sam was tired of the constant petty warfare going on along the Río Grande. Furthermore, the greedy fathers in Washington were looking for a good excuse to "take a run down to Monterrey"—in short, to start a war with Mexico. The trouble in the brand-new state of Texas looked like a ready-made reason for this reprehensible undertaking.

Little difficulty was encountered in raising the war whoop among the Rangers. The memories of Hacienda Salado and the black bean were still fresh in many a free-booting mind like Bigfoot Wallace's and handsome young Sam Walker's. A chance to chase Mexicans under license from the United States government? With regular pay to boot? And plenty of good government food? Not to mention the bonus issue of two of Sam Colt's great new six-shooters to each and every man? It was too much for the border warriors. Perhaps they were growing a mite weary of their little war on the Río Grande. More likely, it was the promise of the new Colts. They were the ones that Sam Walker had been sent up north to have made to Ranger order. They were twice as big as the old ones. They shot three times as hard, and could be reloaded on horseback at a full gallop. No question about it, a man could kill a lot of Mexicans with a gun like that.

For whatever reason, the Rangers flocked into

Taylor's camp. With them came hundreds and hundreds of their wild-riding Texas friends, eager to enlist as Rangers. Some accounts claim that as many as 2,000 men were in the motley "scout corps" that made up Hays's regiment of Texas Rangers. A more conservative estimate places the number at 1,000.

Regardless of their true strength, the Rangers took over the war as their personal, private expedition from the very first. Hays's men, and those of his two principal lieutenants, Captains Ben McCulloch and Sam Walker, led the attack in every major battle from Matamoros to Mexico City. In the crucial assault on the "terrible fortress" of the Bishop's Palace at Monterrey—the victory that marked the beginning of the end for the Mexican Army—Hays's frontier fighters won the day single-handed.

Ordered to take the palace, which was the key to the whole defense, Hays stormed it in the face of the "most galling and withering fire imaginable." Watching the crazy courage of the action through a spyglass on a distant hill, General Worth, who was supposed to be directing the attack, is said to have shouted impulsively: "By the Lord! Hays and those men of his are the best light troops in the world!" A veteran American newspaperman who was much nearer the action reported it better. *The Texas Rangers,* he wrote tersely, *are the most desperate set of fighting men I have ever seen.*

Later, when Hays's Rangers rode into the fallen capital, Mexico City, three more memorable pictures of them were drawn for posterity. The first was by a foreign lady resident, writing to a friend in the United States. . . . *Perhaps,* the good woman suggests, *you would like to know who these terrifying beings are. Well, they are nothing more or less than Jack Hays and his Texas Rangers. With their old-fashioned, maple-stock rifles lying across their saddles, the butts of two large pistols sticking out of their holsters, and a pair of those new Colt revolvers around their waists, they are armed with fifteen shots to the man! There are a thousand men in their regiment, so they have 15,000 rounds which they can discharge in from eight to ten minutes when on the charge! The Mexicans believe the Texans are only semi-civilized . . . half man and half devil, along with a mixture of mountain lion and snapping turtle. They have more holy terror of them than they have of the Evil Saint himself!*

One of Taylor's highest-ranking generals wrote: *Hays's Rangers have come. Their appearance is never to be forgotten. They are not in any sort of uniform, but are well mounted and doubly armed. Each man has two Colt revolvers besides ordinary pistols, a sword, and every man a rifle. They affect all sorts of coats, blankets, and headgear. The Mexicans are terribly afraid of them.*

A member of their own corps, little known at the time but destined to win wide fame in the very next chapter of his gallant company's saga, stated with typical Ranger modesty: *Our entrance into the City of Mexico produced a sensation among the inhabitants. The greatest curiosity prevailed to get a glimpse of 'Los Diablos Tejanos'—'The Texas Devils'.*

The pertinent similarity of these three greatly separated viewpoints is their common mention of the Mexicans' fearful respect of the Texas Rangers. This fear was clearly very real. It must have stemmed from the four years Jack Hays and his intrepid fellow captains rode merciless herd on the "brown-skinned bandits of the border" and, beyond any doubt, it contributed greatly to the early defeat of the Mexican troops. If the "Texas Devils" themselves did not actually win the war, the Mexican people's fear of them almost certainly did.

As usual, an old Ranger has said it best: "I reckon we didn't start the Mexican trouble and mebbe we didn't finish it. But we sure raised up the middle of it higher than a dog-chased cat's back!"

The Mexican War was not a proud chapter in American history. The part the Texas Rangers played in it can best be quietly forgotten. The unfortunate affair is important to the Ranger story only because it set the stage for bitter enemy reprisals on Texas itself, and because it served as a dangerous training ground for the rise of the next great Ranger captain, who was fated to deal with those reprisals. He was a man few historians outside of Texas know to this day, but a man for all loyal riders of the hundred-year-old Texas Ranger trail to remember for at least another century. His name was Major John S. "Rip" Ford.

XIII

"RIP FORD AND THE TEN-YEAR WAIT"

Rip Ford was a patient man. It was a good thing he was. He had to wait a long time for his chance to join the immortal company of Hays and McCulloch and Sam Walker. For ten years following Texas' entry into the Union and the end of the Mexican War, the fortunes of the Rangers reached their lowest ebb. The reason was disastrously simple. For those ten years the United States Army had been trying to take over the work of the Texas Rangers, but the federal troops made a miserable hash of the job. Along the Río Grande they had fair success, simply because the Mexicans were smart enough to suspend their border operations until the war fever had cooled off a bit. It was when the Army attempted to replace the Rangers on the Indian frontier to the west that trouble arose again in Texas.

To begin with, the federal government forced the new Lone Star state to agree to set aside a reservation on the Brazos River for the so-called "peaceful" Indians still living in Texas. "You provide the land," said the United States, "and we will provide the troops to keep the Indians on it."

Reluctantly Texas gave in. Three reservations were established along the Brazos near the Army fort of Belknap. One was for the Anadarkos, Caddos, and Wacos. Another was for the Mescalero and Lipan Apaches. And the third was for the Comanches. All this took a great deal of time.

It was not until 1857 that the Indians were even partly rounded up and settled upon their new lands. By that time it was clear that the Texans' original doubts about the whole business had been borne out. Only the really peaceful Indians had come in to the reservations in any numbers. These were such long-beaten tribes as the Caddos, Kickapoos, Tonkawas, and the like. A few dejected Apaches and Comanches showed up, mostly old men and toothless squaws whose fighting days were over. The real troublemakers—Iron Shirt and his main band of fierce, white-hating Comanche braves— never came near the reservations on the Brazos. They were far too busy.

Things were looking bright up in Comancheland, thanks to Uncle Sam and his orders that the Texans were to keep their hands off the "little red brother". It was now the job of the federal troops to keep the Comanches in line, and the United States Army let it be known that it needed no help from the raging band of rascals, the Texas Rangers. The new policy worked to perfection for Iron Shirt and his wild-riding warriors. They could raid the western frontier settlements once more, safe in the knowledge that "the Grandfather in Washington" would not let the "Texas Devils" trail them down and kill them for their depredations. So the Comanches went back to work at once.

By the following year, 1858, Texas had had enough—United States troops or no United States troops. Governor Runnels reached far back into the records of the Rangers in the Mexican War. The card he pulled out of the dusty files bore the name of John S. Ford. Rip Ford was given supreme command of the hastily reorganized frontier battalion. His orders were right to the point: "Go after Iron Shirt and don't come back till you've got him."

Rip Ford did not wait for details. He gathered his Rangers and started north. The Comanches, hearing that the Rangers were back in business, gathered up their women and children and got out of Texas. They fled across the Red River into the United States Territory of the Indian Nations, later to become Oklahoma. This had been their successful practice while carrying on their new war with the distracted Texas settlers. They would make a raid, burn, kill, and loot to their hearts' content. Then they would run for the safety of the Indian Territory and the protection of the federal troops who were stationed there.

But Rip Ford's orders did not say anything about stopping at Red River. They just said: "Follow any and all trails of hostile Indians. If possible, overtake and chastise them." That was the kind of uncomplicated talk the Texas Rangers understood. On April 29, 1858, Ford struck across Red River. His scouts found the Comanche camp late in the evening of May 11. The surprise attack was launched in the eerie gray daylight of the twelfth.

The first group of buffalo-hide teepees was taken swiftly. The Indians, supremely confident in having pitched their lodges outside of Texas, were stunned. Yet two warriors managed to mount their ponies and escape, carrying the warning to the main camp three miles away. The Rangers pounded after them at an unbroken gallop, but the Indian mustangs were too fleet of foot. When Ford's little force topped out above the Canadian River, they saw "a tremendous congregation of cowhide teepees, literally aswarm with painted braves, either already mounted or running desperately for their tethered war ponies." The battle was shortly joined.

Ford's forces numbered perhaps 200. Of these, fully half were friendly Indian scouts of the Shawee, Tonkawa, and Anadarko tribes, who had joined the Rangers as they passed through the Brazos reservations on their way to the Red River. These were brave and good fighters, as anxious to end the Comanche menace as their white Texas brothers. Iron Shirt's strength has been reported as from 300 to 500 "war-age braves, beautifully mounted and heavily armed after the Comanche custom."

Iron Shirt was a very dangerous leader. Ford knew that. The Indian war chief had taken his name from a jacket of ancient Spanish armor which he had found and which he always wore into battle. The Indians believed that this rusted vest of Conquistador chain-mail made their chief invulnerable to enemy bullets. So far, the legend had held true. Iron Shirt had never been wounded in battle. Rip Ford knew that his first act must be to destroy the Comanches' faith in their war chief's fabled invincibility. There was only one way to do that. Quickly Ford turned to Doss and Pockmark Jim, his two most trusted Indian guides. "You must bring down Iron Shirt," he told them, low-voiced.

Ford's continuing words tell the rest of it with terse Ranger economy: "Iron Shirt was followed by his warriors, who trusted their own safety to his armor. The sharp crack of five or six rifle shots brought his horse down. The chief fell riddled with balls. Our Shawnee guide, Doss, and Pockmark Jim, the Anadarko captain, claimed the first and last wounds."

With their leader dead, the Indians still fought with savage fury but with failing spirit. Again, Rip Ford's spare words put it with the most merciful brevity: "The Comanches would still occasionally halt and endeavor to make a stand. Their efforts were unavailing. They were forced to yield ground in every instance. The din of battle had rolled back from the river. The groans of the dying and the cries of frightened women and children mingled with the reports of firearms. The shouts of desperate men rising from hilltop, from thicket and from ravine, were everywhere."

The pursuit of the broken Indian army lasted until two o'clock in the afternoon. It ceased only because the exhausted horses of the Rangers could run no farther. In the eight hours of its bloody course, Ford's aroused Texans killed seventy-six Comanche warriors. They captured more than 300 horses and took but eighteen prisoners. Their own losses were two killed, two wounded. Ford's official report closed with the deliberately pointed postscript: *The prisoners were mostly women and children.*

It may well be believed that they were. Certainly there were no able-bodied warriors among the prisoners. Rip Ford's men had a forgotten tradition to rebuild. The Texas Rangers were riding again. Let the red enemy understand that. Let him realize that it would do him no good to surrender. Make him know that, if he wanted to save his life, there was exactly one way he could do so—and only one. Get out of Texas and stay out of Texas.

A second grim postscript remained to the destruction of the Comanche camp on the

Canadian River. The remnants of Iron Shirt's band continued to raid the Texas settlements. They did not believe the Ranger warning. Not content with their own villainy, they went even further. They prevailed upon some of the "good Indians" of the Brazos reservations to join them in their scalping and horse-stealing forays along the western frontier. For the crimes of a few weak brothers who were willing to listen to the lying tongues of the untamed Comanches, every Indian remaining in Texas was punished. The reservations on the Brazos were ordered closed. It became the unwelcome job of the Rangers to close them.

On June 11, they began the odious chore. By August 8, 1858, they had completed it. On that date Major Robert S. Majors, the Brazos Agent, wrote bitterly: *I have this day crossed all the Indians out of the heathen land of Texas and am now out of the land of the Philistines. If you want to have a full description of our Exodus out of Texas, read the Bible where the children of Israel crossed over the Red Sea.*

Thus, the final end of the Indian in Texas. From that day no red man had any legal business in the Lone Star state. He was an outlaw and the Texans were determined to treat him as such. The Rangers were given orders to shoot him on sight, and no questions asked. A few pathetic bands continued to test those orders to their unvarying sorrow. At last, no more warriors came.

The red man's eighteen years' war with the settlements, so gloriously begun with the great Linnville raid, was over. "God bless the Texas Rangers," sighed the good folk of Texas, and settled back to enjoy the first real peace they had known since 1836.

But they did not settle very far. They had turned their backs on the Río Grande. It was all that Cheno Cortina had been waiting for. He struck at once and without warning.

XIV

"THE PRIVATE WAR OF CHENO CORTINA"

Brownsville, Texas, was the most important town on the Río Grande in 1859. Its permanent population of over 2,000 was ninety percent honest Mexican and ten percent dishonest Texan. The latter owned and operated Brownsville. They exploited their darker-skinned fellow citizens without mercy. They cheated them freely of their every right as equal-born American voters. The helpless Mexicans lost their homes, their livestock—even their lives—to the first Texan who might want them and who could afford to hire a dishonest lawyer to steal them for him. The Texans had plenty of money and there were plenty of dishonest lawyers in Brownsville. The result was a legal robbery of the good Latin American citizens of the town.

Across the river, in the historic old Mexican town of Matamoros, friends and relatives of the mistreated American Mexicans began to mutter darkly of a new war with Texas. In Brownsville itself, the persecuted Mexicans were more than ready to listen. All they needed was a champion of their own race. History had one waiting.

Juan Nepomuceno Cortina was a self-made rascal of the most colorful stripe imaginable. Born of a wealthy and honorable old family of the highest Spanish blood, he was a complete scoundrel from the start. Faced with every opportunity of culture and education, he refused even to learn to read or write. He had one burning ambition: to raise a rebel army and return Texas to the mother country. An account of the times describes him at the moment fate tapped him on the shoulder for his one-man war with the Texas Rangers: *In 1859 he was living on his mother's ranch on the Texas side some six or seven miles west of Brownsville. Then in the prime of manhood, he bore a striking appearance. He was of medium size, fair in complexion, fearless in manner, self-possessed, and cunning. His brown hair, green-gray eyes, and reddish beard set him apart among his own people. He had inherited personal charm and acquired from his little mother excellent manners. These qualities, combined with a flair for leadership, the disposition of a gambler, an eye for the main chance, and a keen insight into the character of the Mexicans made him a man of destiny.*

"Cheno" Cortina, as his devoted followers nicknamed him, did not keep that destiny waiting. When the American sheriff of Brownsville seized his faithful lieutenant, El Borracho, The Drunkard, and threw him in jail, Cheno did not bother about seeing a lawyer to free his friend. He just rode into town, shot the sheriff, broke open the jail, and galloped off with El Borracho slung across the crupper of his horse.

Having won the opening round in such grand bandit style—the very image of a Mexican Robin Hood—Cheno struck while the simple minds of his admiring countrymen were still glorying in his daring rescue of El Borracho. Gathering a hundred cheering *vaqueros* around him, "General" Juan Nepomuceno Cortina got on with his personal part in the history of the Texas Rangers.

At three o'clock in the morning of September 28, the sleeping citizens of Brownsville were startled out of their beds by the thunder of 400 pony hoofs. In the next instant their pounding hearts were stopped by the wild cries of the invaders. "*¡Viva Cheno Cortina! ¡Mueran los gringos! ¡Viva la republica de Méjico!*" Hurrah for Cheno Cortina? Death to the Americans? Long live the Republic of Mexico? What kind of crazy, drunken talk was that in the middle of the night? It was not funny. The sheriff would hear about this in the morning, the inhabitants promised themselves. Steps would be taken.

But the sheriff had already heard about it. And he was already taking his steps—long and hasty and heading for the safety of the sagebrush. He wanted no part of Cheno Cortina and his self-declared war on Texas. As a result, by daylight the little bandit was in complete control of Brownsville.

His first act was to lead out and execute three Americans who he claimed were "wicked men, notorious for their misdeeds among my people." Next, he broke open the jail again, freeing all the prisoners and declaring a general amnesty for "all helpless victims of the American lawyers." For good measure and in the spirit of things to come, he sentenced the *gringo* jailer to death—and carried out the execution with his own pistol. Then, seizing nearby Fort Brown, the United States Army post, he tried hoisting the Mexican flag over its humbled ramparts. He failed only because the flagpole tackle broke at the crucial moment.

"Thus," bewailed Major S. P. Heintzelman, the Army commander, "was an American city of from two to three thousand inhabitants occupied by a band of armed bandits, a thing till now unheard of in the United States!"

But Cheno was only getting started. Returning in triumph to his mother's ranch, he set up military headquarters on Texas soil and issued his ringing call for revolution. "We will not injure the innocent!" he orated grandly. "But we will strike for the emancipation of the Mexicans. Our enemies shall not possess our land until they have fattened it with their own gore!"

Hearing this, the Texans sat up and took sudden notice. This little man meant business. It sounded as though he actually intended to take over Texas. And not tomorrow, either! A determined force of town militia, proudly calling themselves the "Brownsville Tigers", armed themselves with two brass cannon and set out for Cheno's ranch headquarters at Santa Rita. Cheno, as promptly, gave them a good thrashing. He sent the "Tigers" home with their tails between their legs, "a good deal more like buggy-whipped hound dogs than striped jungle kings."

Sterner measures were clearly called for. Major Heintzelman started for Santa Rita with 165 regular Army troops. But Cheno never slept. When the regulars arrived, he was long gone. The troops next heard of him in Matamoros, and Major Heintzelman did not like what he heard at all. "Cortina is now a great man," he reported worriedly in November. "He has defeated the *gringos* and his position is impregnable. He has the Mexican flag flying in his camp and large numbers are flocking to his standard. He says that he will right the wrongs the Mexicans have received and that he will drive the hated Americans back to the Nueces."

Well, now what? The Red Fox of the Río Grande had whipped the Brownsville volunteers and run rings around the United States Army itself. Who could be found to hunt him down before his revolt got really serious? Who, indeed, but the Texas Rangers. In response to Major Heintzelman's thinly disguised yells for help, Rip Ford and 100 Rangers set out for Santa Rita. Heintzelman and the Army were waiting for the Rangers, but the Rangers did not wait for them. "Follow us, boys!" Ford told the frustrated troopers. "But you'll have to step right along or you'll miss the main show."

Cheno Cortina was a smart man. He did not trust the Texas Rangers as he did the Union soldiers. Away he went up the Río Grande, Rip Ford hot on his retreating heels. Three times the Rangers nearly trapped him, but each time the Red Fox got away. And each time it was because the Rangers were slowed down by Heintzelman's orders not to run away and leave the troops alone.

Finally Rip Ford had had enough. Gathering his captains about his campfire, he said: "Boys, I think if we ride all night, we can cut around this Mexican Reynard and bring him to earth."

"What about Major Heintzelman and his bonny boys in blue?" asked one of his men, grinning.

"Let's not worry about them!" Rip Ford laughed. And away the Rangers went.

That same twilight, convinced that he was far ahead of his clumsy pursuers, Cheno Cortina at last curled up for a good night's sleep. He picked a very poor evening to close his eyes. In the cold, gray December dawn he awoke to find the Rangers in front of him. There was still a chance of retreating to the south. As Cheno considered it, one of his scouts raced in with some great news. The Rangers were all alone over there! The regular troops were far behind them! Cheno at once saw his golden opportunity.

He had beaten the Texas militia and the regular Army of the United States. Now he had the chance to wipe out a whole company of Texas Rangers. Why, the glory of a victory over the hated *"Diablos Tejanos"* would bring every fighting *vaquero* in old Mexico to his side! Excitedly he formed his troops for battle. By this time, he had gathered a real army, complete with cavalry, buglers, battle flags, and all—even a company of artillery! It would be a slaughter—600 stout *vaquero* troops against 100 raging "Texas Devils".

General Juan Nepomuceno Cortina sounded his bugles and rode forth with banners flying. Rip Ford's Rangers were not impressed. They charged Cortina's center and tore right on through it "with a withering fire of Colt revolver and single-shot horse pistol which emptied two-score Mexican saddles in the first sixty seconds." After that, it was the old story of Jack Hays's Salado trap all over again. The Mexicans broke and fled. The Rangers war-whooped after them.

It was a good fight while it lasted, but it did not last long. "Within five miles we had captured all their cannon and had not a thing left to shoot at," remembered one old Ranger. Cortina himself escaped into Mexico and lived on for many a fat year, according to the same informant, "practicing his banditry on his own side of the river." But he, like General Woll before him, found a single taste of the Texas Rangers one large bite too many. He was never again caught on the Texas shores of the Río Grande. According to the old man quoted above: "Major Heintzelman and the United States Army came over the hill in time to get a south-bound glimpse of Cheno's noble charger splashing out the far side of the river and hitting for the chaparral of old Chihuahua. And that was how the Army won the day at the battle of Río Grande City."

As usual, the Army was not bashful about accepting full credit for the victory. Also, as usual, the official casualty lists fail to bear out the claim. Sixteen Rangers died that day. Twenty-three were seriously wounded. Not a solitary United States soldier got a scratch. It is very safe to say that Rip Ford and his Texas Rangers terminated the wonderful private war of Cheno Cortina.

XV

"MCNELLY AND HIS MEN"

After Rip Ford came the Civil War. And after the Civil War came the Reconstruction. When the war began, the Rangers did what could be expected of such gallant fighters and desperately loyal Southerners. They flocked to the thirteen-starred battle flag of the Confederacy. They did so in such numbers that there were not enough of them left in Texas to make any Ranger history for the years 1860 through 1864. For the following ten years Texas was under the "enemy" rule of a northern Republican governor. The Rangers were abolished in favor of a better-forgotten force of "carpetbag badge-toters" called the State Police.

Hence, until the spring of 1874, there was another "no history" period for the heroes of Plum Creek, Salado, and the battle of Río Grande City. Then came McNelly and his men. They were not a moment too soon. The Mexicans, under the old Red Fox of the Great River, Cheno Cortina, had had fifteen years to organize a new kind of border war. This was the highly profitable hobby of running off good Texas cattle for quick, "no-questions-asked" sale in old Mexico.

Cheno himself was far too crafty to get trapped again on the Texas side of the Río Grande. But he had a reckless young lieutenant who lacked his leader's wisdom born of hard experience. Guadalupe Espinosa was too young to remember the Texas Rangers. When he heard that they had been called back to duty, he shrugged. When told that they had been dispatched, under a boy captain, to put an end to Cheno's cattle-stealing campaign, he smiled. He would have done better to have listened a bit more carefully to the name of that "boy captain" and to have taken a good hard look at his record before he came to the Rangers.

Leander H. McNelly had enlisted at the age of seventeen in the Mounted Texas Volunteers. He had won a captain's commission in Tom Green's famous Texas Regiment before the Civil War was a year old. At one time he and a handful of his troops captured 800 Union soldiers twenty miles behind the federal lines. By the time he was nineteen, McNelly was the most feared of the Confederate guerrillas operating along the lower Mississippi. When he came home to Texas in 1865, he was a glittering war hero—and just turned twenty-one! But Espinosa did not bother to read his record. He was only interested in the fact that one twenty-one-year-old youth and eighteen Texas Rangers were coming to punish him and the great Cheno Cortina!

Small wonder Guadalupe Espinosa shrugged and smiled. Old Cheno had built up a band of a thousand faithful followers. He was running the biggest organized ring of rustlers the West was ever to know. He had waxed enormously wealthy doing it. And he was justly proud of his hard-earned title, "The King of the Mexican Cattle Thieves".

More to the immediate point: Guadalupe Espinosa had done such a noble job of stealing Texas cows for his greedy master that old Cheno had just appointed him *mayordomo*, or general manager, of the flourishing "American Beef Company of Matamoros". What had such a hero of the Texas-haters to fear from a thin, consumptive lad who had to affect a big, black beard to make him look old enough to vote? Under the circumstances it was a fair question. But the circumstances were due for a sudden change.

On the morning of June 12, 1875, Captain McNelly and his eighteen Rangers, on patrol west of Brownsville, cut across an interesting trail. It was made by 250 cattle—undoubtedly Texan—and fourteen horses, unquestionably Mexican.

"Well, boys," said McNelly, "I believe we have just found our first honest day's work. Let us get on with it."

McNelly was famous for his strangely soft voice. He rarely spoke above a whisper. Some said it was owing to his painfully shy nature. Others said it was because of his tormented lungs, already wracked by the tuberculosis he had acquired in the war. It did not matter to his men. They never listened to his voice; they always watched his eyes.

They were steel-blue as midnight stars and had a sudden way of snapping like hot coals when he spoke. They were snapping now. Instantly his little patrol "got on with it". They went at a dead gallop, straight for old Mexico. Within the hour, they caught sight of the thieves.

The latter crossed the stolen cattle over a treacherous marshland and dug themselves in on a low hilltop just beyond the swampy ground. It was a very bad place for McNelly and his men. At the same time, the young guerrilla captain had been in far worse situations. He gave the famous old Ranger command without hesitation.

"Follow me, boys," he whispered softly, and plunged his horse into the morass.

A hail of bandit bullets cut about him as he drove his mount, floundering and struggling, through the blue-black mud directly at the outlaw stronghold. Behind him came his men, cursing and blasting back at the hilltop with their long-barreled Colts. McNelly had not yet so much as *drawn* his pistol.

It was "too much *bravura*" for the Mexicans. Abandoning the cattle, they broke and fled for the border. The Río Grande was very close. It was almost in sight—just over the next hill. But McNelly had waited too long for this chance. At last, he had trapped a pack of the swarthy rustlers on the wrong side of the river. There could be no question of mercy. And there was none. Of the fourteen frightened Mexicans, not one lived to see the Great River or to cross over it again into his beloved homeland.

McNelly himself, riding "like a dark angel" in advance of his men, drew first blood. Singling out the Mexican leader, he rode him down, killing his horse from under him with three revolver shots. Unharmed, the bandit leaped up and dived into the tangled brush of the swamp's edge. McNelly was down from his own mount in a flash. Calmly pulling his Winchester carbine from its saddle scabbard, he walked straight into the dense thicket.

His Rangers counted six shots from the bandit chief's pistols. Then they heard a single flat crack of a .44-caliber Winchester. They saw McNelly stalk back out, his carbine smoking, catch up his pony, and gallop on. There was no need to shout any questions about the Mexican leader. They knew where he was—lying in that thicket. They knew what he was doing—staring up at the tangled boughs with a Texas bullet hole between his wide-open eyes.

In the next few miles and minutes of the continuing chase, every one of his followers met the same swift fate. Within the hour of their apprehension, the last of the bandits lay quietly upon the Texas side of the Río Grande. Next, the silent Rangers caught up the escaped Mexican horses. Upon the nervous back of each was strapped the slack form of its late rider. Then the hard-faced procession set out for Brownsville, driving the recovered cattle ahead of it.

The sun was mercilessly hot in the Brownsville plaza that day—July 13, 1875. It stared down with a terrible stillness on the thirteen bodies laid out upon the baked earth of the town square for all to see and take warning from.

"Come and look upon the faces of your friends and loved ones," Captain McNelly invited the muttering crowd of Mexican onlookers. "If any relatives are here and want to claim a body, they may do so. My Rangers are through with them."

His Rangers were through with them! It was all the speech McNelly ever made about his deadly ride. It was all the warning he ever issued the stunned kinsmen of the lifeless *vaqueros*. And it was all the accounting he ever gave them of the thirteen corpses in the Brownsville plaza. It was enough. The awestruck Mexicans understood it.

A dozen and one of their bandit brothers lay dead in the dirt before them. The fourteenth member of the band lay dying in the jail across the square. The young Ranger captain had said no word about who these *bandidos* were. He did not have to. Those were Cheno Cortina's men lying there, looking up at a sun they would never see again. There could be no mistake. The thirteenth body—the one with only a part of its handsome face still showing, a terrible rifle-bullet wound squarely between the eyes—was that of Guadalupe *"El Jefe"* Espinosa.

Beyond the silent bodies stood a row of motionless men in sweat-stained hats and brush-scarred boots. They leaned on their worn-barreled Winchesters, heavy twin Colts sagging their gun belts. These were McNelly's men, watching and waiting, their hard eyes searching the sullen crowd. Waiting, waiting. . . . But not a solitary volunteer moved forward to accept McNelly's soft-voiced invitation. One man left quietly. Then another. And another. Within minutes the thirteen dead bandits lay alone in the fly-droning dust of the plaza.

The free-handed happy reign of Cheno Cortina, self-styled "King of the Mexican Cattle Thieves", was over. His long war with the Texas Rangers was at an end. For another four or five months the old man tried in vain to rally his scattering followers. He sent across a few more raids. Then, in late fall, when McNelly got good and mad and chased them right on across the Río Grande into Mexico itself, the Red Fox knew the hunt was over. He retired deep into the province of Tamaulipas, and was seen no more along the Texas border. With the final retreat of the old bandit, the era of the border-raiding *vaquero* came to its colorful close.

Cheno Cortina was the first and the last of his breed. After him, the others were only cheap imitators, and not very bright. The old man had been smart. He knew when to quit. There was simply no decent profit left in *americano* cattle, for the Texas Rangers had raised the price too high.

XVI

"THE HUNTING OF JOHN WESLEY HARDIN"

John Wesley Hardin was a Methodist minister's son. He had every advantage of a Christian home and upbringing. He was a bright lad, well-mannered, and quiet. He was kind to animals and very good to his gentle mother. In fact, young John Wesley had only one serious fault in his character. He was a merciless, cold-blooded killer. The history and legends of the Old West have always been generous to the dashing badman and brave bandit.

King Fisher, who was such a bandit, is still a hero in Texas. Up in Clay County, Missouri, to this very day, it is unhealthy to insult the memory of Jesse Woodson James. Tom Horn, another badman, has become an outlaw saint on the Great Plains. But nobody mourns John Wesley Hardin. The West, old and young, has never liked a senseless killer. Still, for all his murderous misdeeds, it is probable that John Wesley would have become a hero, too, if he had not made one little mistake, a slight error in judgment which had been fatal to many a better man before him. He tangled with the Texas Rangers.

It was May 26, 1874. The town of Comanche, Texas, was mighty quiet. There was a good reason for that. The town had a good sheriff whose name was Charley Webb. At that time Comanche County was as dangerous a place as there was in the South-west for a man to pin on a star and call himself sheriff. But Charley Webb feared no man, and certainly no badman. He was, moreover, a very courteous man. He never failed to offer the hospitality of the Comanche jail to visiting outlaw notables.

When he heard that the deadly John Wesley Hardin had just ridden into town, he did not hesitate to do his civic duty. He simply reached for his hat and strolled down the street to ask the great man to be his guest while in the city. John Wesley was at the bar of the Yellow Dog, Comanche's toughest saloon. He was having his solitary breakfast of raw, red whiskey. It is safe to say that he was in an unsociable mood at best. When the soft-voiced man came up behind him, he put down his glass but did not turn around.

"I want you, Hardin," murmured the mild-mannered newcomer apologetically. "You're under arrest."

"Wes" Hardin had killed twenty-seven men, not counting Mexicans or Negroes. But no sheriff had ever put him behind bars. He answered not a word to Sheriff Charley Webb. He simply spun around and shot him through the heart. Under the twisted youth's treacherous guns twenty-seven men had died. Yet their killer had still gone free. The twenty-eighth was not to join that pitiful company of the unavenged.

Sheriff Webb's deputy gazed down at the body of the brave sheriff and asked himself a grim question. If the state and local law officers could not arrest Wes Hardin, who could? The white-lipped deputy thought he knew the answer. It was an answer to which frightened and angry Texans had resorted for thirty-eight years, and never in vain. Webb's deputy wired the Texas Rangers.

Back came the terse answer. If it took three weeks, or three months, or three years, the Rangers would get John Wesley Hardin for the murder of Sheriff Charley Webb. They would get him and they would bring him back to Comanche to stand trial at the scene of the crime.

At first, it looked as though it would be the lesser length of time, for within four months Hardin was captured in his Louisiana hide-out and returned to Texas. But on the way to Comanche, guarded by local law officers and not Rangers, he escaped.

Patiently the Rangers started all over again. It would be a long trail this time. Hardin had learned he could not bluff the Texas Rangers. He would be very hard to find. He was.

For three long years the Lone Star state neither saw the least sign nor heard the faintest word of John Wesley Hardin. The reputation of the Rangers began to suffer. Soon the situation became intolerable. Either the force "got" Wes Hardin, or it "forgot" forty-one years of fiercely proud tradition.

Lieutenant J. B. Armstrong was not inclined to be a forgetful man. He had received his early training under Captain Leander H. McNelly. He had been taught to get his man, or die in the attempt. Lieutenant Armstrong suddenly decided that John Wesley Hardin had "disappeared" long enough. He buckled on his single, right-hand Colt and went after him. Right away, he ran into legal trouble. There was a rumor that Hardin was hiding out near the town of Penasacola, in Florida. But when Armstrong tried to get the extradition papers that would let him arrest his man in that state, he was told that such things took time. He would have to wait.

The determined Ranger shook his head. "You can bet John Wesley won't be waiting for any legal papers," he told General William Steele, the Texas adjutant general in charge of the case. "He will be long gone and far away, before ever you sign his extradition. And so will I! You tell the governor to send the papers along," he went on to Steele. "I've got all the 'papers' I need to arrest my man right here!" With those words, he patted the worn handle of his old single-action Colt and set out for Florida.

The shadowy rumor was all he had to follow. It said only that Hardin had gathered together a band of "baggage-car bandits" over in the sunshine state, that he was operating under the assumed name of J. H. Swain, and that he was giving the

Florida railroads a very bad case of hold-up fits, indeed. It was trail enough for a Texas Ranger. The lieutenant followed it swiftly to Pensacola.

Contacting the railroad detectives on the case, he learned something very interesting. "Swain" was known to be riding a certain train that would arrive in Pensacola that very afternoon. Armstrong only smiled, asked the train's number, and said: "Good day, gentlemen. Thank you very much."

At 3:45 p.m., August 23, train Number 29 puffed to a halt at a lonely water-stop station just outside Pensacola. A slender, gray-eyed stranger, neatly dressed and wearing a flowing, imperial beard and leaning heavily on a cane, waited on the station platform. When the cars stopped moving, he limped painfully toward the steps of Coach Four. The five hard-eyed men inside the coach looked him over carefully. Then they shrugged and went back to their interrupted card game.

They were sure none of them had ever seen him before. Besides, it was obvious from his frock-tail coat, ruffled white shirt, and freshly pressed shoe-string tie that he was a city dandy. He was also badly crippled, and, more important to men in their hard profession, there was no one with him.

"Some Florida dude with the gout from eatin' too high off the hawg," growled John Wesley Hardin, turning away from the window. "Whose deal is it?"

Three years before, John Wesley had made his

first great mistake by turning away from a saloon bar and shooting a Texas sheriff. At 3:45 p.m., the afternoon of August 23, 1877, he made his second great mistake by turning away from a train window and not realizing he had been looking straight at a Texas Ranger. For the slim stranger with the steel-gray eyes and the bad limp was Lieutenant J. B. Armstrong.

As he had climbed painfully aboard Coach Four, the Ranger had shifted his cane to his left hand and drew his Colt revolver. A fateful moment later, "J. H. Swain" looked up from his cards into the gaping muzzle of a long-barreled .45.

To understand the incredible bravery of Lieutenant Armstrong in that death-still last minute when he entered Coach Four, one must remember three things. First, John Wesley Hardin was the fastest draw and deadliest shot in the history of frontier gunfighting. No authority has ever denied that. Second, a railroad secret agent and a Texas detective who were supposed to support Armstrong in confronting the gang had lost their nerve in the final moment. The Ranger knew they had already fled when he paused at the head of the car to draw his gun. Third, the four desperadoes with Hardin were all wanted men, with prices on their heads and holstered Colts beneath their coats. There was even a fourth dark fact weighing against Armstrong. He was still suffering intensely from an unhealed gunshot wound and could hardly walk without a cane. Now he pressed heavily upon it as he stared at the five startled outlaws.

That one man should willingly face such odds with a single weapon and the quiet command—"Don't move, you men are under arrest."—seems unbelievable. But that is exactly what Lieutenant Armstrong did, and precisely what he said. Wes Hardin knew guns. He knew more about them than any man alive. When he saw that old model Colt with its seven-inch barrel and worn walnut handle, he knew he was not facing any Florida officer.

"Texas, by gum!" he cried to his companions, and went for his two .41-caliber Colts.

But for once his terrible guns failed him. His right-hand revolver caught and hung for a fraction of a second in his suspender strap. In the instant it took him to free the weapon, his seat companion leaped up, flashed his own draw, and fired at the Ranger. Armstrong was now stalking slowly down the aisle, still not firing but determined to take Hardin alive. He fired back, once. The man who had shot at him screamed and dove through the glass of the car window to the platform outside. He ran five steps, and then fell dead, shot through the heart.

Hardin now had his pistol free at last. But he was staring into the smoking bore of Armstrong's .45, not two feet from his face. The Ranger, still intent on taking the outlaw alive, grabbed for his gun. Hardin lashed out with his boots, kicking his foe backward across the car aisle. Armstrong leaped back at him like a wounded tiger, slashing at his head with the long barrel of his revolver. Blue steel met unbending skull bone. John Wesley Hardin slumped to the floor, and did not move again.

When he recovered consciousness two hours later, the train was speeding through Alabama, bound for Texas. The outlaw's three companions had been captured without a peep and left behind for the Florida authorities. Lieutenant J. B. Armstrong did not want them. He had come to Pensacola for just one man. He had gotten him. That simple fact, and the rest of the story, is swiftly told in a terse telegram which General Steele was at that moment reading in far-off Texas.

To: General Wm. Steele   Whitney, Alabama
Off. Adj. Gen.   Aug. 13, 1877
Austin

ARRESTED JOHN WESLEY HARDIN, PEN-SACOLA, FLORIDA, THIS P.M. HE HAD FOUR MEN WITH HIM. HAD SOME LIVELY SHOOTING. ONE OF THEIR NUMBER KILLED, ALL THE REST CAPTURED. HARDIN FOUGHT DESPERATELY, CLOSED IN AND TOOK HIM BY MAIN STRENGTH. HURRIED AHEAD THE TRAIN THEN

LEAVING FOR THIS PLACE. THIS IS HARDIN'S HOME AND HIS FRIENDS ARE TRYING TO RELEASE HIM. HAVE SOME GOOD CITIZENS WITH ME AND WILL MAKE IT INTERESTING.

J. B. Armstrong
Lt. State Troops

John Wesley Hardin was tried for the murder of Sheriff Charles Webb in Comanche County, Texas, the last week of September, 1877. The jury was out one hour. The outlaw was found guilty in the second degree and sentenced to twenty-five years at hard labor in the state penitentiary at Huntsville. The gray, iron gates closed behind him on October 5.

Thus, the first and worst of the Southwest's famous badmen had been cut down to size. And the man who did the whittling was a Texas Ranger.

XVII

"MAJOR JONES AND THE FRONTIER BATTALION"

The time was now the late 1870s. Texas was having a roaring boom. The reason was the great cattle drives thundering northward to the Kansas railways. The cattlemen, big and little, were making quick millions. The beckoning smell of this sudden wealth reached eagerly waiting nostrils. From every outlaw hide-out on the Western frontier, all the way from Canada to Mexico, the hard-eyed knights of the calico mask and the Colt revolver descended on Texas. The honest rancher had no chance. The few sheriffs and town marshals were helpless. The badmen simply overwhelmed them by sheer force of numbers. Shortly there was no law at all in the outlying cow counties. The outlaw clan rode unchallenged.

Completely without fear of punishment, they shot down those who tried to protect their property. In the settlements, armed robberies of banks, business places, and private citizens took place in broad daylight, Monday through Sunday. On the outer ranges, wholesale rustling of horse and cow herds went on all night, every night. What happened next was inevitable. The tax-paying Texan turned his desperate back on the badly "buffaloed" local officers and sent, posthaste, for the one true friend and fearless law officer who had never failed him. The Texas Ranger.

As usual, the Rangers acted fast. They called in their famed trouble-shooting special force, the Frontier Battalion under Major John B. Jones of Corsicana. The orders Major Jones received were in the best Ranger tradition of coming right to the point. They simply said: "Get out there and clean up those thieves."

Major Jones's response was equally to the point. He got "out there" and went to work.

John B. Jones was the least-known, "littlest" Ranger of them all and, quite possibly, the greatest. He was but two inches over five-and-a-half feet tall. He weighed no more than 135 pounds. Yet he had the heart of a lion and the spring-steel muscles of a stalking jaguar. His hair, fierce eyes, and sweeping mustache were as black as a bat cave at midnight. His whole attitude was one of such dangerous quietness and unquestioned command that no man who ever served under him thought of him as "small". He was the greatest horseman the Rangers ever knew. His fiery bay stallion, Gold Eye, had carried him on more miles of risky frontier patrol than any Ranger before him or after him. Yet Major Jones was a far different man from his more famous fellow officers. And therein lay his greatness.

Where Hays, McCulloch, and McNelly had ruled "by iron hand and steel pistol", the little Major Jones led by soft voice and superior cunning. In his long career as a Texas Ranger, he brought in more badmen than all his better-known predecessors combined. But it was never the number he brought in that set him apart from his famous fellow Rangers. It was "the way" he brought them in. In his entire life as commander of the Frontier Battalion, Major Jones was never personally involved in the death of a single outlaw. His was the highest art of the frontier peace officer—to take his man and deliver him to the proper authorities. No law enforcement officer ever performed that hazardous duty better than Major John B. Jones in his dramatic clean-up of Kimble County, Texas.

On the day Major Jones received his orders, he and General Steele looked searchingly at each other across the adjutant general's desk in Austin. When the latter finished speaking, Major Jones nodded quietly. "I understand the situation, General, and my Rangers are ready."

"Good. How do you propose to go about it?" asked Steele.

"Set them an example, sir," replied Jones without a moment's hesitation.

From the beginning, Ranger tradition had been founded on that simple principle. If your trouble was Indians, get rid of the biggest Indian. If your problem was Mexicans, chase the number one Mexican. If your difficulty involved American badmen, go after the worst one. Major Rip Ford and Iron Shirt! Captain McNelly and Cheno Cortina! Lieutenant Armstrong and John Wesley Hardin! It was the way of the Rangers, and General Steele understood that. Still, he wanted to be sure.

"What do you mean, John?" he asked the black-eyed officer.

The little major thought a moment. "Which, in your opinion, sir," he asked, "is the wickedest county in west Texas?"

General Steele did not have to think before answering. "Kimble!" he cried at once.

"Then, sir," said Major Jones softly, "Kimble County is what I mean!"

XVIII

"THE KIMBLE COUNTY ROUNDUP"

The Rangers closed in on Kimble County in ten tight columns. The utmost speed and secrecy veiled their advance. They moved only during the dead of night, camping under cover through the daylight hours. During the swift nighttime gallops no smoking was allowed. No campfires were permitted for boiling coffee to refresh the men after their hard ride. Not even a match was struck after the sun went down. The result was a complete surprise of the bandit gang, which usually had warning long beforehand of any law force's approach.

John B. Jones, the keen-minded little major, did not confine his surprise to his approach, however. For five perilous weeks, picked members of his company had been carrying out the most dangerous work in the Ranger service—serving as spies in the camp of the enemy. These daring men, whose names are unknown to this day, had succeeded in upholding the established tradition of the force. They had "gotten" their men.

When Major Jones halted the main column on the outskirts of the town of Junction, he had in his breast pocket a most remarkable list. It gave not only the name of every wanted man in Kimble County, but the exact location of where he was living! Each of the other column commanders had a copy of the list. Their forces were poised, at the same instant, outside the towns of Bear Creek, Fredericksburg, and the other known outlaw strongholds along the Llano River. The plan was to advance simultaneously, closing in on the courthouse city of Kimble. Here, District Judge W. A. Blackburn had a secret grand jury in session, waiting to indict the captured criminals.

At midnight, April 19, Major Jones struck with three columns from the southeast. The following day a second force cut in from the southwest. On the third day, their moves perfectly timed to catch the rascals fleeing the southern attacks, the remaining six Ranger detachments galloped down from the north. The outlaws, caught flatfooted in their snug camps, broke and scattered like stampeding cattle. And like stampeding cattle, they were run down and roped by the night-riding Rangers. If a man eluded one squad, he came squarely up against another. There was simply no getting around the widely spread Frontier Battalion. No least chance, whatever, of slipping through the shrinking cords of its ten-column dragnet. Rangers were everywhere. For once, the outlaws found themselves outnumbered and out-marched.

Old men down in Texas, who heard the story from their fathers, will still tell you all about the "Kimble County surround". Major Jones had planned the whole thing, you will be told, exactly like a real Texas-size roundup. Only the little old major was not gathering beef steers. No, sirree! He was bringing in "bandit critters"! Popping them out of the pear thickets and the Llano scrub like so many mossy-back longhorns, and herding them into the hoosegow corral down Kimble-way, peaceful and spirit-broke as any bunch of muley cows on the way to the milking barn! And he was aiming to slap a brand on them, too. One they wouldn't be forgetting the burn of for a considerable spell—a big black Huntsville State Prison cell number, right square between their ornery shoulder blades! For ten days and nights the wild riding went on.

Every house was searched from root cellar to kitchen bed loft. Every patch of river timber was beaten through by narrow-eyed riflemen, riding boot to boot. Every rocky hilltop was scouted out; every brushy draw flushed on foot. Not a square yard of Kimble County cover that would hide a grown man was overlooked. The cringing captives were bunched and driven into Kimble. When all the Ranger "roundup crews" came together there on April 30, even Major Jones was astounded at the size of the "final tally". He had started his historic "gather" with a list of forty-five names of known and wanted members of the notorious Kimble County gang. When he checked his prisoners into the waiting jail, he found that his men had made forty-one official arrests. Of the entire listed number, and in a county bigger than some eastern states, only four outlaws had escaped!

Even more amazing action followed. The emboldened grand jury returned twenty-five true bills of guilt. And the charges were serious. Murder. Theft. Forgery. Assault. These were major crimes. They would mean long and heavy jail terms. These, in turn, would mean the sudden end of organized crime in Kimble County. Major Jones knew that it was a desperate job well done, but the humble little officer would never have said how well done. Fortunately, the official record remains.

In ten days, he had arrested and imprisoned forty-one members of perhaps the most ruthless ring of organized rustlers and gunmen in Western history. He had done it in the toughest county in all Texas. And he had done it without the shedding of a single drop of blood! It is typical of Major John B. Jones that he closed the affair by quietly denying his personal part in it.

I cannot commend my men too warmly for their successful actions in this unpleasant service, he wrote. *The work of shelling the woods for wanted outlaws is extremely trying, as it has to be done mostly at night. No Ranger failed to respond at once and cheerfully to his duty. All credit is theirs.*

As for the weary men themselves, it was all in the day's ride. They did not expect any credit for it. They were Texas Rangers.

XIX

"SAM BASS, THE BALLAD WRITERS' BANDIT"

Sam Bass was a Yankee, bred and born in Indiana. Yet Sam gained his undying fame in the far South. He was the only Northerner ever to have his name memorialized in the folk songs and ballads of the old Texas frontier. For, you see, in a twisted sort of way, people loved Sam Bass down there in the Lone Star borderlands. His daring exploits outside the law, his quiet, friendly manner, and the charmed life he seemed to bear, all combined to capture the Confederate fancy. In time, he became a sort of Texas Jesse James.

Yet, actually, he was a very ordinary example of an entirely common criminal. His history is valuable because it demonstrates so clearly the dangerous ease with which a genuinely bad man can become, through mistaken sympathies, a popular hero. And Sam *was* a genuinely bad man. He was born bad. He grew up bad. He died bad.

In the simple songs and sentimental bandit ballads written after his violent death, he was invariably portrayed as a gallant Robin Hood of the Red River country. In truth, he was never anything more than a petty thief and a bungling, small-time outlaw. He was not even a good hand at his own hard profession. Still, the folk singers of his day insisted on making a great man of Sam Bass. So let us see what it took to make a bandit hero in 1878. Then let the reader decide for himself whether or not he would like to have ended up as Sam Bass did.

The tragic tale may even be told in the willfully favorable way of the old ballad writers of Sam's own time. The final, grim point will still remain the same. Crime did not pay any better in the 1870s than it does today. The best way to prove that truth is to recount the first bad chapter of Sam's wild life by deliberately giving him the benefit of every doubt, just as his misguided admirers did so many years ago. The purposely exaggerated beginning of such a story, told their way, would start about as follows: Sam Bass was a great and noble adventurer, with the soul of a true Southern gentleman. It did not matter where he was born. It was the way he died that counted. And, like any brave and fearless son of the Old South, Sam died for what he believed in. The only trouble was that what he believed in was robbing stages and banks and railroad trains. Still, and no matter, Sam was just about the friendliest bandit that ever stuck up an express car or poked a big Colt pistol at a bank teller. He did his unpleasant work with a warm smile and a courteous word for every one of his luckless victims. If they smiled back and hoisted their hands, all went well. If they did not, Sam not only took their money but pistol-whipped them as well. That's how friendly Sam Bass was.

His early life alone held adventure enough for ten ordinary men. A poor farm boy, he was orphaned at a tender age. He never went to school. Not young Sam. He knew a faster way to get smart. Travel, that was the idea. There was, he felt, nothing in the frontier world to broaden a boy like travel. So Sam Bass took off from Indiana. At a time when Huck Finn was still unborn in Mark Twain's imagination, Sam floated down the Mississippi River on a raft all the way to Rosedale, Mississippi. There, he lingered a year to begin his self-education. What he learned in Rosedale was how to become the youngest cardsharp and crooked gambler in Mississippi.

Presently he ambled on out to Texas. There, he taught himself a second shady profession. When he left to go back north (three jumps ahead of the local sheriff), he was an accomplished horse thief. Never one to waste motion, Sam picked up another criminal degree on his way out of the Lone Star state. This one was from the College of Cow Knowledge. He lifted a fine herd of fat Texas steers and drove them clean up to the Black Hills of South Dakota. By the time he sold the stolen animals in Deadwood, he could proudly call himself a postgraduate cattle rustler. Sam was learning his bad lessons fast. But he was hungry for more knowledge. In quick succession, he studied the high arts of saloonkeeping, running whiskey to the Indians, and buying up gold mines. The latter were sold by sharp-eyed swindlers and were, of course, worthless.

When Sam found he had been cheated, he swore vengeance. Things had reached a sorry stage when one hard-working crook could not trust another! It was time to learn something more profitable. Sam had an idea where that might be done. There was a weekly stagecoach that went out of Deadwood carrying Black Hills gold to the outside settlements. It looked like a paying proposition to young Sam. He gathered around him a little band of brother businessmen with no great respect for the laws of the land.

For the next seven weeks not a stage got out of Dakota with any gold on it. Sam and his industrious men made sure of that. In the process, guns went off and stage drivers stopped bullets. Now Sam was an experienced gambler. He knew that seven was a lucky number. So after seven weeks he quit robbing stagecoaches and moved on. He still believed in travel, you see.

At Big Spring, Nebraska, he acquired another lawless degree. With his trusty bandit crew he held up an eastbound Union Pacific train. Sam and his daring lads were in beginners' luck. The express company messenger was guarding a special shipment of freshly minted California gold. A few minutes later, the carefree outlaws galloped southward with $60,000 in brand-new twenty-dollar gold pieces jingling in their saddlebags.

Young Sam now figured he was well enough educated to go into business for himself. It was time to return to his favorite haunt, Denton County, Texas. He liked it down there, always had. Besides, once a man has struggled hard to teach himself a profession, he has to settle down somewhere and practice it. Sam had heard that new railway lines were radiating out of Dallas like spokes in a wagon wheel. There were said to be a dozen of them, more or less. Surely a bright chap ought to be able to pick up a dishonest living from such grand opportunities—particularly if he did not linger too long between train stations. Sam was right again. In less than two months' time, he held up four trains within twenty miles of Dallas. Two of these trains belonged to the Texas Central Railroad, and the others to the Texas & Pacific. It was no trouble at all for Sam—no more trouble than it took to pull a gun on the express messenger and pack the gold pieces on a waiting pony. The getaways were all as clean as a hound's front tooth. The profits were every bit as handsome as a bay colt with four white feet. The prospects for steady work looked mighty encouraging.

Young Sam sighed gratefully and settled down. He was in business at last. But Mr. Bass had overworked his illegal education. Four daylight train robberies in fifty days were three too many for the angry Texas authorities. The Rangers were called in. Two days after the last job at Mesquite Station, General Steele wired Major John B. Jones. Steele knew the Rangers pretty well by this time. He did not waste words. TAKE CHARGE BANDIT HUNT NORTH TEXAS was all he telegraphed Major Jones. But by now Sam's outlawry had raised a hornet's nest of other law officers.

Word had gotten out that there was a price of $8,000 on his head for the Union Pacific robbery up north in Nebraska. Railroad detectives, Pinkerton operatives, United States special marshals, and a hundred private agents, all eager for the reward, swarmed down upon Denton County. Major Jones let them swarm. He knew how Sam Bass would have to be taken. And he knew that to take him would require time. For Sam had showered around his gold pieces with gay heart and noble generosity. As a result, the grateful poor folks up in the tangled Denton County bottomlands, who had profited from Sam's bigheartedness, would shelter him to the death. He had at last become a frontier legend, exactly like Jesse James. But even though the famous James boys had not yet been brought to justice, Major Jones knew all too well the only way to get to men like Jesse and Sam Bass. It was not a pleasant way and Major Jones did not enjoy employing it. But he had no choice. He could not take unnecessary chances with Sam Bass's kind. He had to get to them in precisely the same way as he had gotten to the Kimble County gang— *from the inside.*

The method Major Jones used to smoke out Sam Bass foreshadowed by nearly four years the traitorous end of Jesse James. And it worked the same deadly way. He hired a spy to betray him. Jim Murphy was his name. And in Texas, to this day, you had better smile when you call a man "Jim Murphy". Jim had been arrested for hiding out Sam Bass. He was a known member of the train-robbing gang. The Rangers had caught him and made him talk. The traitor proved eager enough to save his own skin at the price of Sam's scalp. In exchange for his freedom, he offered to rejoin the gang and warn the Rangers in advance of its next job. In order that Sam would trust him and allow him back in the bandit fold, a dramatic jailbreak was arranged.

Next morning, all the Dallas papers carried the stirring news: *Last night James W. Murphy, a desperate member of the Sam Bass gang, broke jail and fled. It is feared that he will find his old friends, and that his warnings will prolong the chase indefinitely. Major Jones of the Frontier Battalion says that the incident is a downright calamity for the Rangers' long and arduous efforts to apprehend the wily Bass. . . .*

It was a calamity, all right. But not for the Rangers. Sam Bass fell for the deadly trick, hook, line, and six-gun. Jim Murphy was welcomed back warily enough, but soon convinced the happy-go-lucky Sam that he was his best and staunchest friend. His name, according to the old ballad writers, should not have been Jim—it should have been Judas. For Jim Murphy betrayed Sam Bass and led him to his death. But with that betrayal, the work of the old ballad writers is done. Their distorted opening chapter of Sam's short life is finished. From then on the Texas Rangers took over. And they were duly-sworn officers of the law, not sentimental ballad singers. Somehow, they couldn't see anything particularly great or noble about shooting down an unarmed bank teller in cold blood, or anything especially brave or fearless in pistol-whipping an honest railroad baggage man, or anything outstandingly kind and generous about assaulting a poor, ignorant stage driver. Somehow, they just never did get the idea that Sam Bass was much of a hero. So they were out to get him.

✖✖

"THE LAST OF THE GREAT BADMEN"

For many weeks after his "escape" nothing was heard of Jim Murphy. Sam and his gang made but one brief appearance out of hiding, and that was for the purpose of stealing fresh horses for their next job. The Pinkertons and railroad agents still buzzed in and around Denton County as thick as hiving bees, but they buzzed in vain. Sam was not to be so easily stung.

The Rangers sat back and waited. The other law officers began to grin and say that Major Jones had at last met his match. They liked that. There had never been any official love lost between the county sheriffs and the Texas Rangers. The latter had had to come to their rescue too often. It made the sheriffs look bad. Major Jones said nothing. He knew Jim Murphy.

On a sultry day in mid-July, the major got what he had been waiting for. It was a letter postmarked in Denton County. It was not signed, nor did it need to be. Major Jones ripped it open, his black eyes narrowing to steely slits. This is what he read: *We have left Denton. Sam, Frank Jackson, Seaborn Barnes, and me. The party is again very suspicious of me, having once more been warned that I am a spy. I have had no opportunity to com-*

*municate with you until now. They are going to rob
the bank or railroad at Round Rock, unless you get
there in time to prevent it. If you don't come, I will
have to help them, or they will kill me. I beg of you,
in God's name, to be there. . . .*

Jim Murphy did not beg the Lord's name in vain.
The Rangers were there. But first, Major Jones
studied the letter. It gave him very little time.
There was no large force of Rangers near the
threatened town. Jones himself was the closest to
it. He was attending an outlaw trial in which he
was a witness at Austin. He had only three Rangers
with him. Again he counted the names in the letter.
Bass. Jackson. Barnes. Murphy. Four outlaws. He
glanced up, counting his Rangers. Dick Ware,
Chris Conner, George Harrell. He smiled softly,
and added himself to the count. Four badmen, four
Rangers. Good enough. The odds were even.
Major Jones and his men mounted up and rode.

They reached Round Rock on Thursday, July 18,
after a killing ride. Word from Murphy reached
them that night. The outlaws were camped in the
old cemetery outside town. They would ride in
next day to look the bank over, then rob it the following day, Saturday, July 20. Major Jones
decided he would not wait for the boys to take on
another load of bright Texas gold. If Sam showed
up on schedule the next day, he would pick up a
deadlier burden and a duller-colored one, com-
posed of good, gray Ranger lead. Toward this end,

the major was forced to take two local peace officers into his confidence, for he and his Rangers did not know Sam Bass on sight. Deputy sheriffs Grimes and Moore did. The trap was set.

Friday morning dawned clear and hot. The sticky hours dragged by. The dusty main street of Round Rock lay strangely quiet. Not a citizen in town knew of the nearness of the Bass gang. Yet the noonday stillness had an eerie quality to it. The sun was burning mercilessly on. High noon. One o'clock. Two. Three. Still nothing. Then, suddenly, four narrow-eyed horsemen appeared to the north. They jogged their lathered mounts slowly down the street. Each wore a long cavalry coat despite the melting heat. This was understandable, for men who made their living with cross-belted Colt revolvers did not advertise the fact.

Presently the fourth rider stopped and got down off his horse. He picked up the animal's hoof and waved to his companions that he would be along in a minute. There was just a small pebble in the frog of his gelding's foot. He would have it freed with his pocket knife in no time. His three friends nodded and rode on.

"Jim Murphy," whispered Major Jones. Then, tersely, to the two deputies: "Is that Bass in the lead?"

Grimes shook his head uncertainly. "I can't see against this infernal sun. When they get down to case the bank, me and Moore will drift over and make sure, close up. Then we can signal you."

"All right. But whatever you do, don't jump them by yourselves."

"Lookit! Yonder!" interrupted Deputy Moore. "They're going into Kopperal's Dry Goods, next the bank!"

"Let's go," grunted the brave Grimes.

"Remember!" Major Jones's low-voiced warning came again. "Just look them over and give us the signal."

"Sure," muttered Deputy Grimes, and stalked across the street to keep his date with destiny.

In the store, Sam was laughing and joking with the clerk, Simon Jude. Jude later said he never met a better-natured fellow. There is no explanation for what happened next. For at the last minute, Deputy Grimes disobeyed his orders. Perhaps he did it because of the $8,000 reward on Sam's head. Perhaps he wanted the glory of taking the great bandit single-handed, or the professional satisfaction of showing up the Texas Rangers. Two things alone are certain. One is that Deputy Sheriff Grimes was one of the bravest police officers who ever lived. And the second is that he was also one of the most foolish. He gave a warning nod to his friend Moore, and stepped up behind Sam Bass.

"I'll thank you for your gun, Sam," were his first—and last—words.

Sam whirled and shot him dead. Behind him, Deputy Moore went for his Colt. He got off one shot at Sam, nicking him in the gun hand. Sam flashed his other .44 and drilled a shot clear through both lungs of the second officer. Then he said: "Boys,"—nodding to Barnes and Jackson—"I think we had better go. There may be more of them outside. Good day to you, Mister Jude."

As usual, Sam Bass was right. There were "more of them" outside. But the ones out there were not local deputies, and they were not trying to beat Sam Bass to the draw with revolvers. They were Texas Rangers, and they were firing point-blank across a sixty-foot street with lever-action Winchester rifles.

As the cornered outlaws ran for their horses, six-guns blasting, Ranger Dick Ware squinted coolly along his carbine barrel. He fired once. Seaborn Barnes spun into the main-street dust, a .44 Winchester bullet in his brain.

In the same instant, with outlaw lead splattering the adobe wall behind him, Ranger George Harrell laid his sights on Sam Bass. He could see the famous badman's body jerk at every shot. But Sam Bass was tough. Shot through half a dozen times, he still managed to make his horse. Frank Jackson lifted him into the saddle and held him there as the two galloped out of town under a withering blizzard of Ranger lead. The brave and loyal Frank Jackson was never found. But Sam Bass was.

Early the next morning the Rangers trailed him to his last hide-out. It was a gaunt, gnarled mesquite tree standing in solitary loneliness on the level prairie just north of Round Rock. Beneath its dusty shade, his shattered body braced against the rough bark, sat Sam Bass. Texas' beloved bandit had halted his last train, robbed his last bank.

When the Rangers came up to him, he smiled weakly and managed a gallant wave. "Don't bother shooting, boys!" he called, gray-faced with pain. "I am the man you are looking for. I am Sam Bass."

Walter Prescott Webb has left us the best picture of the actual death of the little outlaw: "He was brought to Round Rock and Dr. Cochran was called to attend his wounds. Every attention was given him by Major Jones. Bass lingered until Sunday, conscious to the last. Major Jones was with him, or had others with him, all the time, and made every effort to learn from him the identity and whereabouts of his confederates. All his statements were written down. Bass steadfastly refused to give information, though he talked freely of the men who were killed, and of the facts that were well known. On Sunday Bass's death became a certainty. Major Jones again tried to gain some information.

" 'No,' said Bass, 'I won't tell.'

" 'Why won't you?' asked Major Jones.

" 'Because it's ag'in' my profession. . . . If a man knows anything, he ought to die with it in him.' " And Sam did.

When Dr. Cochran told him the end was near, he

said: "Let me go." And, as he went, he said: "The world is bobbing around!"

Thus passed the last of the great badmen. Many a question has been asked about the life and death of Sam Bass. The one which seems to tell his whole sad story the best appears in the last line engraved on a forlorn granite headstone in the old cemetery of Round Rock, Texas.

SAMUEL BASS

Born July 21, 1851

Died July 21, 1878

A Brave Man Reposes In Death Here

Why Was He Not True?

No man will ever know why Sam Bass was not true, but there can never be any doubt at all about why he was dead. He just crossed trails with the Texas Rangers. It was as simple as that.

John Wesley Hardin was in jail. The Kimble County gang was wiped out. Sam Bass was dead. Thus, the gunman killer had been tamed, the cattle rustler caged, the bank-and-train robber cut down. Before them, the other enemies of the Lone Star state had met as swift a fate at the gun hands of the Texas Rangers. Ben McCulloch and his Plum Creek boys had whipped the wild Comanches. Jack Hays and his Texas Devils had helped win the Mexican War. McNelly and his Iron Men had finished off the Border Bandit. Now, Major John B. Jones and his Frontier Battalion had pretty well pacified the American badman. What real work honestly remained for the hard-riding Texas Rangers? Well, one or two little odd jobs, anyway. . . .

There was, by way of interesting example, the strange case of Sergeant Ira Aten and the dynamite bomb. In 1874, barbed wire was introduced into Texas. By the time the badmen were brought to heel, the open range was being fenced in at an alarming rate. The hated "bobwire" was nearly everywhere. In a few more years, it *was* everywhere, and the embittered cattlemen were up in arms.

Looking about for a weapon with which to fight the "fence-building" homesteaders, who were wiring off the last of the great range, the big "free grass" ranchers found—of all innocent things—a pair of ordinary wire nippers! The Fence Cutters' War was instantly under way. It was easy. All an angry cattleman had to do was have one of his cowboys ride out when the moon was dark, and cut his farmer neighbor's nice new fence into forty-foot pieces! The job was done in minutes and there was no evidence upon which to make an arrest. The gunman could be caught with the murder weapon. The horse thief could be apprehended with the stolen pony, the cow thief nabbed with the rustled steer, the bank-and-train robber trapped with the jingling gold. But the fence cutter? He just threw away his nippers when the job was done, and rode, whistling, on his way. That is, he did until the frustrated fence men sent for the Rangers. And the Rangers sent the fence men slow-drawling Sergeant Ira Aten.

If the expression may be excused, young Ira found his work "cut out" for him. He would spend weeks of dangerous spy work around the big ranches. To have been caught prowling these ranges would have meant the mysterious disappearance of one more Ranger in the line of risky duty. But Ira Aten prowled on. Long days of careful detective work tracking down a certain bunch of fence cutters would be followed by endless nights of "laying out" along the threatened line of barbed wire, waiting for the cutters to return.

Then, while the patient Ranger lay shivering in ambush on that fence line, the cutters would butcher another line forty miles away. Still, Ranger Aten was a man of boundless determination and of considerable inventive genius. After enough weeks of wasting his good time lying out in the cold prairie darkness, he had an idea. Like all Ranger ideas, it was short and to the point. It aimed to set an example to just *one* fence cutter that would serve to encourage *all* fence cutters to throw away their wire nippers.

To accomplish this, Ranger Aten took six sticks of dynamite and wired them to a particular fence that had been cut three times in as many weeks. From the bundle of dynamite, he ran another wire to the trigger of a hidden gun that was nailed to a nearby tree and aimed squarely at the dynamite. The theory of operation was uncomplicated: the fence cutter snipped the fence; the released wire triggered the loaded gun; the gun went off; the bullet hit the dynamite; the fence cutter disappeared.

Content with his invention, Sergeant Aten sat back to roll a cigarette and await results. Presently, on a fine, dark night, there was a range-shaking explosion along the particular fence that had been cut three times in as many weeks. Homestead windows rattled for five miles around.

In the morning the cautiously curious farmers went to find out what had happened. They did not find much. Just the singed brim of a powder-burned Stetson hat. A small piece of a cowboy boot heel. The scorched seat of a pair of Levi Strauss blue jeans. And a fine new pair of barbed-wire nippers—slightly bent from having been blasted halfway through an adjacent fence post. Sergeant Ira Aten said nothing. He just saddled up his pony and rode away. The Fence Cutters' War was over.

Historians will contest the central fact of this fine Texas legend. Let them. Argue as they will over whether or not the dynamite bomb was ever actually exploded, they cannot avoid the all-important result of its ingenious invention: the Texas Rangers had won another signal victory against seemingly insurmountable odds.

Not all Rangers, of course, were as quick to

understand a situation as Sergeant Aten. There was, for instance, the case of Private Ragan Kenedy and his famous "fumigation by six-shooter" misadventure. Private Kenedy was sent down on the border to fumigate a certain hut whose Mexican inhabitants had come down with a slight case of smallpox. His orders were not too clear, and neither was the simple mind of Ranger Ragan Kenedy. When he was told to fumigate the hut, he assumed that the poor souls who lived in it were intended to get the same poisonous treatment. The uneducated *peónes* did not understand the science of killing germs any better than the big Ranger. When he told them to get inside the hut and stay there, they obeyed meekly. But when he lit the deadly smoking formaldehyde candles which he had been given for the job the strangling family at once rushed back outside.

Orders were orders to Private Ragan Kenedy. Whipping out his six-gun, he herded the choking Mexicans back into the fume-clouded hut. Again they broke out, gasping for breath and clawing frantically at their burning throats. Private Kenedy set his blunt jaw. Grabbing his unhappy victims by the neck, he literally dragged them back inside the miserable hovel. This time there would be no slip-ups, by jingo! To make certain of it, he would stay in there with the rascals. Slamming and barring the plank door, the strapping Ranger stood in front of it, glaring his defiance at the cowering occupants.

He did not glare very long. In fact, he led the wild rush back out into the blessed open air. Not even a Texas Ranger could outfight a formaldehyde fumigating candle! But Ranger Kenedy was big enough to accept his failure like the six-foot Texan he was. *I have fumigated the house real good,* he wrote his company captain apologetically. *But I fear as much cannot be said for its inhabitants.*

It must not be imagined that all Ranger work after 1880 was so simple or had such humorous results. Such deserving captains as Lee Hall, John R. Hughes, Dan Roberts, and June Peak ran down many a hardcase criminal and hanged more than a few rustlers and horse thieves after this date. The full history of the force covered almost exactly 100 years. It began with the Texas war for independence in 1836, and did not end officially until the following brief report appeared in the New York *Herald Tribune* of August 4, 1935: *Famous in tradition as the Southwest's most picturesque and most fearless law-enforcement group, the Texas Rangers as now constituted will pass out of existence August 10.* . . . But the real finish had been written long before it was announced in any big-city news item.

The romantic truth is that after 1880 the Forty Year War of the Texas Rangers against the fierce Comanches, the vengeful *vaqueros*, and the gun-toting outlaws was at an end. The Rangers had won every battle, from the ambush of the Linnville raiders at Plum Creek to the trapping of Sam Bass at Round Rock. They had never taken a backward step to any wrongdoer, be he red, white, or brown. They had never surrendered. They had never deserted a comrade. They had never come back without their man. But the Indian was gone, the *vaquero* forgotten, and the desperado peacefully at rest in his lonely grave. A great land, comprising one-twelfth of the total area of the United States, had been made safe and its frontiers guaranteed forever by a little band of resolute men who were willing to offer their lives for an ideal—and who asked no quarter from any foe for the privilege.

And so, good bye to handsome Jack Hays and smiling Ben McCulloch. *Adieu* to young Sam Walker and fiery-eyed Rip Ford. *Adiós* to soft-voiced Captain L.H. McNelly. To fearless J.B. Armstrong and gentle little Major Jones. To sharp-shooting George Harrell and dead-eyed Dick Ware. To sly-minded Sergeant Ira Aten and slow-witted Private Ragan Kenedy, and to all the other big and little heroes who fought and died for $1.25 a day! Good bye to them all, and to each a heart-felt "well done!" The re-organized Texas Rangers, as part of the Texas Department of Public Safety, have done their best to maintain the standards of their long heritage. They remain the oldest law-enforcement agency on the North American continent with a statewide jurisdiction.

THE HUNKPAPA SCOUT

I

"SIOUX WAR SIGNALS"

Clanton's men were as hard as the baked earth under their rawhide infantry boots. Their eyes peering, red and slitted, from the alkali-stained masks of their faces narrowed yet more at the fat column of smoke towering, black and greasy, there to the north beyond the Powder. Funny about smoke. When you first got transferred out to the Territories, you didn't think much about smoke. Why should you? You'd seen lots of it. You'd been with Sheridan down in Georgia. You knew how a house or a barn or a corncrib went up. You'd laid outside Petersburg for nine months while Grant impatiently chomped his cigar at your butt side, and you knew what crawled skyward after your artillery quieted down, to cool its throats. That was smoke. Sure. But out here in Wyoming it was different. After a few months out here you began to *know* smoke. It got so it meant something to you. Like maybe your life, for instance.

You got so you could look off over the plains, maybe ten, twelve miles, at a big, dirty-white mushroom of smoke, and shrug: "Shucks, prairie fire." You got so you could peer off at the hills, say across the fork yonder, watching the ash-gray of that smoke with the orange flame light stabbing at its rolling underbelly, and have nothing more to say than: "Dogged, if they haven't gone and fired the brush again."

And you got so you could look ahead of a long, hot valley like this one, seeing that fat, black smoke you were seeing now, and know what kind of smoke that was, too. And what you knew was that it wasn't grass smoke and that it wasn't brush smoke. From the stunted cedar scrub atop the granite escarpment that shouldered the narrow valley down which Clanton's troops were marching, another pair of eyes gazed north at the snaking smoke column in the air, then shifted to watch the other column moving up the valley below.

This other column was not fat and black, like the smoke, but a thin, dusty-dirty blue. It was not soft and billowing, either, but lean and tough as a tendon. This was a column of marching men, a column all the way from Fort Loring to the south, a wiry fighting column, dirt-caked, red-eyed, bone-weary. These were regulars. No frontier militia of border rowdies, here. These were hard veterans of the War Between the States, and they weren't probing northward up that rock-girt track for exercise, or to broaden their cultural aspects. Watching them from the escarpment, detailing every item of their identity and equipment, the hard eyes above showed no emotion. No surprise, no fear, no relief. Certainly no gladness. Sunkele Sha, Red Horse, knew better than to be glad to see white troops marching north of the Powder when Makhpiya Luta, the war chief, had told them their crossing of it would mean war.

Red Horse knew more. He knew, now, why that black smoke rolled to the north. An hour before he could only have told you what the smoke was. Now he could tell you why. Still, those were white men marching down there. They must be warned, and, if Red Horse didn't warn them, nobody would. There weren't any white men left to do it. Red Horse knew that. It was up to him.

Not that the troops wouldn't guess what lay ahead of them under that reaching smoke spiral. They would. They would also guess what circled the ground around that smoke. But what they wouldn't guess was *who* led the circle and *how many* were riding in it. These were the things Red Horse knew, these were the things he had to tell them. He knew these things because an hour before, the Winchester, now cold and quiet in his right hand, had been hot and noisy with hard firing. The two Colts, now silent in their strapped-down holsters, had been out and talking very loud. The reason he had to tell them, those marching white men down there, of these things he knew was because he, Red Horse, was their friend.

He slid back down off the granite ridge, pushing himself down and back with slow movements of his free left hand. When Red Horse was down off the skyline, he stood up, and you saw him for the first time—a dry, spare Indian, of better than medium height, clean and quick and furtive in movement. As he went along behind the ridge toward his pony, his gait was the ambling, reaching gait of the High Plains Sioux. His wide shoulders were bent forward in that permanent hunch peculiar to those who have spent their lives perpetually half crouched, ready to spring for cover and weapon at the first crack of a dry twig or thin hiss of a war arrow. His face was angular, high-cheek-boned, low-foreheaded, the mouth as wide and cruel as the slash of a hunting knife.

Red Horse was a full-blooded Hunkpapa Sioux, orphaned early, hard-reared among a succession of Sioux and Cheyenne war camps. In his teens, drawn to the side of the white man by the sage counsel of his famous uncle, Spotted Tail, he had learned the ways and walking the trails of the *Wasichu*. But the white way was a hard way for Sunkele Sha. The tracks of the *Wasichu* toed out, the tracks of the *Shacun* in. There was always trouble in the camps of the white man for Red Horse—withal, the young Sioux had fairly earned his reputation as the best wagon guide on the Bozeman Road. Red Horse knew, even as he started down to warn the soldier chiefs, that he was stepping into a deadly noose of prejudice, ready-set to snap around his corded, bronze neck.

The larger of the two officers fronting the troop column raised his right hand, the yellow gauntlet flicking quickly right and left. The column clanked to a halt, and the officers sat their horses, stirrup to stirrup, squinted gazes fixed on the distant smoke.

Major Travis Clanton was a barracks officer, an engineer by training, a disciplinarian with a good military record as a brevet major general in the late war. He was a clean man, honest, open, friendly, and as much out of his element on the frontier as a trout in a dust puddle.

"What do you make of it?" he asked the smaller man.

Captain Riley Maxwell was his commander's antithesis. Short, red-bearded, imperious, Captain Maxwell was a cavalryman who rated himself professionally somewhere between Von Seydlitz and Tamerlane. "Wagons burning, naturally." His words were snappish, impatient.

"I suppose it's that train we sent the convoy after, eh?"

Maxwell looked at his superior, his annoyance just shy of patent. "Yes, sir. Sergeant Stoker and eight mounted infantry. Your own men, Major." This last was deliberate. The older man seemed not to notice it and Maxwell concluded: "It's got to be that train. No other has gone up the Bozeman since Red Cloud sent you the warning at Fort Keene last week. You'll recall I asked you at the time to let me trail the train with fifty men." Here, the younger man paused. "At the time, Major," he added pointedly, "you were of the opinion that a sergeant and one squad would do the job nicely."

Again Major Clanton appeared oblivious of the plain criticism. "There were about twelve wagons, weren't there, Maxwell?"

"Yes. A family train. Women, children, livestock. Going up to Montana to take land. If you'll remember, the wagon captain wouldn't wait for a convoy. Most of our troops were out on woodcutting details and you couldn't spare him a squad for two days. At least that was your opinion. He said his guide wanted to go on up right away. Something about his having heard, the guide that is, that Red Cloud was moving up onto the Bozeman and was not going to let any trains past the Powder. He told the wagon boss that, if they got through on the Bozeman, it would have to be before Red Cloud got into the country. The boss believed his story and decided to try and beat the Sioux up the trail. You issued orders for them to wait, but they went anyway. I guess you remember."

"Yes." The words were as level as the gaze that accompanied them. "I remember quite a few things you may not suppose I do, Captain." Maxwell shifted under the use of the military title. "I remember that train pulling into the fort. I remember two little girls sitting on the tailboard of a Pittsburgh. They had the yellowest curls and shyest eyes I ever saw. I remember a young woman smiling at me and waving as they rode in. She was just a girl herself, no older than my daughter Reno, but she had a baby in her arms and a blue-eyed toddler on the seat beside her. I remember an imp of a boy, about ten, snapping me a grin and a proper salute. Some things I don't forget, Maxwell." The words had softened for a moment, but suddenly they were honed with sharpness. "*Who* was the guide on that train, Maxwell?"

"Red Horse, a full-blooded Hunkpapa. Raised by Red Cloud's Oglalas, I understand. Nephew of old Spotted Tail, they tell me. I don't know him and I didn't get to see him at the fort. He was out scouting the Bozeman, uptrail. But I know his reputation, and, while there's nothing definite on him, folks just don't trust an Indian guide in Sioux country. You can't blame them, as I see it. However, the train had to take him because it's almost impossible to get a white guide to work north of Fort Loring since you had that powwow with Red Cloud and Man-Afraid-Of-His-Horses down there this spring. You remember that powwow, don't you, Major? Red Cloud called you the Little White Chief and wanted to know what the devil you and all the walk-a-heaps were doing in this country when the Grandfather in Washington had just promised the Indians to keep the white men out of the Powder River lands."

Now the major's words were beginning to show an edge of impatience. "Yes. And I also told him why we were here, didn't I?"

"You certainly did, sir. Though you'll remember I advised against it."

"We won't go over that again." Clanton's voice was short. "I was given my orders to come up here and build a fort forty miles north of Fort Keene, and I'm going to do just that."

"Yes, sir." Maxwell's acceptance carried a question. "And while we're up here, what are we going to do about that smoke there?"

"We'll go on up, of course. Nothing else we can do. When you see smoke, it's already too late."

"Too late for the train, maybe." Maxwell's words began to jump with excitement. "But how about the hostiles? There's a little something we can do for them?"

"Such as?" Clanton was a martinet, perhaps, but no fool.

"Major, let me take the horses and go on in ahead of you. Might just catch the red buzzards hanging around snapping their beaks."

"Out of the question, I think. These are infantrymen. They're not your cavalry, Maxwell. They're no good on a horse. You know that. And you've got mounts for only thirty men."

"I could ride through the whole Sioux Nation with fifty men." The red-bearded officer's harsh claim was delivered with that brand of conviction

that comes in packages labeled: CAUTION . . .
PURE IGNORANCE.

"I don't know, Maxwell. I. . . ."

"Major, let me go on up. There can't be many of
them this close to us. They wouldn't dare operate
in force so near Fort Keene. It's probably a raiding
party down from the north, not aware of our presence. Hunkpapas, I'd guess. We know Crazy Horse
is in the Black Hills and we know, now, that Red
Horse was lying about Red Cloud coming up this
way. So that rules them out. Cuss it, Major, if
you'll just let me. . . ."

Clanton's interruption still held strong question.
"Maxwell, that train had about twenty men in it,
plus a tough, experienced guide and nine regular
soldiers. We assume the train is gone. It would
have taken a strong force to wipe it out. Doesn't
that figure to you?"

"Well, yes and no. But not necessarily, sir."

Maxwell hesitated. He had the "Indian itch", that
crazy contention so common to green frontier officers, that a squad of regulars could handle a tribe
of hostiles. His superior didn't share his ailment.
This caused the captain to choose his words carefully. "Look at it this way," he went on, "they probably hit the train when it was noon-halted, maybe
even with the teams spanned-out and grazing.
Another thing. Let's not overlook this Red Horse.
Blood is thicker than a scout's pay, especially red
blood. You know that. What about this Sioux guide

245

leading the train into a set trap? That was a fat train. Lots of livestock, good weapons, big mules, plenty of horses."

"The Lord knows, you may be right." The thought of a plotted ambush, involving treachery on the Indian guide's part, had not occurred to the phlegmatic Clanton. "Go on up, Maxwell. But keep your flankers out wide, and, if you run into Indians in force, retire on me. Stay clear if you see more than a hundred hostiles. That's a direct order. Are you straight on it?"

"Yes, sir!" The younger officer's answer hopped with eagerness. Wheeling his horse to return to the resting column, a frown whipped across his face. "Now, what the devil?" His scowling glance was directed, with his question, upvalley. Following his gaze, Clanton, too, saw the approaching horseman.

II

"MY HEART IS WHITE"

Watching the stranger come up, the two officers saw a reed-slender figure dressed in the grease-blackened buckskins of the frontier scout. The shirt and leggings were heavily fringed, the moccasins flashily quilled and beaded. The man rode bareheaded, his lank, black hair hanging shoulder-long and straight. In the saddle scabbard under his knee snugged the latest spring-plate Winchester.

Cross-belted over the hips, tied down at the thighs, two worn Colts rode low and handy. The rider was long-armed and long-legged, his face as narrow and keen as a lance blade. He sat his pony, a keg-headed, potbellied paint, Sioux-style, legs dangling straight down, back rounded, shoulders hunched forward. He drew up to them making the palms-out sign of peace.

Maxwell returned the sign, but it was to Clanton the scout spoke.

It was now you got your second surprise about Red Horse. From the looks of him you'd be ready for any kind of a voice but the one you heard. True, it had the male timbre you'd expect from a figure of such wildness, but otherwise it fooled you. It was as soft as a woman's, gentle as a drawing master's.

"*Hau*! I'm Red Horse."

In his astonishment that any such figure could turn out to be the suspected wagon guide, Clanton forgot to return the inevitable—"*Hau!*"—of prairie politics, stammering, instead: "Red Horse! Red Horse, the wagon guide?"

"And an evil-looking weasel, if I ever saw one," interpolated Maxwell evenly, then added, his stare as challenging as the question: "Where the hell have you been, Indian, and what's happened to your train?"

The Sioux scout looked at him a long three seconds before deliberately turning to address

Clanton. "Major, my train's gone. Everybody in it wiped out."

The column commander just looked at him, unable to match the soft English with the savage looks he saw and the evil reputation he'd been told about.

"I suppose you're just lucky?" broke in Maxwell, stung by the scout's calculated ignoring of him. "We'll be interested to know how you got away."

This time Red Horse didn't even give him the weight of a look. "It was partly my fault," he went on, talking to Clanton. "I made a bad guess."

"Worse than you've got any idea," growled Maxell. "You're in a tight, Indian."

"Did my soldiers catch up with you?" Clanton ignored his fellow officer.

"Yes, Major. Sundown last night. A sergeant and eight men. They died well, especially the sergeant. He and I were the last ones left. He rode out with me. When they shot his horse down, he flopped behind him and fired to cover my getaway. *Woyuonihan.* He was plenty man. I kept going."

"Naturally," snapped Maxwell. "You couldn't be expected to stay and die like a white man."

"That will do, Maxwell. Let's not convict this man before we've heard him. We haven't got him on a drumhead court-martial and we're not interested in his lineage."

"My heart is white," said Red Horse, and that was all he said.

Major Clanton started to question the newcomer further, but Maxwell interrupted. "Major, I'll go along now. Do you want me to put this man under arrest before I leave?"

"No, I'll talk to him a bit yet."

"Good. Well, I'll move on up ahead and see if I can't catch a few of our guest's little red friends still watching the bonfire."

"I wouldn't, if I was you," Red Horse said. "You won't get back." The scout's observation was easy and drawling but it hit Maxwell like a slap in the face.

"What the devil do you mean?" The captain shouldered his horse into the stranger's pony, thrusting his square, red-bearded jaw up toward the tall rider's thin face.

"I mean there's upwards of four hundred Sioux riding a victory gallop around those wagon embers right now."

"Four hundred!" Incredulity rang out in Clanton's exclamation.

"Impossible!" snorted Maxwell simultaneously.

"Closer to four hundred and fifty," went on the tall Sioux. "Mostly Oglala Bad Faces, and under a pretty salt-tailed chief."

"What chief?" This came from Maxwell, the question rasping with pugnacity.

"Makhpiya Luta, no less."

"And who the hell is Makhpiya Luta? I never heard of him."

"Oh, I think maybe you have, Captain." The Sioux's black eyes appeared to slit still more as they fastened on the irascible Maxwell. "Only you probably call him Red Cloud."

"Red Cloud!" Again Clanton was incredulous, his methodical mind apparently running on legs too short to keep up with the conversation.

"The one and only," offered Red Horse laconically.

"It's a lie!" Maxwell was livid now. "Major, Red Cloud wouldn't dare pull such an attack even if he were around. And by the way"—whirling on Red Horse—"weren't you the bright scout who said he *wasn't* around? Weren't you the smart guide who was going to get that train up the Bozeman before he *did* show up? How about that, Major? You remember me telling you what this Indian told the wagon captain, don't you?"

"Yes. How about that, Red Horse? It doesn't look just right, you know."

"I told you I made a bad guess. That was it. I had information the war chief was coming but that he was five suns east. I know now my information was wrong. It came from an Indian, and Lord knows I ought to know Indians. I told you I thought this wipe-out was partly my fault. Well, it was. I fell for a bait. They got me into a *wickmunke* . . . that's their word for a trap. They just trapped me good, that's all."

"You'd be lucky if it was." Maxwell's comment

was acid. "But I don't think that's all by any means. I think there's plenty more. What do you think, Major?"

"I'm afraid Captain Maxwell is right, Red Horse." Clanton spoke thoughtfully. "You must see it doesn't look right, from our view, for you to get clean on a wipe-out like this. You being a full-blood, that is. Especially when you admittedly went up the trail without an escort. In fact, you actually went ahead against my express orders. Captain, Red Horse was informed of that order, was he not?"

Captain Maxwell scowled at the scout, then slowly shook his head. "Not directly. I told the wagon captain. Red Horse was up the trail at the time, scouting. We know now what he really was doing was chinning with his Sioux relatives about their dirty *wickmunke*."

"Red Horse, did your wagon captain tell you about my order?" The major's voice was patient, plodding.

"He did."

"And you advised him to go, anyway? Against my orders? Without a guard?"

"Yes. I told the wagon captain there was only two things to do . . . go ahead, fast, or turn back to Fort Loring and go out the old Oregon Trail. It's getting autumn, Major. They had not time to go back. Early snows would have caught them in the mountains. Such as the choice was, they took it themselves."

"Oh, that's pure manure," barked Maxwell. "It's a bald-faced lie and he knows there's no way to prove it, one way or another. Major"—wheeling quickly to his senior—"I'm charging this red rascal with deliberately steering that train into a trap. That's flat, sir." As Clanton hesitated, the captain urged him tersely: "Look at him! Not a mark on him. He probably left the train on some rotten pretense, long before it was attacked. I say put him under arrest."

Major Clanton looked at the scout steadily, regret plainly evident in his ensuing agreement. "Red Horse, I'm afraid I've no other course. You're under arrest. The charge is murder, and complicity in inciting and abetting hostile Indians in an attack on peaceful white settlers. In either event, you know what the sentence will be if you're convicted. You'll go to the Dry Tortugas for life. I'm not saying you're guilty, and I'm not even saying I think or feel you are. But the circumstances look bad. You can see that, I hope."

"Sure." The narrow, dark face held no visible emotion. "I guess I knew all about that before I rode down here to warn you."

"He's a hero, can't you see that, Major?" Maxwell's short laugh was a sneer set to mirth.

"My heart is white," said Red Horse simply.

III

"A CHANCE FOR ESCAPE"

Major Travis Clanton was a big man, precise, cautious. A West Pointer, he fought his wars by the book, and the book said: "When in doubt, go slow." Now, thinking of Red Horse, he was in doubt. As soon as the scout had ridden in with his report on the burning of the emigrant train by Red Cloud and his Oglala Sioux, he had remanded his order permitting Maxwell to take the mounted troops forward and had, instead, thrown the whole company into a tight camp.

"We'll stay here until morning," he had told Maxwell. "Then we'll see what develops. Meantime, you and Captain Benton get the camp set for trouble. I want double flankers out at one hundred and three hundred yards. I want no fires after dark. I don't want to see any rifles stacked or any stock grazing off picket. When you've got everything in order, I want to see you and Benton up at my tent. We've still got Patterson to worry about, you know. And send Red Horse here. I want to talk to him."

Now, with dusk coming in fast and the cooking fires winking out quickly, the major was ready for his renewed talk with Red Horse. He instinctively liked the dark, scowling Hunkpapa, just as Captain

Maxwell apparently held an intuitive distrust of him. Still, the man's story, in view of the circumstances, was very thin in spots, and Maxwell's sharp accusations had gone largely unanswered.

Hands tied behind his back, the prisoner squatted, dour and silent, by the small fire that still guttered before the command tent. Major Clanton, sitting opposite him, wondered what ideas were flicking past behind the narrow, black windows of those hard eyes. In his turn, Red Horse was sizing up the officer, but with more luck.

He felt sorry for Clanton but his sympathy was tempered with the bright steel of realism that alloyed all his own thinking and character. Red Horse had been born on this frontier and had sucked hard at its dry breasts. His weaning years had been spent with his mother's people, his knowledge of the Indian way of seeing and doing things hence being a very real one. Looking at Major Clanton, the scout's red past let him see the man with a judgment almost factual in its assumptions. The Indian learns one thing if nothing else— to read the nature of a man or an animal quickly, unerringly.

Red Horse saw the big man across the fire from him, a clean man, decent, honest, slow with caution in both manner and fact. He was obviously by nature too soft for the frontier, by training too set in the tradition of white military supremacy. The thought crossed the Sioux's mind that the white soldier chiefs in Washington couldn't have picked a man better suited to lead troops into Red Cloud's country—and into disaster.

"Red Horse," Clanton began, "perhaps I could put more faith in your story if I knew something about you. Care to tell me anything before Captain Maxwell and Captain Benton show up?"

Briefly, then, Red Horse sketched his life, concluding with a statement put forward to be taken or left just as it was. "So, that's the way it's been, Major. From the time I was about seventeen, when I listened to Spotted Tail, my uncle, I have followed the white man's road. But while I call myself the white man's friend, the Indians call me Sunkele Sha, and say I am red, and the whites call me Red Horse and say I am a dirty, sneaking Sioux. I am telling you this because I think you're in a bad country, and because maybe you'll believe me and turn me loose so I can go away from here. And maybe it's because,"—here, for the first time, the ore of his voice flashed a thin stringer of iron-bearing malice—"I know plenty well the reason I'm under arrest isn't because my train was burnt."

As he finished, Clanton waited a moment, his brow furrowing. Shortly he spoke: "I don't follow you, Red Horse. You say we don't have you under arrest because of the massacre? Let me ask you a question. Just what the devil do we have you under arrest for?"

The scout, in turn, waited a moment before

answering, his bright, black eyes holding the Army man's wide, blue ones. "Let *me* ask you a question, Major," he suggested, his strange voice as powder-soft as the fall of a moccasin in deep trail dust, "if the guide on that train had been a white man, would you have arrested him on sight?"

Clanton flushed, started to stammer, stopped in mid-sputter, announced manfully: "Damn it all, I don't suppose I would have, Red Horse. No, I probably wouldn't have thought a thing about it. But where does that get us?"

"It gets us right where we are now," said Red Horse quietly. "I'm a full-blooded Sioux and I can't help it. But remember this, Major Clanton"—here the black eyes sparkled like chipped obsidian, the soft voice purring upward to a plane of hard vibrancy—"I didn't lead that train into that ambush and you're not going to send me to Florida for it." He paused a minute before dropping his tones back to their old quietness. "I saw every man, woman, and child in that train die. When they were all dead and there was still a chance to save my own life, I took it. I'm a Hunkpapa, not a hero. I did what I could. My tongue is straight. I'm through talking."

Red Horse was a literal man. Clanton couldn't get another word out of him. He was still trying when Benton and Maxwell came up. The three officers began at once to discuss their situation. The nature of that discussion, the blond, gray-eyed, taffy-haired nature of it, lifted a last, desperate hope before the narrow eyes of the listening prisoner. The captive sat by unnoticed, apparently unnoticing, but when the conversation shortly introduced the predicament of the heretofore-mentioned Lieutenant Patterson, Red Horse swung his head instantly to the group by the fire. Here, perhaps, lay his one chance to escape trial for the ambush with its certain sentence to the Dry Tortugas. Red Horse had seen too many Sioux disappear after summary Army trials not to know that his own fate hung in the balance of the officers' low words. He listened intently.

Clanton was talking. "Naturally, our first consideration is the men, but some of you know my daughter Reno, and will therefore understand my feeling in this matter."

"No one would fail to, sir." It was young Captain Benton. "Your only child and. . . ."

"And," interrupted Maxwell feelingly, "the most beautiful girl I ever saw!" The aspirations of Riley Maxwell in the direction of the major's daughter were well known.

"Thank you," said Clanton quietly with a nod. "Our problem remains to decide the probable whereabouts of Patterson's troop, and the possibilities we have of contacting them, considering our own situation."

"I suppose the fool's lost." Maxwell's bitterness was compounded by uneasy thoughts of Reno's being alone with the attentions of a dashing second lieutenant of cavalry. "Lord! We ask for six troops of cavalry and they send us one. And under a wet-nosed shave-tail who couldn't find his way to his own tent without a compass. When was he supposed to report, anyway?"

"A week ago," answered Clanton. "The last we heard was the wigwag message I got from Squaw Point, saying he had Reno with him."

"That's one hundred and fifty miles south of here," asserted Captain Benton. "It looks as if something must have happened."

Mention of the major's daughter set a desperate plan afoot in the fertile mind of the listening Red Horse. If he could somehow convince Clanton that he, Red Horse, could guide the relief to Lieutenant Patterson, there might yet be a chance to win freedom. The thing was to get the commander to send a small relief party right away, tonight. Then, in the darkness of the downtrail journey, with Red Horse in the lead, guiding, many things might happen. . . .

Clanton's solemn conclusion interrupted the scout's thoughts. "Our problem, now, is to decide what we're going to do about finding Patterson, in view of what we know about Red Cloud's being out in force."

"What you've been told by that lying Sioux, you mean," interjected Maxwell.

Clanton gave his opinion quietly. "I've talked

with Red Horse fully, Captain. As to his report on Red Cloud, I see no reason to doubt him. In fact, I'm inclined to believe his whole story. At any rate there's little point in aggravating the precariousness of our own position, and that of Patterson and Reno, by prejudice based on this man's failure to be a European. We'll break camp in the morning, as soon as it's clear that Red Cloud doesn't intend to attack us. We'll back-trail till we meet up with Patterson. I can see no other course and unless a better suggestion is forthcoming, gentlemen, that's it."

IV

"INDIAN VISITORS"

Neither Benton nor Maxwell seemed to have such a suggestion but one came, nevertheless, and from a forgotten quarter.

"I've got a better suggestion, Major." The purring voice of Red Horse fell across the little group in the lull that followed Clanton's announcement.

"Oh, for the love of . . . ," began Maxwell, before Clanton cut him short.

"Go ahead, Red Horse. Let's hear your suggestion."

"First off," the scout said quickly, earnestly. "Red Cloud won't attack this column. He's not ready for any such big medicine. He sure aims to drive you whites out of the Powder River country, but his big attack won't come till this winter, after the fall buffalo hunt's over and the meat's all in and dried. He. . . ."

"Major, what's the use of listening to this scoundrel? We can't believe a word he says. Now, I. . . ."

"Captain Maxwell, your attitude is commendably alert, but I happen to want to hear what this man has to say." Maxwell took his reprimand with a bristling—"Yes, sir."—and Red Horse continued.

"As I was saying, you've got too much force in this column for Red Cloud to fool with." The scout could see that Clanton was listening to him carefully. Hope for the success of his plan grew. "He's not the war chief of the Seven Tribes for nothing. You'll hear a lot of commotion about other chiefs, but they're mostly talkers. Red Cloud's different. He's a crazy kind of an Indian, moody, spooky, proud as a bull elk with six strange cows."

"What the devil are you getting at?" Maxwell's question was angry, defiant. Red Horse continued, ignoring him.

"He told you down at Fort Loring what he'd do if you came up here. Well, he'll do it. The next time you hear from Red Cloud will be when he lifts your hair and runs off your horses. He's through talking."

Clanton's interruption labored with his usual heaviness. "I don't see precisely what you're getting at myself, Red Horse. You just told us he wouldn't attack us, now it sounds like you're telling us he will. What *do* you mean?"

"Just this. Red Cloud won't attack your strong column of regulars, but you say you've got a green lieutenant and forty replacement pony soldiers running around without a wet nurse. In fact, lost somewhere between here and Fort Keene, with your own daughter with them."

"Yes, yes, that's right. Lieutenant Patterson and G Troop of the Eighth, up from Fort Loring. My daughter informed me she was coming up to Fort Keene with them. Thank God, Murphy and Moriarty are along."

"Who're they?" The scout's question was terse.

"Two regular sergeants."

"Well, that helps. But forty green pony soldiers and a damp-eared second lieutenant make a supper just cooked to a turn for Red Cloud and four hundred Oglala Bad Faces. A white girl, daughter of the big soldier chief, won't slow down their appetite any."

"So?" Major Clanton's query was strained.

"So, what do you think Red Cloud will do to get his hands on the daughter of the soldier chief who has broken the Fort Loring treaty and come north of the Powder?"

"Well?" Clanton couldn't seem to get the picture.

Red Horse, feeling his chance of scaring him into sending out a night column slipping, fired his final shot. "Well, unless you want Lieutenant Patterson and his forty to join Sergeant Stoker and his eight, you better find him right now. Break camp and start back tonight. Send Captain Maxwell and his thirty mounted infantry on ahead. Don't waste twelve hours sitting here waiting for Red Cloud. He's not coming, but"—the scout's slanted black eyes gleamed suddenly—"he may be going. And where he may be going is after your new lieutenant. *And* your daughter. This whole country is belly-button deep in hostiles. It's almost impossible that some scout band won't get their noses on Patterson's trail. When they do, they'll have the war chief down on top of him like a travois load of hot, red rocks." The lean Sioux's last words were ominous. "Your only chance of doing that is to let me guide the mounted relief party."

Clanton nodded gravely. "You may underestimate Patterson and overestimate the hostiles, Red Horse, but I can see your point. I'm half a mind to let you do it."

"I can see his point, too," burst forth Maxwell excitedly. "But not the one *you* see. Major, I think this murdering redskin is trying to get us to break camp and go into a forced night march for the sole purpose of getting us strung out in the dark for his friend, Red Cloud, to jump us. The whole thing points that way. Sending me out ahead, you following, out of contact, him guiding. . . ."

"By George, Maxwell, you may be right!" This possibility had not occurred to Clanton.

Encouraged, the younger officer again swung hard at the suspected scout. Red Horse saw his chances go glimmering. "Not only may I be right, but I suggest we all remember this man is under direct suspicion of one ambush already, and that he himself is a red Indian."

"Lord, yes," agreed Captain Benton fervently. "Let's not let him walk us into one."

"Exactly my point!" snapped Maxwell.

"All right." Clanton's voice was flat with finality. "We stay here as planned. Maxwell, you and Benton check the outposts and see that every man in camp is sleeping on his rifle. Red Horse, you. . . ." The major's orders broke in mid-delivery, his glance widening as it fell on the Indian scout. "What the devil's ailing you, now?"

Red Horse paid no attention to the question. He was half rolled on his side, his bound arms awkwardly twisted behind him. His head lay on the ground, right ear flat, pressed to the bare earth. Clanton started to repeat his question, but Red Horse raised his head, scowling savagely. "Shut up!" he commanded. "All of you be quiet."

The three officers looked at one another in surprise. Maxwell, laughing with nervous quickness, muttered something that sounded like: "Insolent

263

redskin beggar!" His words were lost in the heavy silence that followed the scout's abrupt order.

"What is it?" asked Clanton, leaning forward, his whisper sounding loud in the stillness.

"Three, maybe four horses. Yes, four. Coming this way. Were running, now they're walking. Barefoot ponies." He lifted his head, rolling his body back to a sitting position. "Tell your down-valley pickets to hold their fire. Don't let them go blasting up the landscape. Those are Indians coming in, but there's only four of them."

Captain Benton ran off to alert the pickets.

"Shall we douse the fire?" Major Clanton's question was openly put to the bound prisoner.

"No, there's nobody with them. Just the four of them. Hold up and see what they want. They aren't blundering into you, you can bet on that. They know you're here and they want something."

Out of the darkness, downvalley, came a sudden calling out of voices. Major Clanton could recognize Captain Benton's voice in challenge, but the answering tongue was a strange, guttural one. He didn't place it as Sioux, the only hostile language with which he was even vaguely familiar.

"Cheyenne," vouchsafed the copper-skinned prisoner. "And if I remember that voice, you've got big company." A moment later Clanton heard the sibilant intake of Red Horse's breath. "Bigger than I thought, by damn."

The figures of four mounted Indians loomed out

of the blackness beyond the fire glow. In their lead rode an old chief, very dark-skinned, ramrod straight, long-braided hair as beautifully silver-gray as an old badger. A single, black eagle feather worn vertically at the back, Cheyenne-wise, adorned the braids. From the high choker of five-inch bear claws that circled his neck, to the extravagantly beaded moccasins of white elk that cased his feet, every lineament of the old man's body and bearing bespoke the savage patrician, the nomad commander, the hereditary chief.

V

"A VINDICATION"

Out of the side of his mouth Red Horse spoke soft words to Clanton, never taking his eyes from the approaching warriors. "That's Dull Knife," he said. "The stiff-backed old bird in front, the one with the black feather and the claw necklace. He's *the* Cheyenne chief." To the red men, now drawn up, sitting their ponies, tight-lipped, just outside the fire's light, the scout addressed a more formal comment. Rising gracefully despite his bound arms, he inclined his head deeply to the old man.

"*Woyuonihan*," he said, using the Sioux greeting word of respect for the warrior of reputation. "My father will forgive it that I cannot touch my brow, but as you see. . . ." Red Horse left the statement up in the air, ending it with an explanatory shrug of his pinioned arms, as he concluded: "The white soldier chief bids me tell you *hohahe* . . . welcome to his teepee." Turning to Clanton, the scout added: "I have told him we respect such a great chief and that he and his friends are welcome in your tent."

The major nodded, smiling at Dull Knife, half raising his palm as he hesitatingly announced: "Uh-er, how. How, chief!"

"*Hau*," grunted the Cheyenne without changing expression by so much as a nerve-end twitch. The other three savages sat as he did, graven, red gargoyles under the feeble lances of the restless fire.

Clanton shifted uncomfortably, glancing at Red Horse for help. Maxwell for once held his tongue while Benton, who had come up behind the chiefs, stuttered: "Th-the old man, the chief, I mean"— indicating Dull Knife—"he can talk English. He said he wanted to talk to the Oak Leaf Chief."

"Well, who the devil's the Oak Leaf Chief?" Clanton wanted to know.

It was then, had you been watching, you'd have seen the third strange thing about Red Horse—his smile. It was rare and bright, that smile, as fleeting and warm as a sunburst past the hard edge of a coming storm front. It ran over the clouding of his expression like summer lightning shooting the dark face of a thunderhead. Then it was gone just as quickly, seeming again like lightning to leave the scene of its passing darker than ever. You caught the quick flash of the snow-white teeth behind the hard mouth, the sudden lambency of the piercing eyes in their still mask, and that was all. After that, the face went passive again.

"Why, that's you, Major," Red Horse responded to Clanton's broadcast query. "You're the Oak Leaf Chief. They call you that from your emblems of rank. Just like they call your friend, General Crook, Three Stars."

"Well, what does he want?" asked Clanton haltingly.

"You can talk to him direct. He savvies English. But first it would be a good idea"—the scout's words dropped to an undertone—"to shake hands with him. They love to shake hands."

Squaring his shoulders, the major stepped toward the motionless Cheyennes. Red Horse walked with him, calling out clearly: "This is the big white soldier chief, Major Clanton! His oak leaves have seen much war and they are watching you now." Dull Knife and his companions sat impassively, not furnishing a face-muscle flutter among them. Indicating the famous Cheyenne with as much of a flourish as his bonds would permit, Red Horse announced dramatically: "Dull Knife, head of the Cheyenne nation, war chief of all the Cut Arm People." This was the Indian's name for the Cheyennes, taken from their habit of cutting off the left arms of their victims.

Clanton offered his hand uncertainly, being amazed when the old chief at once hopped down off his pony, seized the extended member, and pumped it furiously.

"*Hau! Hau!*" said Dull Knife, his shy grin more suited to an agency boy than to the war chief of all the Cheyennes.

"How!" Clanton returned the greeting stiffly, meanwhile trying to retrieve his hand from the wind-milling the old Indian was giving it. "You are welcome in my camp."

Dull Knife's companions had now dismounted to stand in turn for handshakes from the Oak Leaf Chief. The first one up was another oldster, a patient-faced chief, short of stature, plainly dressed.

"Two Moons, a great chief, a famous horse thief," intoned the scout soberly. So far none of the Indians had given Red Horse any recognition, but at his reference to the old chief's pony-lifting pro-clivities, Two Moons turned to him with a wry smile.

"From Sunkele Sha this is high praise. But let us say no more about it." He spoke in Cheyenne, Red Horse answering in the same tongue.

"Do not worry, uncle, the Oak Leaf Chief doesn't know you are the one who ran off his horse herd down at Fort Loring this spring."

"Aye, but he will if you do not put a hobble on that wagging tongue of yours."

"He knows no Cheyenne, uncle."

"Maybe not," broke in one of the two chiefs still waiting to be introduced, "but if you and old Two Moons are going to stand there all night with your tongues flying loose on both ends, he will have time to learn it."

"Even so, my brother"—nodded Red Horse in serious acknowledgment—"let us get on with this business."

As he turned away, Clanton queried brusquely: "What's going on, Red Horse? What are you talking about?" The scout shrugged aside the questions, saying the chiefs were wrangling over the order of introduction. Quickly he presented Red Arm and Black Horse, both well-known fighting chiefs in the prime of manhood. They applied their considerable vigor to the Oak Leaf Chief's right arm.

"Hang it, Red Horse!" The major's complaint held obvious appeal. "How long does this go on? I won't be able to use this arm for a week now."

A gleam sparked the scout's dark eye. Speaking in Cheyenne, he addressed the visitors: "The Oak Leaf Chief says he loves to shake hands with his red brothers but that he does not want all the joy for himself. He says the Two Bar Chief"—pivoting here with a sweeping bow to the frowning Maxwell—"would rather shake hands than eat young dog!"

"*Hau! Hau! Hau!*" called out the Indians, descending on the captain.

"Blast you, Red Horse," Maxwell began, backing with such haste as to step unwittingly into the fire, "you red son-of-a. . . ." But by this time Captain Riley Maxwell's self-possession was as singed as his toasted posterior. The chiefs, having seized both his hands, two on each member, now stood pumping heartily, uttering unbroken strings of *Hau*s as they worked Maxwell's captive arms. The captain wasn't man enough to stand up to the punishment. Face flushed, fuming, flank smoldering, he fought a successful retirement, ending up safely behind Clanton, both arms at last free of Indians, both luckily still partly in their sockets.

While the Cheyennes had been hand-pumping Clanton's junior around the fire, Red Horse had addressed the major briefly.

"You may think they're playful by nature," Red Horse said. "I can assure you they aren't. They're putting on the friendly act for a reason. My guess is they've got something unfriendly to say and want to get you clear on how good their hearts are before they spring it." Red Horse's opinion was no sooner given than borne out.

Leaving the red-faced Maxwell as abruptly as they'd attacked him, the Cheyennes stalked over to the fire, seating themselves cross-legged before it, with scrupulous attention to the order of the sitting.

"You can always tell Indian rank by the way they sit at a fire for council," Red Horse explained.

"They're rank-proud as sin." Clanton looked at the dark-faced Hunkpapa with new interest.

"Where did you see service, Red Horse?"

"Scouted some for General Price down in Texas."

"A scout for Price, eh? Well, you look skinny and dirty enough for a Confederate at that. Now, then, what about these Indians?"

Following Red Horse's instructions, the three white officers seated themselves opposite the Cheyennes. There were no smiles now, no friendliness. Red Horse noted that Dull Knife and Two Moons both carried ceremonial pipes but that neither offered to light his. Dull Knife opened the talk.

"Today Makhpiya Luta made war on you. He had many warriors." Here the old chief held up his right hand, clenching it, and flicking it open four or five times.

"Each flick is a hundred," the scout said in an aside to the officers.

"He burned your train. He killed your soldiers. Red Cloud did this. He had American Horse with him. The Sioux did it."

"Are you telling us that the Cheyennes had no part in burning those wagons?" Maxwell's demand was suspicious.

"I am telling you that you cannot travel through the Sioux hunting grounds. It is the treaty. No white wagons will roll north of the Powder. I, Dull Knife, tell you this."

"*You* are telling us?" Maxwell took the rôle of spokesman for the officers.

"No, I am telling you for Makhpiya Luta. He says you are going to build a great fort. Is that true? Is his tongue straight?"

Clanton took over, having grabbed the tailgate of the conversation. "I can answer that question for you. His tongue is straight. We are going to build such a fort." There was silence then. For a long minute the only talk was between the quarreling coals of the dying fire. At last old Two Moons spoke.

"A fort will mean war. Makhpiya Luta said you would build it. We thought he lied. Now there will be war. You can still go away. Go away now. War is coming."

"When it comes, where will you be, uncle?" The soft question came from Red Horse.

Dull Knife answered for Two Moons. "We shall be at peace if the Sioux will let us. But you, Sunkele Sha, know how it is with them. Maybe Makhpiya Luta will not let us have peace."

"He won't," predicted the scout flatly.

"Well, where are we now?" said the puzzled Clanton. "As far as I can see, you've told us nothing Red Cloud didn't tell us at Fort Loring months ago."

"Yes," Maxwell stepped in, quick-worded, his old impatience at work. "You heard Major Clanton tell Red Cloud and Crazy Horse we were going to

272

come up here and build a fort. You talk with a big mouth, Dull Knife, but we remember you. When Red Cloud and Crazy Horse walked out on the peace talks, you walked with them. You were big for war then!" Maxwell paused for breath, plunged recklessly on. "If you're through talking loud, get on your ponies and ride! We won't be bullied by a bunch of red. . . ."

"Shut the fool up!" As Red Horse's tight-lipped phrase went to Clanton, the hard-faced Cheyennes were already on their feet.

"Yes, hold on, Maxwell. I'll talk now." Addressing Dull Knife, the column commander spoke with his usual bluntness: "We know you are not threatening us and that your hearts are good." The four chiefs hesitated, their narrowed eyes staring past the fire, not looking at any of the white officers. "But if the Sioux want war, they shall have it. And if the Cheyennes are with them, they will get war, too."

Dull Knife slid the long ceremonial pipe into its buckskin cover.

"We came to smoke the pipe with the Oak Leaf Chief"—his words going to Clanton, but his eyes holding on Maxwell—"but the Two Bar Chief would not let us light it."

The Cheyennes were boarding their ponies. The talk was over. As usual, the white man had covered his ears. Maxwell, stung by the old chief's singling out of him as scapegoat for the conference's failure, sprang forward, seizing the hackamore of Dull Knife's pony. The old man's hand flashed to his shirt, coming away with a bared knife. Before he could strike with it, a lean form shot under his pony's neck, driving a hunched shoulder into the officer's restraining arm, breaking its hold on the pony, sending its owner staggering backward.

"You fool!" Red Horse's exclamation lost none of its contempt for its quietness. "Don't you know enough not to touch an Indian? You *never* lay hands on an Indian."

Maxwell, shaken, livid with humiliation, rasped hoarsely: "You lousy Sioux! If I had a gun, I'd shoot you where you stand. As it is"—the attempt to regain control was successful—"this gallant display of concern for your red cousins will serve to get right at what I had in mind asking the chief." With a quick nod to Major Clanton, he hurried on. "I was just going to ask the chief to give us the thrilling account of your heroic part in the defense of the wagon train. Major Clanton seems inclined to credit your story, so I thought it would be a shame to pass up this chance to interview four undoubted eyewitnesses. Their testimony will surely tend to clear you, Red Horse."

Clanton, entirely missing the irony of his second's speech, at once agreed. "Of course! Good idea, Maxwell. Perhaps these savages can help you at that, Red Horse. I hadn't thought of it."

"I had," said Red Horse flatly.

"Well, go ahead, then," the officer instructed him, "ask them about the fight. I'd like to hear what they have to say."

"No." Red Horse's refusal was blunt. "Get your own information. Then maybe you'll believe it."

"All right, Maxwell," Clanton said with a nod. "Go ahead."

The captain, with a forced bow to Red Horse, turned upon Dull Knife with clear relish. "The Oak Leaf Chief wants to know about this great fighter here"—jerking a thumb at Red Horse—"how he defended the wagon train, how he slew the Sioux by hundreds, how he. . . ."

The old Cheyenne looked at the truculent white officer, contempt as plainly painted on his features as the vermilion and ochre which otherwise daubed them. "The Two Bar Chief thinks to make a fool of me. Now we shall see." The old man's phrases dropped with precise devastation into the breath-held silence. "We were not at the fight. I did not see it. But Makhpiya Luta has placed a price of fifty ponies for the scalp of Sunkele Sha. And American Horse has sworn he will get those fifty ponies. Let that tell you how well your prisoner fought this day." There was a slit-eyed pause during which Dull Knife stared at Clanton. "I respect the Oak Leaf Chief," he said at last, "so let him hear this. The scouts have flashed the glass from the south. Makhpiya Luta knows about your pony soldiers. They are lost. A one-bar chief. A young white squaw. All lost."

He and the other chiefs wheeled their ponies toward Red Horse. "*H'g'un!*" The deep voice of the Cheyenne war chief went to the scout, rolling out the Sioux word for courage, a lifted, right arm salute accompanying it.

"*H'g'un. H'g'un. H'g'un,*" echoed his followers, each in turn saluting.

"*Woyuonihan,*" responded the scout, his face as expressionless as theirs. Then, as they turned their ponies' rumps to the fire, he called out after their retreating figures: "*Mani Wakan Tanka,* walk with God." The Cheyennes acknowledged this farewell with backward hand waves as the darkness reached out and swallowed them.

Clanton stared after them for a moment, then turned to Maxwell, his blue eyes for once lighted with decision. "Cut Red Horse loose, Maxwell. We'll have to keep him under technical arrest till this matter is cleared up, but I think fifty ponies is price enough to at least take the ropes off a man." As the dour captain stepped toward the prisoner, the column commander concluded: "And get your thirty men mounted up, Maxwell. You're going down the trail tonight. And don't worry about losing your way." Clanton enjoyed his brief moment, his concluding words spinning Maxwell around in disbelief, bringing Red Horse to his feet, eyes shining with fierce hope. "You'll have the best guide on the Bozeman Road."

VI

"RACE WITH DEATH"

The night was ringing-clear as a temple bell. On a ridge above the trail, To-Ke-Ya, the dog fox, left off his business of mouse hunting to flick his keen ears northward up the star-brightened Bozeman Road. For a moment he froze, his big ears working the evening breeze. Quickly the warning sound swelled, grew presently into a staccato rhythm even a dull human ear could not fail to catalogue— the drumfire roll of hoof beats galloping in the night. To-Ke-Ya watched the pony of the loose-swinging rider pound past his hiding place and disappear down the gloomy Bozeman. For a moment he wondered idly what the ugly little spotted *sunke wakan* and her Indian rider had been in such a hurry about. Then he silently dismissed the whole subject.

What did he care about a lone Sioux rider pounding down the Bozeman? Or about the young Army lieutenant and the beautiful white girl lost in the hills of the trail thirty miles below? Or about that other group of figures moving in the night ten miles to the east? That group going at a jingling trot? That group whose unshod ponies shuffled by the hundreds through the silent dust? Whose red riders went, slit-eyed, through the night, feathered war bonnets and tasseled lances bobbing and glinting in the starlight? No. The dog fox had no time for Indian wagon guides, or green lieutenants, or white squaws, or Sioux war chiefs. Not tonight. Not just now. To-Ke-Ya had a mouse to catch. . . .

It was 2:00 a.m. when Red Horse slowed the rat-tailed paint out of her hours-long gallop. The little mare was beginning to run rough and the scout knew she had no more than ten miles left in her. She had carried him thirty miles from Clanton's camp, twenty past To-Ke-Ya's ridge. Ahead now, a black ribbon athwart the trail, lay Squaw Creek.

Coming down the long decline of Connor's Ridge, the scout walked, hand-leading the mare, letting her get her breath on the rock-strewn down-grade. At the ford, he led her out into the shallow stream, letting her drink a little before tying her muzzle up so that she could take no more. Then he scooped handfuls of dripping moss and mountain cress from the stream's floor, sponging these over the little paint's laboring flanks. The cool creek water quieted her, and shortly he led her away, putting her to graze in a patch of hay along the stream. He watched her closely, then seeing her begin to eat, he nodded to himself. Good. She would be all right now.

"*H'g'un*, Ousta," he called softly to her in Sioux. "Your heart is big."

The little mare left off her grazing to look up. Ousta, The-One-Who-Limps, was quite a mare and she knew it. Despite the injury that had inspired her name, a Crow arrow through the left hock, she could outgo any pony on the plains. Now, looking at her master, she decided flattery wasn't going to get him anywhere. Soft words didn't make up for hard riding. With a flick of her rump she returned to her grazing.

Red Horse grinned, knocked out the pipe he had lit, ground the coals with a twist of his moccasin. It was time to ride. A look at the shift of the stars told him dawn was two hours off. Briefly he calculated his position. Two things he knew, two he assumed. He knew Clanton had broken camp and was night-marching down the Bozeman. He knew Maxwell was out front of Clanton with the thirty mounted infantry. He assumed Lieutenant Patterson and the major's daughter were somewhere on his front, lost in the hills flanking the trail. He assumed Red Cloud was somewhere in the hills, too, but definitely not lost.

Red Horse, although freed of his bonds, had still been under technical arrest when, hours before, he had deserted Maxwell's column. To Red Horse the desertion was logical: he had made a smart plan and bluffed the white commander into falling for it. Now he was free by his own brainwork, and by the same token he was going to stay that way. He had done nothing. Why let them punish him?

To Maxwell, the desertion was treacherous, wholly vindicatory of his original suspicion of the scout. Furious with Clanton for having technically freed the Sioux guide on the testimony of the Cheyenne chiefs, furious with himself for letting the hated scout outwit him and give him the slip on the trail, 2:30 a.m. found Captain Riley Maxwell blundering down the Bozeman two hours north of Squaw Creek.

Two-thirty a.m. found other things. It found the smoke of Lieutenant Patterson's banked campfires curling, thin and white, up out of the hilled-in meadow where he and his forty troopers slumbered peacefully—slumbered with their rifles stacked, their horses grazing far off picket. Once it had climbed up past the sheltering hilltops, that thin, white smoke lay, hard and clear, against the prairie skies, visible for miles in every direction. Letters of fire as tall as ten warriors couldn't have advertised Lieutenant Patterson's position any better. To eyes schooled in the ways of the High Plains, that thin, white smoke clearly spelled: "Quiet, please. Many foolish men sleeping. Approach without caution. Slaughter at will."

Red Horse saw that smoke ten minutes after he remounted and left Squaw Creek. Curses flew then with an evil fluency never learned in the war camp. That had to be Lieutenant Patterson. Who, but an Army man, would leave night fires smoking in the heart of hostile Indian country? Red Horse shrugged. It was nothing to him. He was well out of the whole mess. Let the fools die. But how about the girl? How about her, Red Horse? Your friend, the major's daughter? The one Maxwell had said was the most beautiful girl in the world? What about her? Let her die, too? Did you owe the major anything? Like maybe the fact you were free right now? *Woyuonihan. Wowicake.* So it was true. Did an Indian pay his debts? A Hunkpapa Sioux? A chief's son? *Waugh!* Did the rain fall down and the grass grow up?

Ousta grunted in pained surprise as the moccasined heels pistoned into her ribs. Flattening her belly to the ground, she went up and over the low hillside to the left of the trail, her hoofs scrambling like a scared cat's. On the other side she found a narrow, level gully, running easterly toward the smoke. Red Horse pointed her down this tortuous track, letting her have her head. "Go on, you spotted she-mustang," he whispered savagely into the mare's pinned-back ear. "Run your heart out."

Ousta ran then and she ran fast. But ten miles to the east other ponies were running, and they were running fast, too. The eyes of Makhpiya Luta were as bright and black as those of Red Horse. He had seen that smoke even better than the scout. After all, the war chief had been miles closer to it when he saw it.

Within a mile of the smoke, Red Horse brought the mare into a walk. He had seen nothing, heard less. But that sky-crawling smoke was such an inviting signature of helplessness that he knew, if the Sioux were within ten miles of it, they would be riding it down as hard as he. So he had the mare walking, and walking very softly. It was well he did.

As the diminutive paint picked her way through the black of the gully, her rider kept his glance fastened tightly on the best signpost available. He could just make out the little beast's bobbing head in the trace of starlight, filtering down to the gulch's bottom, and not for an instant did he take his eyes from her flickering ears. Back and forth they moved, in regular cadence with her head. Forward and back—then, suddenly—staying forward, sharp-pricked. Red Horse stiffened, leaning along her wiry neck, right arm reaching up along her head, hand clawed, tense, ready. In a moment the ugly jughead swung up, following the point of the ears. Ousta flared her nostrils, sucking in the cold air blowing fresh to them from the east. As she got her nose full of it, the scout felt the little stiffening that raced down her back. Instantly his poised hand dove for her nose, clamping it hard. Another second and he was off her and had wrapped a turn of the hackamore around her muzzle. Then he stood with her, both man and mount straining their senses through the darkness.

Although Red Horse's nose was not as good as Ousta's, it wasn't much less so. Softly he blew out through his nostrils, clearing them two or three times. Then his head swung back and forth across the breeze. Not thirty seconds after the mare's ears first shot forward, Red Horse had the scent himself. It was pungent, sharp, almost acrid, and to the scout it smelled of one smell—many ponies, close-packed, warm with traveling. No forty-odd, cooled-out cavalry mounts were going to put that potent a flavor into the night air. Red Horse felt the small hairs at the nape of his neck lift. Somewhere ahead of him, between where he stood and Lieutenant Patterson's campfires, were several hundred Indian ponies, and, unless Red Horse missed his guess, each one of them was carrying a rider of other than white hue. When you were born in a skin lodge, weaned on a rawhide cradleboard, cut your teeth on an eagle-bone whistle, and grew up with the delicate effluvia of wood smoke, boiled meat, tanned hides, and pony dung constantly in your nostrils, you got so you could "smell Indian". Red Horse was "smelling Indian" now. Lots of it. Very close.

He couldn't have more than minutes left to do whatever he was going to do. Dawn came early in that northern country. With the first streaks of it the Oglalas would go pouring down on that cavalry camp from every gully flanking it. Red Horse reckoned the time now to be somewhere after 3:30. On a night as clear as this, faint gray would come at shortly after 4:00. The scout had not time to go around the Indians. If he were going to get into that sleeping camp ahead of them, he would have to go through them.

VII

"THROUGH ENEMY LINES"

Keeping his tight wrap on the mare's nose, Red Horse led her forward through the dark, his eyes straining over the dimness of the gully floor. Shortly he saw a dense clump of poplar scrub. Urging the mare into this cover, he snubbed her up tightly to a four-inch sapling, cinching down the nose wrap with cruel hardness. You didn't play with tenderness in this company. Unbuckling both Colts, he wrapped them in their belts and hid them under a tangle of dry twigs. The Winchester followed suit. Next, the fringed buckskin leggings and hunting shirt.

When Red Horse came out of that poplar clump, he came out naked save for three things: the chamois-soft moccasins on his feet, the deerskin breechcloth about his loins, the thin Spanish knife in his right hand. You didn't see him go up the ridge out of the gully. One minute he was standing outside the clump, the next he appeared along the top of the ridge—not the top, either, but just below the top. And that is where he went along, just below the top, crouching and swift as a hunting cougar. Red Horse knew enough to stay off the skyline even in apparent darkness. You may think a night is black, but no night is as black as the sudden bulking of a body atop any elevation backed by sky.

As the man went slinking along the shoulder of the ridge, that feeling began to get into him that always did when he knew he was cat-and-mousing it with *Yunke-lo*. *Yunke-lo* was the Sioux Shade of Death, and, when he got into the game, Red Horse never felt quite like the wagon guide he so seriously considered himself to be. There was something about the clean feel of the wind on the nakedness of your body, in the feel of the hard muscles running, taut and springy, through every inch of being, to the firm, sure feel of the friendly ground under your stalking moccasins, to the power feeling of the knife haft in your hand with its beautiful balance of blade thrilling your hand as though it held something alive. There was that very smell that got in your nostrils when the play tightened up like this. Red Horse never really knew what it was, this smell, but it shrank the membranes of the nose, flaring the passages and making them feel stinging clean. Sometimes he thought maybe he did know what it was. Sometimes he thought maybe it was the body scent of old man *Yunke-lo* himself. Sometimes just like now, he wondered, even as he was wondering now, if he didn't know how death smelled. And more. If, knowing the smell, he didn't like it? These were the times he knew his blood, knew his color, his heart, the wildness that was always there just beneath the thin veneer of the *Wasichu*. That instinct to hunt, to stalk, to destroy that ran so closely beneath the hard, invisible shell he had built up so carefully around himself. These were the times Red Horse knew what he was. The Oglalas beyond the ridge weren't the only Indians abroad that frosty morning.

After paralleling the ridge for about 300 yards, the scout topped it. The odor of men and horses was now so thick it could be felt. Belly-flat, Red Horse lay on the spine of the ridge, peering down. Spread before him was a cup-like little valley, perhaps a half mile in diameter. Out in the flat of the valley, closer to the other side, loomed the white cluster of the Army tents. Over against the far side of the valley was a clump of tree growth backed up against overhanging, low cliffs. Another clump choked the ravine immediately in front of and below his position. Otherwise, the ground was open and clear all around the campsite.

By the first signals and sounds which came up to him from the grove below—the jingle of metal harness, the dust-deadened stamping of ponies' hoofs, the occasional flash of a white feather headdress, or dull glint of a gun barrel or lance blade in the starlight—Red Horse knew the growth crawled with Indians. After a few seconds he began to believe the whole group was down there. The sign that kept coming up to him spelled hundreds. Apparently Red Cloud was so sure of this camp he hadn't circled it. It appeared the Oglala leader had kept his command intact, probably planning one big frontal rush as soon as there was a streak of light to run by.

Red Horse showed his white teeth. The quick grimace could pass for a grin only by the rarest stretch of charity. It pleased him even more that *Wakan Tanka*, the Great Spirit, had given it to Red Horse, the Hunkpapa, to show the vaunted war chief the error of his ways, if, indeed, the Oglala leader *had* neglected to fill that other grove across the valley with warriors. Not that there still wasn't a hazard or two between the scout and his first goal: reaching those tents ahead of, and unknown to, Red Cloud. Yes. A hazard or two. Like say, for instance, those 400 Oglalas down there.

Silently Red Horse cursed the shortness of time. Given twenty minutes he could have circled the little valley, coming into the soldier camp from the far side. As it was, he had to go straight in from where he was—straight in and wading arm-pit deep through a bunch of trigger-nerved hostiles. Withal, he wasn't on the ridge three minutes before he went gliding down its far side and into the hidden hundreds below. His medicine was good. Scores of other figures, as naked and red as his own, were crouching or moving about in the cover. At first he went forward rapidly. Once he bumped squarely into a sneaking brave, as the two of them rounded the same tree simultaneously.

"*Wonunicun*," grunted Red Horse. "It was a mistake."

"Who is it?" whispered the other.

"High-Back-Bear," Red Horse responded, using the name of a minor chief he knew to be along. "And keep your flapping mouth closed. You jabber like a squaw. Makhpiya Luta will cut your wobbling tongue out!"

"*Ay-eee!* Even so. Good hunting, brother."

"Be still!" growled Red Horse, and turned quickly away.

When almost free of the woods, his reaching foot landed soundly in squirming flesh. A hoarse rasp came from the ground: "If you must go strolling at such a time, keep your big foot out of my mouth!"

"*Wonunicun*," apologized Red Horse.

"Who is it?" The challenge came swiftly.

"High-Back-Bear."

"Oh. Well, many coups, cousin."

"*Shhh!*" admonished Red Horse, going quickly forward.

Another moment and he felt the waist-high grass of the valley around him and knew he was out of the woods. With a long sigh, he dropped to his belly, beginning to snake out toward the cavalry camp. He had gone ten yards when his outstretched hand closed over a human leg. He felt the flesh contract, then the guttural voice grunting.

"Who is it, there? Who touched me?"

288

"*Kila, tahunsa*," muttered Red Horse. "A friend, cousin. Is this the last line out?"

"Aye. Forty of us with American Horse. One every three-pony lengths. We lead the attack."

"I come from Makhpiya Luta. He wants me to go up a little way more. *Mani Wakan Tanka*, brother. May your arrows not wobble."

Slithering past the other Indian, Red Horse felt the hand reach for him and lock like a vise on his left arm. The deep voice fairly purred with suspicion. "Who did you say you were, brother?"

"Shut up, you *heyoka*! You want to wake up all the pony soldiers? I didn't say."

"You are saying now. I don't like the sound of your voice. Too soft. Who is it?"

"High-Back-Bear." As Red Horse uttered the name, he heard the quick intake of the other man's breath. Instantly the scout knew the masquerade was over. His right arm whipped backward and up, flashing the thin Spanish knife into poised readiness.

"A small world, brother," the unseen enemy's heavy voice was barely audible. "I, too, am High-Back-Bear!" With the Oglala's words, Red Horse felt the hand on his left arm tighten spasmodically, knew what it meant. Had it been broad daylight he couldn't have seen the knife coming any more clearly. He rolled into the Indian, feeling the enemy's striking arm thud across his bare back, feeling the knife miss, feeling its vicious blade graze the skin of his far side. At the same time he hurled his own blade down and forward, whipping it straight in. He heard the tunk! as the knife went home, felt the hot blood gush over his hand and wrist. An instant later the grip of the hand on his left wrist slackened, fell open, then flaccidly away.

"*H'g'un*," whispered Red Horse, twisting his blade free. "It's a bad night for high-backed bears."

Ten minutes later he lay alongside the tent of Lieutenant Patterson, listening to the breathing of its occupants. That was a little strange, Red Horse thought. He hadn't expected to find anyone sharing the lieutenant's tent. Must be another officer along, after all. Commissioned men weren't in the habit of tent sharing with troopers. Sliding around to the front of the tent, he parted the flap and eased in. Behind him the first thin tinge of gray picked out the gleaming peaks of the Big Horns.

VIII

"RENO CLANTON"

Sneaking into that tent was like wriggling into the cave of a grizzly—it was that black. But it wasn't the blackness that caused Red Horse to freeze just inside the flap. It was the smell! That smell had no right to be in an Army camp two hundred miles north of the last civilized post on the frontier. It was a smell that made every nerve fiber in the scout's body go singingly tight. It was purely delicious, that smell. A smell that any man of Red Horse's untamed nature would recognize instantly. There was a woman in that tent.

Red Horse trembled, sudden perspiration breaking over him like a warm breath. His stomach drew inward on itself till it felt like a clenched ball no bigger than his knotted fist. The great muscles of his back tensed aching-tight down the long arch of his spine. His chest felt compressed, his throat constricted, his nostrils pinched. A moment before, a naked red Sioux had slipped through that tent flap. Now, in his place, a confused wagon guide. Red Horse knew the sensation that gripped him was a new one. The mood that had seized him when he started in through the Oglalas was gone. In its place was this strange, nerve-tingling unrest, a deep, good-feeling thing he had never known before. He went forward into the tent, high-strung as a panther on colt tracks.

It was no trick to find the man. It was easy to smell a man out in the dark. First, you had just the male smell, which was good enough for any stalker, but then you usually had the cloying fragrance of tobacco, too. In this case, the scout noted, there was another designator present, not unfamiliar to the frontier or to Red Horse—trade-whiskey fumes! What a breakfast dish to be setting before the noses of 400 hostile Sioux—a sleeping camp of forty green men and a lone white woman, in charge of a raw junior lieutenant heavily at work snoring off a fine drunk.

As soon as he smelled the whiskey, Red Horse was afraid to touch the man. *Wakan Tanka* knew it was touchy enough awakening any soldier sleeping in Indian country. To arouse a green officer out of a liquor stupor could be suicide. Still, there was no time to go prowling the camp looking for someone else. It was going to be the woman, then? And God help them all if she made an outcry. Even as he went toward her, Red Horse wondered at the odd morals of the whites—a major's daughter sleeping in the same tent with a strange lieutenant! True, they were bedded separately, but. . . .

"Ma'am," whispered Red Horse. "Wake up, ma'am." His reaching hand touched bare flesh, warmer and softer than spring wind. He felt rather than heard the indrawn, stiffening gasp from the woman, and brought his hand away as though from a hot stove lid. "Ma'am, for God's sake don't make any noise. If you do, we're all dead. Don't talk, just listen." He could see the whites of her eyes now, staring wide at his bulking shadow, could feel the quick, sweet breath of her on his bare arm.

"Who are you?" she whispered. "Quick, or I'll cry out!"

Red Horse knew there was great fear in the voice, knew the whole thing hung in the balance on his next words. "John Red Horse, government scout with

Major Clanton." He pulled the name out of the air, hoping it would sound right. "Are you Miss Reno?"

Her voice was controlled, steady, letting Red Horse know his gamble had succeeded. "Yes, I'm Reno Clanton."

"Your father sent me," the scout lied. "Listen to me and make your answers straight and fast. There are four hundred hostile Sioux in those hills west of here. They'll attack this camp in about ten minutes. Do you understand that?"

Her answer was a stifled gasp, then the quiet words: "Yes, yes. Go on."

Red Horse nodded to himself. This white squaw was no *heyoka*. She would do to ride the river with. "Listen. The lieutenant is drunk, isn't he?"

"Yes."

"All right. I want the sergeants, then, Murphy and Moriarity. Where are they?"

"The next tent, I think. I'm not sure."

"I'm going," Red Horse warned. "Now, listen. You're a white woman. You sleep in a tent with a strange man. Is that right?"

"I don't know what you mean. I. . . ."

"All right. I'll be back for you. While I'm gone, I want you to get the lieutenant awake. You know what I mean. Wake him up like a woman. That'll bring the blood, flush his mind out, maybe. Keep him from yelling out, anyway. There's no time for anything else."

"I . . . I don't know. I. . . ."

293

"Don't ask me what I mean, white girl! You're all woman. Get over there and wake that drunken slob up. And wake him up quietly." Red Horse went out of the tent in a running crouch, not waiting to see what she did.

Slipping into the next tent, he called out, voice low but no longer whispering: "Sergeant? Sergeant Murphy! Wake up. Where are you?"

"Yes, sir?" The voice sounded encouragingly alert. "What's up, sir? Who is it?"

"I'm John Red Horse. Regular scout with Major Clanton." He repeated the lie. "We ran into Red Cloud up north. He's out in force. Wouldn't tackle Clanton's column, but he found out about your outfit. . . ." Red Horse broke off abruptly. "Are you other men awake? Listening?"

"Yeah."

"Sure."

"What's the matter?"

"All right." Red Horse's voice raced now. "Red Cloud is out there in those west hills. There's four hundred Oglalas with him and they're going to be down on this camp in five minutes."

"Lord Almighty. . . ."

"Shut up. If you want to keep your scalp on straight, just listen. There's no chance to save anything but your hair. No horses, no supplies, nothing. Now, get this. East of here, two hundred yards, there's a big alder clump up against some low cliffs. Do you mark the spot, Sergeant?"

"Yes, sir, I do."

"Good. The bunch of you in this tent get out and wake up every man in this camp. As you wake them, start them moving for that alder clump on their bellies. Each man takes his carbine and all the ammunition he can carry. There'll be no orders, don't wait for any, just hit for that clump. Any noise and the Sioux will be on us. If we make the trees, we've got a chance. Major Clanton is on the way and Captain Maxwell is just two hours behind me with thirty horse. We've got maybe five minutes now. Let's go. And let's go fast. I'll get Lieutenant Patterson and the girl."

The troop commander may have been grass-green, but Sergeant Murdo Murphy was that color by nativity only. "All right, yez hairy-chested apes. Yez heard Mister Red Horse, didn't yez? Git goin', and the first one ave yez which so much as breathes noisy is goin' to git his barkin' backside knocked off by me, Murphy, personal. Danny, yez wake up the south half of the camp, I'll git the north."

Sergeant Moriarity, Murphy's opposite number, responded cheerfully: "Jest as ye say, Murdo, me bye. Soft and easy."

The tent was cleared in seconds, and, as Red Horse went running, bent over, back toward Lieutenant Patterson's tent, he could see some figures already snaking out into the tall grass, headed for the alder grove. Good. This thing might yet work out a mite different than Makhpiya Luta had it figured.

"Ready, ma'am?" His low voice went in at the tent flap.

His answer came from the lurching figure of Lieutenant Arleigh Patterson. "Listen here! What the devil's going on around here? By heaven, I. . . ." The voice was loud, blatant. There was a trace of light now, allowing Red Horse to see the bulk of the officer's body—and Patterson to see Red Horse. The scout saw the lieutenant's face drain white as he realized he was looking at a naked Sioux, knew the next instant would bring the drunken officer's befuddled yell of—"Indians!" Red Horse shot through the tent flap, circling and coming up fast, his left arm seeking and finding the lieutenant's neck from the rear. Throwing his knee up hard into the man's kidneys, Red Horse bent him far back over his braced thigh.

"That's a knife in your ribs, friend." His white teeth chopped at the words. "If you make one more drunken sound, you'll get it all the way into your liver. This camp is going to be under Sioux attack in about three minutes. I've ordered all your men out and I've come back for you and the girl. We're going to try for those trees against the east bluffs. You're either coming or you're staying here. What do you say?" Here, easing the iron forearm away from the throat, the scout concluded: "If you stay here, it'll be with this knife between your ribs."

"Let's go. I don't understand all this, but let's go. I. . . ." His voice started to rise again, and Red Horse stepped back and struck him, palm flat across the face.

"Get out!" the scout snarled, shoving the stumbling officer through the tent flap, tripping him on his face as he went out. "And get down on your belly and stay there! Come on, ma'am," he murmured, all the old softness back in his voice. "Down on your hands and knees! Right out through this tall grass here." The girl, who had been watching the Sioux, fascinated as a child staring at a tiger, obeyed him without question. "Crawl straight for those cliffs up ahead, ma'am. We'll keep the lieutenant between us, so's not to lose him. Hurry up, ma'am. We're the last ones out."

The girl slid ahead as instructed, Lieutenant Patterson, cursing and grumbling incoherently, crawling after her. Before following them in, Red Horse took a last look and listen, east. The dawn streak behind the Big Horns was a luminous gray now, although the hills surrounding the little valley still crouched in darkness. Even as Red Horse watched, the grayness broke out from behind the distant peaks, tipping the near hills with silver. A fox barked querulously in the grass near the east grove. Another answered him from within the grove. A poorwill whipped sleepily farther along the hills. Its mate called dolorously back. Red Horse couldn't resist the temptation.

To the straining ears of the Oglalas, nerve-keyed for the go-word from the war chief, an eerie howl came drifting from beyond the dark soldier camp—long, low, incredibly sad, the hunting song of the buffalo wolf, the signal call of the Hunkpapa Sioux. Hearing it, Makhpiya Luta stiffened. Under him, his pinto stud, hearing it, too, pinned his ears and walled his eyes. For a moment the war chief hesitated.

"It is nothing!" Elk Nation spoke from the shadows to Red Cloud's left. "Truly a *sunke manitu*, a wolf, nothing more."

"Aye," agreed Buffalo Runner, looming up on the war chief's right. "No Hunkpapas around here. Just a wolf. Let's go."

"No doubt you are right," growled the Oglala. "But for a moment there, I thought. . . ."

"*Hookahey* . . . come on . . . let's go," urged Elk Nation. "This is the time."

"All right, here we go." Red Cloud tightened his knees on the pinto stud, threw back his head, rolled his deep war cry down the waiting line: "*Hiiii-yeee-ahhh! Hopo*, let's go!"

"*Hookahey! Hookahey! Hookahey!*" echoed snarlingly from 400 throats, before all human sound was drowned in the hammer of the ponies' hoofs.

IX

"FIRST SKIRMISH"

In looking at Reno Clanton you would miss her just as far as young Arleigh Patterson had when he'd met her in St. Louis the month before—or as Red Horse had when he'd whispered to her in the blackened tent. To see her you would say, first, that she was beautiful, and you would be as right as sun in August or snow in January. Beauty sparkled in every clear feature of her face, in every feline curve of her body. Peaches and cream, flaming gold, and sea-foam gray would describe her skin and hair and eyes no more tritely than truly. She was a flashing blonde, tall, fair, fascinatingly handsome, full-formed, strong, graceful as a cat. Then, second, you would say she was wicked, and you would be wrong, as surely wrong as the difference between wickedness and wildness. Actually knowing her, you would say something else. Maybe something like Sergeant Murdo Murphy was saying to Red Horse, as the two lay in the east grove, waiting for Red Cloud to charge the deserted camp.

"Jest between I and yerself now, Red Horse, I don't know as they wuz ever married. Lieutenant Patterson brung her along when he reported in at Fort Lorin' two weeks ago. Story goes they was married in Saint Louie. But I don't know. For all she's the old man's daughter, she's a wild one. Wild eyes and wild ways. When Lieutenant Patterson first got to the fort, yez could see right away he wuz a boozer. But, mind you, nothin' like he soon was. At first, the two ave them acted fairly decent. Then he begun drinkin' heavy. Been drunk as Flannegan's goat ever since. If you ask me, that red-headed gurl is the cause ave all this trouble. Seems she run away from the convent in Saint Louie, took up with the lieutenant, come West with him to the fort. Then she wired the old man she wuz comin' on up to Fort Keene when Patterson come up. Of course, the old man wired back to Colonel Boynton to hold her at Fort Lorin'. Yez kin see what good it done. Like I wuz sayin', if you ask me. . . ."

"Well, I didn't ask you, Sergeant. All I asked was if Lieutenant Patterson was very drunk last night."

"Last night and every night. They wuz trouble between him and the gurl. They kept to the tent together but was sleepin' separate."

"I know that, too," Red Horse said quickly. "But all I wanted to learn was if you thought Patterson was too drunk to fight his command. Right now, I mean."

"Absolutely."

"That's your opinion?"

"Yes, sir!"

"Well, you just remember it, Sergeant, because

I'm taking over this command. You know what the Army thinks about its commissions and you know what insubordination is."

"Yes, sir."

"It's safer to pull a sucking cub off a cow grizzly than to steal a command this way. You're liable to get yourself busted clear back to a buck for taking orders from me instead of Patterson."

"Yes, sir."

"Well, what do you say? Will you take them?"

"I'll not only take 'em, Red Horse, I'll see that every wet-eared scut in the company takes 'em!"

"All right. Now, listen, you take half the men, Moriarity the other half. Lay 'em out along the front of the woods, yours to my right. Moriarity's to my left. No firing till I give the word. And pay no attention to Lieutenant Patterson, no matter what."

"Yes, sir."

Satisfied that the sergeant would co-operate, Red Horse grinned. "Get going. The light's on the hills. We'll hear from our friends across the way any minute." As if in answer to Red Horse's prediction, a long-drawn—"*Hiii-yeee-ahhh*!"—broke the quiet of the opposite hills.

"That's him! That's Red Cloud!" Eyes shining, for once excitement came into Red Horse's voice. "Watch 'em come now."

Come they did. Whooping and *hii-yee*ing down on the empty camp, the thunder of their ponies' hoofs rolled across the valley like the drumfire of wheel-locked artillery. Sergeant Murphy took one look before he jumped and ran for the rear. "Holy Mither ave Mary, lookit them heathen banshees ride!" Too much the old cavalryman, Murdo Murphy, even in such a moment, had to admire the great Sioux horsemanship.

Red Horse watched the howling Oglalas hit the camp. The first wave rode right over it, firing into the tents. Those would be American Horse's picked group of forty, carrying every serviceable rifle the Oglalas possessed. The second, main body of the Sioux, haunch-slid their mounts to dust-showering stops in among the tents, piling off the ponies, and diving in through the tent flaps intent on knifing or clutching whatever soldiers survived the rifle charge. In a matter of seconds they discovered they had been duped. The camp became a scene of the utmost confusion. The Indians milled their ponies among the trampled tents, many still jamming their lances through tents or piles of duffel, hoping to find some hidden trooper. Scores of others were running about on foot among the supply dumps, hungrily plying the rapacious Sioux appetite for loot in any form. Half a dozen chiefs surrounded Red Cloud, gesturing and arguing heatedly.

Watching them, Red Horse knew he had a rare opportunity for an Indian shoot. He also knew Red Cloud wouldn't be long figuring where the troops had gotten to. If Murphy would only move his Irish hulk fast enough. . . .

"All right, Red Horse!" The sergeant's cheerful voice came out of the scrub to his right.

"Hey you, Moriarity!" Red Horse's words cracked with tension. "You all set, over there!"

"All set. Say the word, General!" Moriarity's answer echoed Murphy's cheerfulness.

"All right. Here goes a three count for a volley. Fire on the count, then fire at will. One. Two. Three!"

The volley crashed out, followed by a piling fire of free shots. The new Spencer carbines were accurate, the men behind them unexpectedly cool for green replacements. Several ponies went down, kicking and screaming. Others broke loose, running wildly down the valley. The hostiles, after a minute's mad scramble, raced for the cover of the west grove. Many of them went riding double, the double riders in most cases hanging over the ponies' withers like very sick men. A ragged fire from Patterson's troopers followed them but the range was too great. No more ponies went down as the savages got safely back to the trees.

"Cripes!" bawled Sergeant Moriarity disgustedly, "we didn't get a single one of them. Look there. There ain't a body lyin' in that camp."

"They never leave bodies lying around," called Red Horse. "You got some of them, all right. Eleven, by my count."

"Hooray!" yelled Sergeant Murphy. "We'll give them red heathens a sweat, now!"

"You mean they'll give us one," Red Horse corrected. "Look over there." The two sergeants followed his pointing finger. Up out of the west grove, two long files of gaudily feathered warriors were climbing into the backing hills, one file winding southward, the other north.

· "Yippee! They're goin'!" Murphy was jubilant.

Red Horse shook his head. "Not quite. They're coming. Around the valley, Sergeant. One column each way, behind the hills."

"Whut do yez reckon they're up to?" Murphy's question came uneasily.

"Some of 'em'll get up on the bluffs above our grove here. The rest will sneak out in the grass on our front and flanks. We'll likely take some casualties, but we're not in bad shape . . . if we keep cool, and they don't rush us."

"Yez reckon they will?"

"I reckon." Red Horse's answer was a flat statement of certainty. "An ordinary Indian wouldn't. But Red Cloud isn't ordinary. He'll come after us. I only wish I knew *how*."

"What happens when he does?" Moriarity's query jumped with nerves.

Red Horse didn't answer, but Sergeant Murphy felt compelled to offer his countryman some manner of solace. "Well, now, Sargint Moriarity, me fine, skinny broth of a lad, whut kind ave posies will yez be preferrin'? And whut'll I be tellin' that fine widdy woman of yers, back in Fort Lorin'? Aye, 'tis a poor, sad colleen she'll be, me bye, with yer back all bristly with Sioux arrers and yer fine red scalp a bouncin' on Red Cloud's belt. But Murphy's the lad to cheer her up, Danny, me son. Never you fear fer that."

"You black Irish scut"—Moriarity's Hibernian pedigree was as clean as the meadow turf in Donegal—"I'll live to bury the likes of you fourteen times over. And as for Kathleen, Murphy, me lad, you ain't the boy fer it."

"Kathleen won't have to worry about either of you," broke in Red Horse, "if you don't get to shooting off something besides your flannel mouths. We've got company!" Out in front, the sergeants could see the grass moving where the scout nodded. "Get back to your men. Tell them not to fire at moving grass. Only at gun flashes, or if they see part of an Indian. Murphy . . . !" Red Horse called the sergeant back. "What's become of Lieutenant Patterson?"

"The last I saw of him, the gurl was arguin' with him back there ag'in' the cliff. He still acted drunk."

"I told her to keep him away from us. We're in enough trouble now." Verifying the scout's claim, the soft hissing of arrows began to come down through the trees. "Oh, oh. That means Red Cloud has got American Horse and his rifles out front in

305

the grass, or does it, by damn? Say, listen, Sergeant, I've got a hunch. You see how these cliffs bulge out into the valley? With our grove sitting on the bulge? What's to keep a bunch of horsemen from coming around that bulge, on either side of us? We couldn't see them till they were within sixty yards."

"Ye're right." Murphy was paying very soldierly attention, as Red Horse went on.

"Those aren't riflemen out in the grass, they're decoys. You'll see. They won't fire a thing but maybe a couple of old muzzleloaders or ball pistols."

"What'll we do?"

"Get Moriarity up against the cliffs on the flank, you on the other. When they come in, we can hold our fire till they're up close, then knock their heathen brains loose. That's it. Get a move on."

The interrupting voice came from behind them. "You're not going any place, Murphy!"

Red Horse and the sergeant wheeled to see Lieutenant Patterson swaying on braced feet, curly hair hanging limply, face flushed, eyes red-rimmed and wild. Gesturing toward Red Horse with the long cavalry Colt in his right hand, the officer sneered unsteadily. "No red-skinned son-of-a-squaw is going to steal my command. By the Lord, I'll. . . ."

Red Horse didn't try to talk; he just went for him. Lieutenant Patterson fired blindly at him but the scout was under the flash, driving his right arm up, fast. The clenched fist was hard as horn, the arm and shoulder behind it tough as a pack mule's hind leg. Patterson's head shot back like a cracked branch. He hit the ground hard and lay still.

"It's a turrible thing to strike an officer," breathed Murphy, white-faced.

"Get to your men." The white teeth flashed in the dark face. "If American Horse gets into us around those cliffs, we're done."

"Yes, sir," assented the sergeant, backing away. "But, faith, I do hate to think of losin' me stripes."

"Prefer to lose your hair?" asked the scout sarcastically.

"You have a fine point there," admitted Murphy, heading for the brush. "Moriarity! Moriarity! Where the divil are yez, ye bog-trottin' Irish gazoon?"

"ATTACK OF THE HOSTILES"

A twig snapped behind Red Horse, and he whirled to see the gray-eyed Clanton girl standing by the fallen lieutenant. In her hands was a Spencer.

"Here," she said, holding the carbine out to him. "It's his. But I see he won't be needing it. Is he dead?"

Red Horse took the weapon, levering it to check

the magazine. There was something about the quiet way the girl watched him, the complete disregard she showed for the unconscious Patterson, that upset the scout. "You don't seem very disturbed about your husband." There was challenge in the statement.

"I don't care what happens to him. Or to me, either. I've been a fool." Her expression was unsmiling but her strange eyes were beginning to glitter in a way that set Red Horse's breath to catching. "And he's not my husband. We were never married. I joined up with him because he promised to bring me out here to my father."

"Well, ma'am"—Red Horse moved uneasily—"we can go into that later. We all make mistakes, and, if you want me to forget yours, you've come to the right country. As far as I'm concerned, you're Missus Patterson."

"Thank you, Red Horse," the girl said simply, her eyes never leaving the dark face. "We'll leave it that way for the others. For you, I'm Reno Clanton." The tall Sioux heard the words, refused to admit their clear implication. In the world he'd known, a white girl didn't talk to an Indian like that.

"Right now, ma'am"—the words were an order—"I want you to go back against the cliff, where I put you, and stay there. We're going to have it hot and heavy around here."

Reno looked at him with a directness no man

could miss. "I'm going with you," she said. "I like you, and I like it hot and heavy."

Red Horse felt the blood pile up in his temples, pounding like drums. What the devil did she mean? This creamily beautiful white woman couldn't possibly . . . ? "Do you mean that?" His hot stare swept her with a heat-lightning flash.

"I mean it," was all she said.

The Sioux stepped over the unconscious lieutenant and seized her. One arm went around her waist, the crook of the other cupped her white neck viciously. It was a long, hard kiss, and the girl came to Red Horse with it, like fire to a piece of dry wood. When she twisted her mouth away from his, a thin line of blood ran from the full lower lip.

"Let me go!" Her words were strangled, angry. "I can't breathe."

Red Horse moved away from her, his arms and all his muscles strung, bow-tight, with the cords of suppression. When she spoke again, he watched her eyes.

"I didn't mean that," she murmured resentfully. "Not what you thought. Oh, Red Horse, I'm sorry." He watched her another instant, before turning away.

"Come on," he grunted, soft voice gutturally deep. "Let's go. You meant it, all right." She didn't answer, and together they went through the trees, back toward the cliffs, the girl following the man, her cat's-paw lightness of foot almost as neat and sure as his. Behind them, Second Lieutenant Arleigh Patterson lay alone, his only company the whispering of the arrows probing the grove with their flickering fingers.

Where it based up against the bluffs, the grove was perhaps forty yards wide. Red Horse lay on the north flank, with Moriarity and his half of the troop, Murphy and the other half, forty yards away, on the south flank. A minute stretched itself nervously to five, then ten. Half an hour went by. Still, no attack.

Red Horse cursed the wily Red Cloud. It appeared the war chief figured he had all day to get them, would let them dangle on the hook, knowing full well the tension each minute's delay would cause. The attack might come in five seconds or ten hours. This was Makhpiya Luta's advantage. He would enjoy it to the last nerve twitch.

The sun was climbing now, beating into the thick foliage of the grove with the force of a molten hammer. The scout guessed an hour and a half had passed since he had aroused the sleeping camp. If he hadn't lost the trail or tried any short cuts, Maxwell should show up within the next thirty minutes. The knowledge of the captain's approach was Red Horse's advantage, he in turn getting what enjoyment he could from it. If Red Cloud would just stall a little while longer. . . .

But the war chief was through stalling. The

assault came now, and it came in such a way as to catch the wary Red Horse off guard. The scout had been waiting for the usual preludes to an Indian attack, the owl hoots, fox barks, bird calls, and other nature sounds by which the red men customarily talked back and forth over the heads of their intended white victims. Even after these sounds there was always the last-second warning: the screaming war whoops that inevitably preceded the frantic, rapid-fire galloping of the ponies' hoofs. But Red Cloud had heard a wolf howl just before he had raced down on the empty camp. The others had thought it was a wolf, but Makhpiya Luta had not been sure. Now he was sure. He was sure it had not been.

Red Horse had turned to say something to Moriarity, taking his eyes from the front along the bluffs for a second's fraction. The next thing he felt was the tremble of the ground under him. Whirling, he saw fifty or sixty warriors already in the open, no sounds issuing from their clamped mouths, their ponies straining their flying bellies to the grass tops. In their lead came American Horse, his careening black stallion easily marked among the piebald and motley colored horses of his followers.

"How about it, chief?" asked Moriarity, cool as a butter pat in a well house. "They're pretty close."

"Go ahead," said Red Horse, levering his own carbine and aiming at American Horse's black stud as he spoke.

"Fire!" yelled Moriarity, the twenty Spencers crashing so close on the word as to cover it. At such point-blank range the effect was devastating. At least fifteen horses went down, including the war chief's black.

The other riders came on, right over the neighing, kicking scramble of their companions' fallen mounts. They were within ten yards of Moriarity's men when the second volley went into them, and the third right on top of it. Down went another clotted tangle of horses and riders, and still the hostiles came on.

Half a dozen actually careened their mounts into and through the hard-firing troopers, but the others, about thirty of them, had had theirs. Turning, they swept off to the left, out into the open valley. The six warriors who got into the position lasted long enough to down four troopers, Sergeant Moriarity among them.

"Hold your fire!" yelled Red Horse to the soldiers still shooting after the fleeing hostiles. "Let them go. Keep your eyes on the ones we've got down out here along the bluffs. There's some injured out there, playing 'possum. Fire into every body you can see, whether it looks dead or not." As he talked, Red Horse was callously following his own instructions. Proving his contention, some of the "dead" warriors began to crawl or struggle away. Carefully the troops shot these, one by one.

Soon there were no more crawlers and Red

Horse called out sharply: "All right! Hold it. Get these injured back in the trees. Where's that girl? Oh, all right, ma'am. Take care of these men. See what you can do for them. Never mind the sergeant, he's done. You, there"—the scout addressed a tall Kentuckian whose carbine had been hotter than a two-dollar pistol—"take over here. And keep your eyes peeled. I'm going over to see how Murphy made out."

"Yeah," drawled the trooper, "go ahead. Reckon Ah cain handle this heah side foh a spell."

Red Horse bent over Sergeant Moriarity, who lay where he had gone down, knees drawn up to his chest, hands pressed into his stomach. "In the belly, eh, Sergeant?" The dying man moved his head. "We won't move you," said the scout softly. "I saw you get it. I guess you know where your number is."

" 'Tis up, chief." Moriarity got a white smile out with the words. "I ain't got no more strength left than a sick cat. Tell Murphy. . . ." Red Horse could hear the teeth grind as they clamped to keep the blood from coming through. "Tell Murphy not to wipe his nose on any more poison ivy."

"I'll tell him," said Red Horse, and went quickly away. Sergeant Moriarity didn't hear the scout's agreement. His relaxing hands fell away from the sodden jacket front. He turned a little on one side, and lay still.

Red Horse had heard Murphy's men firing all the

while his own were repulsing American Horse. He soon found the Irishman had pulled through it fairly easy.

"They come in a big wave," Murphy said. "Didn't seem to have many guns. Must 'ave been a couple hunderd of them, but they was jest firin' bows and arrers. We give them two volleys and they veered off acrost the valley. I think I seen Red Cloud. Big scut, ridin' a paint studhorse?"

"Yeah, that's him. The old coyote fooled me. Didn't split up his rifles. Sent American Horse and all the guns in on our side. Near got us, too. He's a cute one. We lost Moriarity and three men wounded."

"Moriarity?" Murphy's question was slow with apprehension. "Not Danny Moriarity? There's another Moriarity over there with yez, ye' know. One ave the troopers. . . ."

"Your Moriarity," said Red Horse. "Sergeant Moriarity."

"Aw, no." The tears sprang, unashamed, to course down the sun-cracked cheeks. "Not me bye, Danny."

"In the body," said Red Horse unfeelingly. "He died quick."

"Did he say anythin' now, before he went?"

"Said to tell you not to wipe your nose on any more poison ivy."

"Ah, me nose, indeed," murmured Murphy wistfully. "The little scut once handed me a fistful ave

314

poison ivy when I asked him like a gentleman fer some soft grass. 'Twas a dirty Irish trick and the saints preserve us. I was the talk of the camp fer six weeks. Me nose, indeed. Bless the bye's little heart." Murphy sniffed lugubriously before concluding: "Well, anyway, we put a spoke in the red heathens' wheel that'll have them runnin' lopsided fer a week. When do you figure them to come back?"

"Take a look out there and figure it for yourself." Red Horse gestured grimly.

Murphy looked and saw a long line of warriors approaching them from across the valley. There were a couple of hundred of them, spread out five yards apart, making a bent sickle over half a mile long. A dozen chiefs rode the line, yelling war cries and shouting battle orders wholesale. Conspicuous among them, Red Cloud, the war chief, wheeled and dodged his nervous pinto.

"Those are the ones we just ran off," growled Red Horse. "Now, look down there." Pointing south.

"Heaven help us. Another hunderd of them!"

"Yeah, and there'll be a hundred more on my side. They've come down off the bluffs."

"Faith, ye're right. There ain't no more arrers comin' down."

"That accounts for all four hundred of them," added Red Horse thoughtfully. "And by the way they're fixing to come at us now, I'd say they'll get

315

us this time." There was no despair in the statement, only hard opinion.

"Do yez really think so, Red Horse?"

"Sure. They're going to make the big rush. There's thirty-eight of us here, four hundred of them out there. Carbines or no carbines, if they come at us without breaking, our meat's roasted."

"Where do yez suppose Captain Maxwell is hidin' his smilin' byeish face right now?"

"Who knows? He's due now. Murphy"—the scout's voice went suddenly low and fast—"spread your men around this edge of the grove till they meet mine on the other side. The hostiles are coming in from the front and both flanks. All we can do is spread out thin to cover all of them. Tell your boys to keep firing low and getting the horses down. Don't fire at the riders till they get right close in. And pound it into them to keep blasting away till the Indians are right on top of us. An Indian will break his charge at the last minute, close up, nine times out of ten, *if* the fire keeps coming into him. They don't like it in the guts."

"Yes, sir. Neither did Moriarity. I'll remember that, Red Horse, and I'd like to shake your hand. Ye're a first-class fightin' man, red or white."

"All right, Sergeant." The Sioux gripped the old soldier's big paw, knowing from the warm pressure of it and from the earnest squint of the blue eyes behind it what all men know who have been there: that, when the last raise has been made and called, all men are the same color. "Good luck. Remember. Fire low and get the horses down." The men parted, each going at a lope back through the woods.

XI

"LAST CARTRIDGES"

Red Horse got his men spread, ordering them to hold their fire till the Indians were 150 yards out. Looking around, he saw nothing of the girl, or of Lieutenant Patterson.

A drawling voice spoke at his side: "Ah reckon they'll fry our fat foh us this time." The big Kentuckian levered a shell into his Spencer as he talked.

"Yeah. And about all we can do is spatter as much of it on them as we can while they're frying it." As Red Horse spoke, the red lines approached within 200 yards of them, and a single warrior rode out of the leading group. He was a lean, dark-hued Sioux, garbed in black buckskin leggings, wearing a solitary spotted-eagle feather slanting through his braids. When he saw him, Red Horse's breath came sucking in, sharp as an arrow's hiss.

"Cripes!" Red Horse said. "I thought so."
"What's the matter?"
"That's him."
"Who?"

"American Horse . . . the one in the black leggings. The son-of-a-skunk has more lives than a six-toed cat."

"Well, let's see if we cain't get about nine of them lives away from him," said the grinning, lanky mountaineer. "Ah feel lucky."

"You've got your chance to push that luck a little right now," announced Red Horse. Across the valley, Red Cloud threw his carbine up, firing it four times. "That's the signal. Four's their good-luck medicine number. Here they come."

The hostiles broke in a running wave toward the grove, the cavalry carbines taking them in from around the perimeter of the grove. "The boys are shootin' good," commented the Kentucky private, as the Indian ponies began to go down, hock over forelock, all along the line. But even as he spoke, and with the range shortening to eighty yards, the fire going out from the grove slackened noticeably.

"I'll be hanged!" ejaculated Red Horse, lowering his carbine to listen.

"Yeah," groaned his companion, at the same time throwing down his own carbine and pulling a long Bowie knife from inside his jacket, "it's the cussed ammunition. Mine's gone, too."

"I hate to think it"—Red Horse's quick grin flashed—"but I allow you're right. Kind of slows a man down, too."

With a wry grin, the Kentuckian consoled him: "Well, you done a good job while you lasted, mistuh. You fought like a swamp cat with a coon dawg crawlin' him. Say, now, do you reckon that's Gabriel's trumpet I heah blowin?"

The question was the kind of jest a man will put out when he figures the last chip has been shoved into the middle of the blanket. In this case, Red Horse missed the humor—for good and sufficient cause. A trumpet *was* blowing.

"It may seem like Gabriel to you," he said with a grimace, "but it sounds like Captain Maxwell to me."

"Well, Ah'll be a razorback pig! The U.S. Cavalry to the rescue!" The mountaineer's words were no less fervent for their sarcasm. "Man, oh, man! You cain say all you want to, but a troop of hoss comin' thataway, with the guidons flyin' and the bugler blowin' his heart out, is really some-thin'!"

Red Horse, watching Maxwell's galloping troop coming across the valley, felt compelled to go along with the larger sentiments of his companion's heartfelt observation. Others were inclining in the same direction. Forty yards short of the grove, Red Cloud swung wide, heading south, downvalley. The rest of the Sioux, sweeping around from the north side of the grove, streamed off after him.

"Looks like my red friends agree with you," commented the scout, allowing himself the luxury of a broad smile.

Well earned as the smile was, it was premature. The forgotten Lieutenant Patterson chose the instant of its spreading across Red Horse's face to make his belated and final contribution to the day's disasters. As Red Horse spoke to Kentucky, he was startled to see the disheveled figure of Lieutenant Patterson burst from the cover of the woods about thirty yards to his right. The officer was stumbling and running out into the open grass lands, waving his arms and shouting to the approaching Maxwell, still a quarter of a mile away across the valley. "Help us! For God's sake, help us!" he screamed frantically. "We're being shot to pieces!"

"He's out of his haid!" cried Kentucky, leaping to his feet. "I'm goin' out aftuh him."

Red Horse grabbed the mountaineer, shoving him down hard. "Get down! You can't go out there. Patterson is not only out of his head, he's going to be out of his scalp, too. Look there!"

Following the scout's gesture, Kentucky cursed softly. "Mah Lawd! Ah thought they was all gone."

Coming from the north side of the grove at a belly-stretching gallop, the riders straining far over their mounts' lathered necks, a last group of Sioux charged around the edge of the woods. Lieutenant Patterson heard the rush of their ponies' hoofs and possibly the first two or three shots, no more. A literal blast of rifle fire knocked him sprawling, face forward, arms flopping grotesquely, into the long grass. Red Horse and Kentucky were so close they could see the dust puffs fly from the crazed officer's jacket as the Sioux lead ripped into him.

"Lawd," breathed the mountain man, "they sho' weighted him down for the big jump."

"He picked a poor time to go for a trot," commented Red Horse. "That was American Horse's bunch he tied into."

"What do you suppose ailed him to go runnin' out thataway?"

"I don't know. Happen a man'll do many a funny thing when his nerves are pickled in whiskey and he's had his pride humbled."

The Sioux had now disappeared downvalley, and Maxwell, who had switched off to chase them, was coming trotting back up the meadow.

"Ah guess the poh devil's done foh," said Kentucky, scanning the grass where Patterson had fallen. "Ah don't see no movin' around out theah."

"Well," observed his companion dryly, "if he's going to die, I hope he's already dead."

"Yeah, Ah reckon you do. One of the boys was tellin' me you done slugged the lieutenant back theah in the woods."

"Had to. He was wild. Tried to gun me down."

"Anybody see it?"

"Murphy."

"You're lucky. The sergeant'll back you up. He's got more spunk than a guv'ment mule."

"We'll see quick enough. Here comes the cavalry."

Watching Maxwell ride up, Kentucky drawlingly opined: "Nevah did like that officuh. Lookit the little cock rooster fluffin' his feathahs. Man, he's done already give hisself credit foh savin' ouah outfit."

"Let's get a blanket and go bring Patterson in." Red Horse made the suggestion abruptly. "He could be alive."

"Sho', be back in a minute." A few seconds later, bending over Patterson's body, Kentucky muttered: "Your tough luck, mistuh. He's still breathin'."

"Maybe his lamp'll go out before we get him in," said Red Horse casually. "Roll him in the blanket easy-like. He's so full of holes you could read week-old sign through him."

The scout's optimism was unfounded. Patterson lived long enough to talk.

Red Horse and Kentucky had no more than gotten the stricken lieutenant into the blanket, than Maxwell cantered up. "It's a long trail that leads nowhere, Indian," he sneered cheerily to the scout. "It looks like you'll still make that court-martial. Is that Lieutenant Patterson?"

"It's him," replied the scout. "But it won't be long."

Dismounting, Maxwell slid his arm behind the dying man's neck, propping him half up. "Patterson, can you hear me? Can you talk, man?" The youth's eyelids flickered, and Maxwell shouted to his sergeant: "Bring me a canteen, Jensen. Hurry up!" When he had the container, he sloshed its contents over the lieutenant's head. "Come on, Patterson, brace it, man. I've got to know what went on here. Can you hear me, Lieutenant? I'm Captain Maxwell. I want you to tell me what happened here." Patterson nodded weakly, the words coming with a rush when they began.

"I had a good camp out in the valley. Just before dawn, an Indian came into my tent. He said he came from Major Clanton. Said we were surrounded and had to get out. I refused to go and he knocked me down. Then he forced Reno and me to. . . ."

"Reno?" Maxwell interrupted, quickly. "Reno Clanton? Major Clanton's daughter?"

"Reno Patterson." The young officer made his dying bid for decency. "My wife."

The words hit Maxwell like a sledge, but he took them in stride. "Go on. Hurry up, man. Then what?"

"The Indian put a knife in my back and made me crawl over here to these trees. When we got into the woods, the Sioux attacked. I was still confused from the blow the Indian gave me in the tent. When I recovered, I tried to take over the command and he knocked me unconscious. When I came around again, I staggered up to the edge of the woods. I'd been disarmed while unconscious and I found Murphy taking orders from this Indian. I didn't know what to do. I was afraid the crazy Indian would come at me again. Then I saw the Sioux turning off, and you coming across the valley. I started to run out to meet you, and. . . ."

Patterson's head fell back over Maxwell's arm. The captain's free hand jerked the head back up again. "Patterson! Can you still hear me? Can you hear me, Patterson?"

"He can't hear anybody." Red Horse's soft voice broke the answering silence. "He's dead. *Mani Wakan Tanka.*"

XII

"DRUMHEAD COURT-MARTIAL"

Gently Captain Maxwell laid the body back on the blanket and stood up to face Red Horse. "Yes, Indian, he's dead. But I think he lived long enough to hang you!"

"You're touched." The scout shrugged. "Patterson was drunk on duty, had been for days. He couldn't command his own two legs, let alone a troop of cavalry."

"You lying, red scut," gritted Maxwell, and struck the scout with his gloved hand.

Red Horse didn't move. He knew where he stood as a lone Indian among white Army troops. He knew, also, that, if Maxwell could make

Patterson's charges stick, he would do it. He knew, too, that the next few minutes could mean the difference between freedom and the Dry Tortugas for him. His wide mouth remained as clamped as a sprung trap.

"The lieutenant was drunk," Kentucky spoke with labored slowness, knowing his words marked him with insubordination, "jest like Mister Red Horse said."

"Sergeant Jensen, put Red Horse under arrest." Maxwell ignored Kentucky's statement. "We'll attend to him when Major Clanton comes up. And this time, by heaven, we'll have our drumhead court-martial!"

"You can have your court-martial, I'll take the woods," drawled Red Horse easily. "Let's get back in there before Red Cloud realizes the infantry isn't right behind you. I know that Indian. He'll be back the minute he savvies there's no support following you in."

Maxwell started to turn angrily on the scout, but his action was interrupted by a bellowing shout from the grove.

"Yez better git yer men under cover, Captain. Red Cloud is comin' back up the valley."

The dust cloud rolling with the galloping Indian ponies was clincher enough for Murphy's warning. The captain's men scattered for the trees like a flushed-up covey of quail. Once in the grove, Maxwell took over the command, first ordering

Red Horse securely bound. Sergeant Murphy, panting up to get his orders, was in time to see the troopers seize and bind the scout.

"Beggin' your pardon, Captain, but yez better let him have a gun till the shootin's over. He's handier with. . . ."

"You better worry about yourself, Sergeant. Lieutenant Patterson accused you of outright insubordination."

"Yes, sir." Murphy made the admission and saluted. "He was drunk, poor bye, may the Lor-r-d rest his soul."

By now the Sioux were racing back and forth across the front of the woods, riding and firing wildly. At the same time the rate of fire going out from the grove was growing heavier. The Indians couldn't seem to agree on a charge. American Horse started in once but veered off sharply while still well out.

The hostiles now drew off about 500 yards, milling and wheeling around in obvious argument. While they were still palavering, a high dust cloud became visible about five miles west, in the direction of the Bozeman. As Red Cloud showed hesitation, three riders came whooping down out of the hills, fanning their lathered ponies across the valley toward the war chief. Seconds after their arrival, the hostile band departed eastward for the Powder, their pace such as to indicate the three scouts had reported Clanton's approach.

· · ·

An hour later, Clanton marched in with his musicians blowing the daylights out of "Garry Owen" and his supply, ammunition, and baggage wagons rumbling and banging impressively. A secure camp was set up, rations issued, the minor wounded cared for, and Lieutenant Patterson read under the ground. Following these duties, Major Clanton and his daughter were closeted in his tent for better than an hour.

It was early evening before Red Horse was brought before the commanding officer, and Maxwell presented the charges made by Patterson: unauthorized seizure of a command in the field, assaulting an officer, responsibility for the casualties suffered by G Troop. Sergeant Murphy was present under charges of insubordination and being an accessory after the fact of Red Horse's command seizure, with Kentucky along as a material witness. Reno Clanton was present on her own invitation and under no charges save those repeated ones leveled by the appraising glances of Captain Riley Maxwell. The girl didn't miss the warm evidence of the officer's wandering eyes, doing nothing more to encourage them than to return them with a level, calculating stare that, to the watching Red Horse, seemed to do all but set the place of the assignation. The Sioux didn't miss so much as an eyelash tremble of this optical conversation, but what emotion it might be creating within him wasn't visible in the narrow, dark face. With his own fate hanging on the major's decision, Red Horse figured he had more immediate worries than the golden-haired Clanton girl. Withal, though—fiercely as he might close his mind to her—Red Horse was suffering. The memory of that smashing kiss over the unconscious form of Lieutenant Patterson would not down. Never having been shot with the love arrow before, the savage scout, even while feeling its deep twinge, failed to understand the nature of the wound.

Maxwell outlined his case with a great deal of earnest conviction, and Major Clanton at once asked the scout for his story in rebuttal. The towering Sioux looked long and hard at Reno Clanton, his simple warrior's heart offered in the level gaze. The girl, wild and adventurous as she was, was as clean of actual love-lance scars as the red man himself. Now, meeting his burning stare, her bold glance wavered and fell, her creamy skin flushing darkly. For one of the few times in his life, the Sioux misread trail sign, assuming the falling glance and rushing blood to spell shame. He had counted on the girl. She had seen the whole thing, from the time he had entered Patterson's tent. Her evidence, freely given, could have cleared him. Now he felt she would not support his story at the cost of exposing her own shameful rôle in the tragedy. Looking at Major Clanton, the Hunkpapa shrugged. "I have no story," he said. "My heart is bad. My tongue is dead. Let the others speak. White ears are uncovered only when white tongues speak."

It was then that Red Horse got the surprise of his life. Kentucky told what had happened, his story being agreed to, in detail, by Murphy and the girl. The sergeant then told his story, and, lastly, Reno Clanton, her wide-eyed gaze on the somber scout the whole while, her words sparing nothing of her own shame, nor of his bravery.

Major Clanton sat for a long minute, his blue eyes studying the accused Sioux. When at last he spoke, his words opened Red Horse's slitted stare with amazement.

"It is obvious," he announced slowly, "that Lieutenant Patterson was guilty of dereliction of duty. As a matter of routine we will verify this testimony with that of the rest of the troopers, but to me it is quite plain we owe Red Horse a debt of gratitude and, that far from castigating him for the precipitation of four casualties, we should congratulate him for the prevention of forty." Turning to the Hunkpapa, Major Clanton concluded, simply: "Red Horse, I want to thank you. There has been tragedy and disgrace enough here, as it is, but I think thirty-eight men and one woman owe you their lives. That's a considerable debt and one I hope we all appreciate." With these words his gaze found the uncomfortable Maxwell, who had been quick to gather the implication.

"Perhaps you're right, Major." The admission came from the captain reluctantly. "I don't believe this man, but it would seem that evidence of a completely disinterested, that is, from the military responsibility standpoint, of course . . . like Missus Patterson"—here a gracious bow to the bereaved widow, who was at the moment affecting a coy humility that brought the quick wolf-grin to Red Horse's lips—"cannot be disregarded. It is clear from her testimony that Lieutenant Patterson had been drinking. I'm ready to withhold judgment."

"The very least you might do, I should think, Captain," said Clanton stiffly. "And now we'll close this court. Red Horse is clear in the matter. And," he added, meaningfully, with a nod to Maxwell, "I want him treated that way."

The Sioux scout thanked Major Clanton briefly and, as the others departed without further comment, asked permission to leave the camp.

"Of course," Clanton rejoined briskly. "You're free to do as you like. But I would like very much to have you stay on with me in the position of chief of scouts. The job will carry a sergeant's stripes and three hundred dollars a month. It's all too hard to find reliable men who know the country and the Indians as you do, and with the building of the fort in immediate view I'm sure you can earn your pay. You have a job, if you'll take it, John Red Horse." The offer came wrapped up in the major's frankest smile and was extended with the right hand he held forth to the listening Hunkpapa.

As Red Horse started to decline the offer without consideration, his flinty eyes caught the figures of Captain Maxwell and Reno Clanton. The two were standing by the officer's tent, Maxwell talking animatedly, the girl smiling provocatively, apparently much taken with the captain's dash and character. But at the minute Red Horse's vision found her, her eyes left the captain's conversation, locking hard with the lean Sioux's fierce glance. Red Horse could feel that look go into him like a six-inch skinning knife. Ten minutes before he couldn't, for his scalp, have read the sign in that knife glance. But love learns fast.

"You've got a scout," said the Hunkpapa suddenly, his hand closing on Major Clanton's.

ABOUT THE AUTHOR

Henry Wilson Allen wrote under both the Clay Fisher and Will Henry bylines and was a five-time winner of the Spur Award from the Western Writers of America. He was born in Kansas City, Missouri. His early work was in short subject departments with various Hollywood studios, and he was working at M-G-M when his first Western novel, *No Survivors* (1950), was published. While numerous Western authors before Allen provided sympathetic and intelligent portraits of Indian characters, Allen from the start set out to characterize Indians in such a way as to make their viewpoints an integral part of his stories. Some of Allen's images of Indians are of the romantic variety, to be sure, but his theme often is the failure of the American frontier experience and the romance is used to treat his tragic themes with sympathy and humanity. On the whole, the Will Henry novels tend to be based more deeply in actual historical events, whereas in those titles he wrote as Clay Fisher he was more intent on a story filled with action that moves rapidly. However, this dichotomy can be misleading, since *MacKenna's Gold* (1963), a Will Henry Western about gold-seekers, reads much like one of the finest Clay Fisher titles, *The Tall Men* (1954). His novels, *Journey to Shiloh* (1960), *From Where the*

Sun Now Stands (1960), *One More River to Cross* (1967), *Chiricahua* (1972), and *I, Tom Horn* (1975) in particular, remain imperishable classics of Western historical fiction. Over a dozen films have been made based on his work.

"I am but a solitary horseman of the plains, born a century too late and far away," Allen once wrote about himself. He felt out of joint with his time, and what alone may ultimately unify his work is the vividness of his imagination, the tremendous emotion with which he invested his characters and fashioned his Western stories. At his best, he wove an almost incomparable spell that involves a reader deeply in his narratives, informed always by his profound empathy for so many of the casualties of the historical process.

ADDITIONAL COPYRIGHT INFORMATION

Center Point Publishing

600 Brooks Road ● PO Box 1
Thorndike ME 04986-0001 USA

(207) 568-3717

**US & Canada:
1 800 929-9108**
www.centerpointlargeprint.com